Death Rides Again

Also by Janice Hamrick

Death Makes the Cut

Death on Tour

Death Rides Again

JANICE HAMRICK

Minotaur Books ⚬ New York

F
HAMRICK
T

www.minotaurbooks.com

ISBN 978-1-250-00555-7 (hardcover)
ISBN 978-1-250-03157-0 (e-book)

Minotaur Books books may be purchased for educational, business, or
promotional use. For information on bulk purchases, please contact Mac-
millan Corporate and Premium Sales Department at 1-800-221-7945
extension 5442 or write specialmarkets@macmillan.com.

First Edition: June 2013

10 9 8 7 6 5 4 3 2 1

For my parents and my children,
who mean everything to me

Acknowledgments

No novel is written in a vacuum (it would be far too noisy and the cat hair would stick to the keyboard). With all sincerity, though, I am deeply grateful to the many people who made this book possible.

My heartfelt thanks go to my editor, Matt Martz, for his sound judgment, impeccable instincts, and mad editing skills. I'm grateful to all the amazing people at St. Martin's Press, including Justine Gardner, who copyedits with the eyes of an eagle, and Sarah Melnyk and Cassandra Galante, who have done so much to promote my work.

I'd also like to thank my amazing agent, David Hale Smith of InkWell Management, for his ongoing support and enthusiasm, and Kristan Palmer, who keeps us both on track.

Scott Montgomery, who is the best moderator ever, has my gratitude for making my book launch a roaring success, for throwing me softballs on panels, and for introducing me to so many marvelous books and writers. I'm also deeply grateful to John Kwiatkowski, Hopeton Hay, Douglas Corleone, Norb Vonnegut, and Martin Porter, who have been beyond generous with their time, support, and advice.

And finally, my thanks go to Cindy Marszal for reading those imperfect first drafts and talking things through with tiny hands.

Death Rides Again

Chapter 1

FAMILY AND FIREARMS

The day Eddy Cranny got himself murdered started bad and went downhill from there . . . especially for Eddy. My first indication things weren't going well was waking to the unmistakable snick of a break-action shotgun snapping shut.

I'd been lying in bed in a pleasant half-drowsy state, just listening to the murmur of voices rising from downstairs and thinking that I really ought to get up and help with breakfast preparations. Mornings at the Smoke Quartz ranch were the best part of the day even in November when the chill breeze carried with it the faint echo of far-off northern winters, but the frost of morning usually gave way to mild sunny afternoons. The light from the single window on the far wall slowly changed from soft gray to gold, illuminating three sets of bunk beds in the big room. From my position in the bottom bunk nearest the door, I could see the only other occupied bed, on which an unmoving lump under a mound of feather blankets told me that my cousin Kyla was still fast asleep. The other bunks would be occupied by evening with an assortment of cousins of varying degrees, all under sixteen, and probably none too happy to have two adults bunking with them. They would just have to get over it. This Thanksgiving weekend, the Shore family was holding a reunion in honor of my uncle Herman's ninety-fifth birthday, and every Shore in the state of Texas—and quite a few from beyond—were in town to celebrate.

I slid out of bed and through the door, closing it behind me as quietly as I could. Downstairs, another door opened and then shut just as gently, a sure sign that some of the family were already moving to the porch to drink their coffee and watch the birds fly to water as the sun broke over the horizon. In the bathroom, I slipped on sweatshirt and jeans and pulled my hair into a ponytail as quickly as I could, already anticipating strong coffee and homemade biscuits. I had just come out onto the landing again when I heard a shout, a crash, and then the unmistakable sound of shotgun getting ready for business.

Gripping the banister, I took the stairs two at a time and ran for the kitchen, which is not as brave as it sounds. On a Texas ranch, at least outside of hunting season, the primary purpose of a shotgun is predator control, and the primary predator is the western diamondback rattlesnake. It would be unusual to see one on a November morning, but occasionally a snake slithered inside seeking warmth and reappeared at an inconvenient time. My expectation upon rounding the corner into the kitchen was to find someone in a standoff with a serpent. What I actually saw was my uncle Kel staring down the barrel of a 12 gauge pointed directly at the narrow chest of his son-in-law, Eddy Cranny.

Which meant I hadn't been far off, although it wasn't very flattering to the snake.

Eddy stood with hands half raised, his face as white as paper, his body stiff as day-old roadkill. A skinny weasel of a man, Eddy had thinning dishwater hair and the watery eyes of an overbred Chihuahua. Give him another minute and he'd roll on his back and piddle the floor, a not unreasonable reaction considering the brick-red color of my uncle Kel's face. Kel was a big man, tall, brown, and muscular from years of hands-on ranch work. The last man who would need a shotgun to subdue someone like Eddy Cranny, whom he could have simply picked up and shaken like a terrier killing a rat. In all the years I'd known Kel, I'd never seen him raise a hand to another living creature, but now he was so angry that the arm supporting the shotgun trembled visibly. I felt my heart begin to pound in my chest.

At the kitchen table, Kel's daughter Ruby June huddled low and small in her seat, hands over her eyes as though she couldn't bear to watch her father shoot her husband. I couldn't help thinking that she would have done better to put her fingers in her ears. If Kel actually pulled the trigger in that enclosed space, we'd all be deaf for days and Eddy would be little more than a red mist on the cabinets. Uncle Kel regularly won the Lion's Club sharpshooting tournaments, but he wouldn't even need to have his eyes open to hit Eddy at that distance and with that weapon.

Out of the corner of my eye, I noted Kel's business partner Carl Cress and one of his ranch hands standing slack-jawed near the refrigerator and knew there would be no help from that quarter. From the radio playing softly on the kitchen

3

counter, an obnoxious voice began spouting something about low, low prices. I snapped it off.

"Uncle Kel," I said, keeping my voice low and quiet. "Has Eddy been bothering you?"

Kel quivered, but didn't speak. At the sound of my voice, Ruby June raised her head, and I saw with some shock an angry red welt high on her cheekbone. She'd be sporting an impressive shiner within a few hours, and I no longer needed to ask Kel why he wanted to kill Eddy.

Taking another step closer to Kel, I started again, "You can't shoot Eddy in the house, Kel. Think about the mess. You'd never be able to get the curtains clean."

At this, Eddy swallowed visibly, pale eyes darting to me in one incredulous and horrified glance.

I went on. "And consider how hard it would be to explain in court. You'd have to hire a lawyer. You might even miss the winter dove season if the trial dragged into December, which it would since you know how slow these things are. He's just not worth it."

At the last bit, Eddy nodded vehemently. He probably would have nodded at anything I said, and after all it could hardly be the first time he'd heard that particular statement.

Another few seconds ticked away, and then as though awakening from a dream, Kel drew in a shuddering breath and lifted his head from the stock of the gun. The tip of the barrel still pointed squarely at Eddy's midsection, but Kel's finger no longer hovered over the trigger. The look in his eyes should have made Eddy run for the hills, but Eddy had never yet managed an appropriate response to any situation.

"Eddy," I suggested, "go. Now."

Eddy took one final glance at Kel's face, then fled. The door banged behind him, followed a few seconds later by the roar of an engine and the crunch of gravel spurting under tires.

My aunt Elaine appeared in the doorway wrapped in a fluffy robe, coffee mug in one hand, empty plate covered in toast crumbs in the other.

"Where's Eddy off to in such a hurry?" she asked through the screen, trying to balance plate on cup so she could open the door. "He almost knocked me down."

No one answered her, and her cheerful expression turned to one of puzzlement and then concern. Taking another step, she moved past the refrigerator and finally saw her husband, the shotgun still gripped in his shaking hands. Her eyes widened in surprise, but in one fluid movement, she set the plates on the counter, took the gun from her husband, and set it in its usual place beside the door. Taking Kel's hand, she led him outside like a child. The screen door slapped shut behind them.

Carl Cress stirred at last. He was a big man, about forty years old, whose narrow hips and ample gut vaguely reminded me of John Wayne, assuming John Wayne had somehow been possessed by the unholy spawn of a used-car salesman and revival tent preacher. Carl was my uncle Kel's business partner and the two of them together owned a herd of some thousand or so beef cattle. I suppose it was my own suspicious nature that made me keep an eye on my purse whenever he was around.

"Guess we'll be on our way then. I'll catch up with Kel some other time," he announced to no one in particular.

Which was just as well because no one answered. He and his ranch hand Manuel followed Elaine and Kel out the door,

Manuel holding the door so it would close quietly. Manuel was Carl's polar opposite, a small man with work-hardened hands and a soft voice that, on the rare occasions he used it, would have pleased even a cranky librarian. Now he gave me a sheepish look before following Carl to their pickup truck.

Alone in the kitchen with Ruby June, I found my own hands starting to shake with the reaction. Opening cabinets at random, I finally found Elaine's stash of baggies, filled one with ice cubes, wrapped a towel around it, and handed it to my cousin. She took it without a word, pressing it to her eye as I poured us each a cup of coffee and sat down.

A single tear slipped down Ruby June's cheek. She was a pretty little thing, who couldn't have been much older than nineteen and looked younger than the kids I taught in my high school history classes. With some surprise, I realized I didn't know her well. A ten-year age difference meant she'd been too young to have much in common with my brothers or with me on our summer visits to her home. We'd been kind to her, in the careless way of teenagers, occasionally taking her with us in the truck or letting her join us when we went fishing, but never really feeling more than a casual interest in her. I'd attended her wedding last year, and considered that by giving her a toaster oven and refraining from telling her that she was being an idiot for marrying so young, I'd more than fulfilled my cousinly obligations.

"He didn't mean to, you know," she said abruptly, rubbing the tears away from her bruised face with the knuckles of a small clenched fist.

I didn't say anything.

She flushed pink, then grew pale again just as quickly.

Drawing breath, she tried again. "He isn't like that. He wouldn't hurt me on purpose."

"What is he like then, Ruby Juby?" I asked quietly.

A little smile twitched at the corner of her lips at the old nickname. "He's not like us—not like folks who have good families, I mean. His daddy is meaner than sin, and his older brothers aren't much better. Eddy never says or does the right thing at the right time. Like then. He didn't mean to hit me, it just happened. He's clumsy, and he feels awful about it after."

Sounded like a classic abuser to me, and hearing her defending him while her eye darkened and swelled made me sick to my stomach. Telling her so wouldn't do any good, but I had to try.

"It doesn't matter why he does it or how bad he feels after or how many times he promises to stop. Even one time is once too many. And you're going to have to do something about it if you don't want your dad to kill him. And I don't mean the threatening, kick-his-ass kind of kill. I mean really, truly kill him."

"Daddy should stay out of my business," she burst out suddenly. "I'm a married woman now. I can do what I want. He's always trying to tell me what to do." She gave me a defiant stare.

I frowned. "Ruby June, your dad just saw a man hit his daughter in his own house. I think that makes it his business. You can't honestly expect him to look the other way."

"I told you, Eddy didn't mean to. And Daddy never gives Eddy a break. He never even tries to understand."

"Again, I'm not sure what there is to understand. That shiner seems pretty self-explanatory to me."

"He doesn't hit me. Besides, even if he did, it's still my business." Now she sounded sulky, like the rebellious teenager she apparently still was.

"Then you need to handle it. If you're going to be an adult, you need to act like one. And adults don't let other people hit them."

"Yeah," she said, but she didn't meet my eyes.

I was trying to think of something useful to say to her when she cast me a sidelong look, and asked, "You ever done anything stupid, Jocelyn? Something you wish you could rewind and do over?"

I opened my mouth to run through the long list of things I'd like to rewind starting with the man I'd divorced and ending with the man I'd killed. Then I paused. Ruby June was family and undoubtedly knew my history almost as well as she knew her own. Seeing the little gleam in her eye, I grinned at her, glad to see there was a bit more to my cousin than I might have guessed.

"Hell, no," I answered. "I'm so frickin' perfect the sun shines out of my hiney. Hope you have a pair of dark glasses, kiddo, 'cause I'm about to turn and leave the room."

An hour later, dressed and fed, Kyla and I dropped Ruby June off at her little house on the edge of town. Pulling the big red pickup to a stop, I looked around, but there was no sign of Eddy's truck or Eddy himself. The house was barely more than a shack, white paint faded and peeling in places to reveal the gray wood underneath. The tiny yard was sere and yellow in the November morning, and a couple of sad rosemary bushes and a double row of newly planted pansies lining the path were the only splash of color. The pansies, no doubt bought on sale at the grocery store, weren't looking too good this morning after the first hard frost. In the window, homemade and uneven flowered curtains hung limply from a pressure rod. I had a sharp impression of children playing grown-up in an only slightly oversize playhouse and felt an unexpected lump in my throat.

"I don't like leaving you here alone," I said, as Kyla opened the truck door and stepped down. "You sure you don't want to tag along with us today?"

Ruby June hesitated only briefly before hopping out to stand beside Kyla. She leaned back in to answer me.

"That's okay. I need to get this over with."

She must have seen something in my expression, because she added, "You don't need to worry about me. It won't come as a surprise to Eddy—I told him that things couldn't go on this way, and he knew I wasn't foolin' around."

"We could wait while you pack and take you back with us," Kyla offered unexpectedly, shooting me a glance over Ruby June's head for confirmation. I nodded.

"Pack?" Ruby June said. "I'm not moving home."

Her stubborn expression and the lift of her jaw changed her from a beaten young girl into one of the Shore women. It was a look that did not bode well for Eddy. Unfortunately, it faded all too quickly into doubt.

Kyla did not seem to notice. "Well, all right then," she said, climbing back into the truck.

I gave Ruby June an encouraging smile. "We'll see you this evening at dinner."

She didn't answer, and I thought she looked evasive. Glancing in the rearview mirror as we drove away, I could see

Ruby June still standing in her driveway, hands on hips, eyes unfocused.

"Do you think she'll really be all right?" I asked.

Kyla shrugged. "I think the one you ought to be worried about is Eddy. That little bastard," she added. "I can't believe I missed all the fun this morning. If he makes it through this weekend without one of us beating the snot out of him, it'll be a miracle. I wouldn't mind a piece of that myself."

I glanced over at her then returned my eyes to the road. Kyla's bulldog expression was a little wistful as though she really meant the last statement, which she probably did. I shot a second sideways glance at her soft leather purse and wondered if it still held her little Glock 19 that had once saved and taken a life with a single shot. I decided not to ask.

Although we were first cousins, the two of us looked enough alike to be sisters, the resemblance courtesy of our fathers, who were identical twins. Kyla, who would never admit to more than a remote family likeness, preferred to think of herself as unique and resented comments about our similarities. For my part, I would have been glad to look more like her because in her a trick of genetics had somehow transformed the family looks into real beauty. It didn't hurt that she had an innate and classic sense of fashion and the income to support her taste. Even now, dressed for a Texas ranch, she somehow managed to look cool and stylish, long dark hair falling in perfect waves around her shoulders, a gold necklace looking rich against her soft yellow cashmere sweater. Even her jeans looked crisp and pressed. My hair was still yanked back in the same ponytail I'd made when I first woke up, my rumpled sweatshirt bore the University of Texas longhorn on a burnt orange background, and my jeans had a small stubborn coffee stain just above the knee from a long ago breakfast incident. I told myself that I didn't care. I was, of course, lying.

I turned back onto the highway heading toward the Sand Creek feed store because, ever practical, Elaine had asked us to pick up a load of cattle cubes after we dropped Ruby June at her house. On the left side of the highway, an enormous green tractor was busy plowing the brown stubble of shorn winter wheat back into the earth, leaving a trail of rich dark soil behind it. On the other side, a single Mexican buzzard traced a lazy circle over a field dotted with goats and cacti, its primary feathers fluttering like fingers at the tips of black wings. In front of us, coming from the opposite direction, the driver of a white pickup truck lazily lifted a couple of his own fingers from the steering wheel as he sped by. I mimicked the laconic gesture.

"That someone we know?" asked Kyla.

"Didn't recognize him," I answered.

She rolled her eyes but then grinned. "You think they'd get tired of doing that. Still, it's nice to be back out here. I forget sometimes how much I like it."

"That's because you don't."

"I like it," she protested. "Lots. I just don't like every single thing about it the way you do. I have discriminating taste."

"You don't like the heat or the cold, the bugs or the animals."

"Well, who does?"

"You don't like riding, hiking, hunting, fishing, camping, or picnicking."

"Again . . . who does? Besides, I like picnicking okay."

11

"Except for the heat, the cold, the bugs, and the animals."

"Yeah, except for them. But so what? I'm here, right?"

I grinned at her. "You're here."

And right now, "here" was the town of Sand Creek. The single-lane highway widened into two lanes, and I slowed the truck to the posted speed limit of fifty, then forty-five, and finally thirty-five. Along the shoulders, small houses mostly painted white gave way to shops, restaurants, and gas stations in no particular order, followed again by a sprinkling of larger, older houses, some with mansard roofs and gingerbread trim and all surrounded by massive oak and pecan trees, limbs adorned by gray clumps of ball moss. We bumped across an abandoned train track and passed by the old train station, currently being restored to its former glory by an active, if underfunded, historical preservation society. Thanksgiving might be tomorrow, but that retail holy of holies, Christmas, was only a month away, and the storefronts lining the square were having an identity crisis. In one display, pilgrims nestled under boughs of holly, in another Frosty the Snowman towered over a faded turkey that looked as though it had just molted and wasn't feeling well. In the center of the square, the courthouse, a massive buff-colored sandstone building complete with rounded turrets and a red roof topped by a clock tower, presided over the town as it had done for the last hundred and twenty years. The old hanging tree, famous as the site of countless legitimate hangings as well as a few lynchings, was located conveniently on the grounds. Workmen swarmed the area armed with staple guns and ornaments.

I sighed happily. "Nothing says Christmas like twinkle lights in a hanging tree."

I maneuvered the truck around the square, pausing twice to wait for pedestrians to amble across the street, and then we were free and clear and picking up speed on the other side of town. On the western outskirts, we passed a funeral home with a marquee out front with the catchy slogan, "Drive Safe—We Can Wait."

Kyla, who'd been unusually quiet, spoke at last. "So are you ever going to tell me what's up with You-Know-Who?"

"Lord Voldemort?" I asked, knowing full well whom she meant.

The breadth and depth of her profanity was truly impressive and had, if anything, improved since our trip to Egypt. I waited until my ears stopped ringing and vision returned, then said, "If you mean Colin, then yes, thanks to you, he's going to join us later."

She sniffed. "Well, someone had to invite him. The boy was going to spend Thanksgiving alone."

"You don't know that. He could have gone to see his family, and I'm sure he had invitations from friends as well."

Kyla half turned in her seat to stare at me.

"What is going on with you? You're dating him, right?"

"We've been out a few times," I admitted.

"And?"

"And nothing. We're dating. But it's only been a few weeks. Too soon to expose him to the Shores, that's for sure."

"He didn't seem to think so. He accepted pretty promptly as I recall."

I thought about that awkward little scene. We'd gone on a double date with Kyla and her current boyfriend, and the dinner conversation had turned to the upcoming holidays.

13

Upon learning that Colin had not yet made plans for Thanksgiving, Kyla had issued an overexuberant invitation to the ranch, complete with gushing descriptions of the first-class quail and deer hunting, the party atmosphere, and the joy of family. Considering that she loathed every single thing she'd described and usually had to be dragged kicking and screaming the entire way, she'd done a good job of making it sound fun. It had been the look in Colin's eyes, the half-wary, half-hopeful expression that had forced me to smile and second her invitation. Even then, I hadn't actually expected him to accept, but he'd done so with pleasure. Too much pleasure. I had my doubts whether he understood the concept of taking things slowly, which was my condition for dating at all. And I was positive that Kyla did not.

She now proved it by saying, "I don't get it. You're not really still considering that idiot Alan, are you?"

My boyfriend Alan Stratton—the man I'd thought I might love. I'd met him while taking a tour of Egypt about six months earlier, which despite being interrupted by two murders, one robbery, and the machinations of a ruthless smuggling ring had turned out to be one of the best vacations of my life. Although I'd suspected Alan of being a criminal for a while and of being interested in Kyla for even longer, eventually he convinced me that I was wrong on both counts. We'd been dating since we returned, but things had not been going smoothly recently. And then, of course, I'd met Colin.

"Alan is not an idiot," I said automatically. "He's a good guy. I know it's hard for you to believe, but I actually care about him. A lot. But that's not the point here."

"There's a point?"

"Yes! The point is that Colin and I have only been dating—in a very casual way, I might add—for a few weeks. Sort of quick to take him home for Thanksgiving, don't you think?"

"No, I don't. I invited Sherman, but he already had plane tickets to go see his folks. Anyway, what's the big deal? Seems like it would be nice for the two of you to have some extra time together."

"Maybe," I said, "but it gives the wrong impression."

Her blue eyes widened in mock horror. "Oh, no! Not the wrong impression. The family honor will be compromised. Whatever shall we do?"

I gritted my teeth and fleetingly wished that the truck had a passenger eject button.

"Anyway," I said coldly, "Colin's going to join us late this afternoon or early this evening. He had a few things to wrap up."

"What kind of things? What could possibly be more important than the Shore family reunion?"

I hesitated, then finally decided on the truth. "He's applying to the Texas Rangers. He's taking some kind of test today."

Kyla blinked. "You're kidding. That's kind of cool—Texas Ranger. I assume you mean the cop kind and not the baseball kind."

"Yes, the cop kind," I said. "When have you seen Colin playing baseball?"

She shrugged. "How would I know what he does in his spare time? He'd look good in those tight pants, though."

That was true, but I was not going to give her the satisfaction of agreeing. "Anyway," I said pointedly, trying to steer the

15

conversation away from Colin's pants, "he'll be here as soon as he's done."

I could feel her beady eyes boring into my skull and kept my own virtuously on the road.

"You don't sound pleased. About the test, I mean."

I shrugged, unable to deny it. "Being a Texas Ranger isn't a job, it's a life. No fooling, those guys are on call every day, all day, always. Plus, being new, chances are he'll be assigned to some region out in the boonies."

"The boonies, huh? Is that anywhere near Bumfuck?"

"If only. People in the boonies dream of one day getting to go to Bumfuck."

Kyla met this with a sympathetic click of the tongue. "That sucks. Why's he trying to get into the Rangers anyway?"

I sighed. "It's his childhood dream. You know, the goal of his life. Other kids wanted to be firemen or astronauts. He wanted to be a Texas Ranger."

"Yeah, but he's a big boy now. Doesn't he have other better goals at this point?"

"No," I answered shortly.

I could feel her looking at me again, but I didn't say anything more. I didn't quite know how to say that although Colin himself felt that a career change and move would not interfere with a potential relationship, I was not so sanguine. That even though I couldn't bring myself to discourage his career aspirations to his face, secretly I was hoping he would fail his tests so spectacularly that future applicants would be warned against "pulling a Colin." And that even as I hoped for it, I knew that he wouldn't. There were few people as competent. Now I found myself in the completely unbelievable position of having two fairly spectacular men interested in me, and the worst part of it was that I had no idea what I wanted to do about it.

Fortunately, we arrived at our destination before Kyla could probe any further. I pulled into the parking lot of the Sand Creek Feed and Supply, a long, low building with a tin roof and two doors, one an open double-wide set of sliding doors that you could literally drive a truck through, and the other a more traditional size. No one was visible on the feed side, so I led the way through the smaller door.

This half of the Feed and Supply was a tack store that looked as though a small and surprisingly clean rodeo had set up inside and then exploded. Half a dozen saddles topped an assortment of sawhorses, which were jammed between racks of jeans, jackets, and work gloves. Bridles, bits, ropes, and other gear hung in random order from hooks on rough-hewn wood paneling. One corner was devoted to a diverse selection of cowboy boots, including an incredibly ornate pair in ostrich leather with a distinctive pattern of bumps and an equally distinctive price tag. I breathed in the clean smell of new leather and denim with pleasure.

Kyla, to my surprise, looked completely disgusted. Following her gaze, I saw the reason. Near the cash register, Carl Cress lounged against the counter and next to him stood Eddy Cranny. Eddy saw us enter and now stood as stiff as an ROTC cadet getting dressed down by a general. Carl hadn't noticed. He was leaning on one elbow chatting up the cashier, a middle-aged woman wearing too much eye shadow who was twirling a strand of dyed auburn hair and giggling. Kyla moved forward, a barracuda gliding toward her prey, and I followed, reluctant to participate in a confrontation in a feed store but also

17

unwilling to abandon my cousin. Or, more accurately, unwilling to let Kyla loose on Eddy unsupervised.

"Aren't you bad, Carl?" the cashier said in a breathy, teasing voice. "You didn't really."

"I surely did. Had my Mexicans take 'er apart and load the pieces on my flatbed. Told the buyer it was seasoned lumber. That warn't no lie, neither. Not my fault the fool never thought to take a look to see just how seasoned it was."

Carl threw back his head and laughed, a big genuine laugh, the kind that made other people laugh with him even if they hadn't heard the joke, or as in this case, only if they hadn't heard the joke. He had, however, inadvertently managed to divert Kyla from Eddy. She swerved and stopped right behind Carl's left shoulder.

"What fool are we talking about, Carl?" she asked loudly. "Not my uncle Kel, right?"

He jumped and turned, swallowing his laughter with a gulp. "Why, girls. Nice to see you. Everyone over at your place recovered from this morning?"

"More or less," I answered, trying to nip that particular topic in the bud. I didn't want Ruby June's private business spilled all over the feed store like a torn sack of grain.

Kyla wasn't going to allow herself to be distracted. "Who'd you sell old lumber to, Carl?" she asked again.

Carl's eyes darted back and forth in shifty little twitches.

Kyla slammed her fist down onto the counter, making us all jump.

The cashier gave another giggle, this one considerably higher than her previous offerings, and said, "Carl's been con-

18

tracting out at the racecourse. They're putting up new stands. Nothin' to do with Kel Shore, right Carl?"

Kyla's smile was icy. "Oh, I see. So you're selling inferior materials to a public venue where people's lives will depend on the soundness of the construction? Is that it?"

"Whoa, whoa. You got entirely the wrong idea," Carl protested, holding up his hands. His eyes had finally settled, and I knew the lie would be a good one. "One of my friends is puttin' up a hot dog stand out there is all. That lumber is plenty good enough for that, and anyways I'm just repaying him for some shifty dealing he did with me a while back. It's just good fun between the two of us. Nothin' at all for you pretty ladies to worry about, and I surely wouldn't do nothing illegal. Y'all know me." He grinned at us and winked.

Kyla made a sound like the one used by the monster in all the best horror movies just before it attacked and ate one of the minor characters. My attention, however, was still on the cashier, who looked confused and worried, which made me suspect the hot dog stand had not figured into the original story. Carl was already edging away.

"Well, if you ladies will excuse us, me and Eddy will just be getting on with our business," he said.

Kyla remained motionless as Carl passed, his cowboy boots loud on the plywood floor, but when Eddy attempted to follow, she stepped into his path, blocking his way.

Keeping her voice low, she said, "I heard about what you did to Ruby June this morning, you ugly little piece of shit. I suggest you go home, pack your things, and clear out of this town permanently."

Eddy's eyes flickered away nervously. "But I didn't mean . . ."

Kyla cut him off. "I don't give a rat's ass what kind of excuses you've got. But you better believe that if I ever hear you hit Ruby June again, I will personally hunt you down and put a bullet in your head." She emphasized her point by poking him hard in the chest as she said each of the last three words.

Eddy reeled back a couple of paces, then scuttled sideways between a rack of jeans and a saddle display and followed Carl out the door with a single frightened backward glance.

The cashier gave Kyla an approving if somewhat nervous smile. "Those Crannys have always been a mean bunch, but I'm sorry to hear Eddy's turning out that way. He never seemed quite like the rest, but I guess snakes don't breed kittens, do they?" She clicked her tongue, then added, "So, what can I do for y'all today?"

Ten minutes later, we drove away with thirty sacks of feed cubes in the bed of the pickup and a bad attitude in the cab. I signaled left and turned very slowly at the corner of the town square, conscious that we'd had to leave the tailgate of the pickup open to accommodate the load.

"I can't decide which one of them I want to kill most," Kyla fumed.

"You gave Eddy a good scare," I consoled her. "Now it's up to Ruby June."

"I suppose. Do you think she'll actually kick him out?"

"I'm not sure she means to." I thought back to the conversation I'd had with Ruby June, feeling as though I'd missed something important. "It's weird—she wasn't nearly mad enough about being hit. She kept making excuses for him."

Kyla was silent for a moment, then she said, "Why the

hell would she put up with him? It's not like she's used to see-ing anything like that at home. She ought to know better."

"I can't tell you—I've never understood it. It's sad, but I see it at school more than you'd think. A nice girl taking up with some creepy loser and then taking his jealousy and abuse. Instead of her helping him away from a bad element and onto a better future, he usually drags her down, cuts her off from her friends, and destroys her self-confidence. It's terrible."

Kyla, who was a dedicated backseat driver, took her eyes from the road to stare at me. "You see it? Why don't you do something about it?"

I shrugged. It was a teacher's eternal dilemma. "Do what? Unless I can tell there's been physical abuse, I have no author-ity whatsoever. Every year I do my classic 'come to me if you need help' spiel and run through how to identify abusive rela-tionships. If the girl is one of my students, I'll call her aside and talk to her, especially if her grades are slipping."

"And? What does she say?"

I slipped into my breathless high-pitched sixteen-year-old girl voice, "You don't understand, Ms. Shore. He's not like that. He's had it hard. He's wonderful."

Returning to my normal voice, I added, "The only thing they're right about is that I don't understand. I guess for some of these girls, having an abusive boyfriend is better than hav-ing no boyfriend at all."

"But Ruby June? She was always such a happy little kid. She doesn't need her own pet asshole."

"No. But I don't think there's much that we can do about it. It's her life. If we're lucky, she'll figure it out before Kel kills Eddy. Anyway, that's not the biggest problem here right now."

"It's not?"

I shook my head. "Carl Cress."

"What a weasel."

"Worse than that. I'm positive he was lying about the hot dog stand. He probably did sell inferior lumber to the racetrack. Plus, did you see his face when you asked him if he was ripping off Kel? He looked like a dog that just got caught drinking out of the toilet bowl."

"That's just his normal expression," said Kyla automatically. "But you're probably right. What are we going to do about it?"

I considered as I made another turn. "You want to go out to the racetrack?"

The narrow road leading to the R. "Blackie" Roberts Memorial Fairgrounds and Racetrack had been freshly paved with glistening black asphalt and the acrid smell permeated the truck. Loose gravel pinged off the undercarriage with a sound like marbles falling on a pie plate. I was glad we were driving the ranch truck, which could only be improved by splashes of hot tar, rather than my little blue Honda. Out here, Thanksgiving had been skipped altogether. Pairs of Christmas wreaths lined the road in preparation for the weekend's festivities, interspersed with candy canes and wire deer dripping with lights. However, as we drew closer, even Christmas gave way to complete chaos.

In one corner of the parking lot, a giant yellow bulldozer pushed gravel from a massive pile onto a newly mown field to extend the available parking. White caliche dust billowed around it like smoke and coated everything downwind. Near the rodeo stands, workers were assembling large portable animal pens, while two men herded a dozen protesting goats into one of the new corrals. On the other side of the stands, the white fence surrounding the racetrack gleamed in the sunlight, the rich loam on the newly smoothed oval track looking as soft and deep as a featherbed. All around, the air was filled with shouts in both English and Spanish, punctuated by the frequent staccato bursts of a power hammer.

Kyla and I parked and then walked along the edge of the lot, trying to avoid the dust thrown up by the bulldozer. As we passed a pen containing a pair of enormous white Brahman bulls, a young man wearing worn jeans and a cowboy hat glanced our way. I guessed him to be in his early twenties and definitely heterosexual if his second and overtly appreciative look at Kyla was any indication. He caught my eye, realized he was staring, and blushed.

"You all might not want to get too close to them," he suggested, still looking at Kyla. He indicated the bulls with a lift of his chin.

Kyla frowned. "Why not? They're in a cage."

He grinned. "They only stay there because they don't know they could bust out as easy as a hot knife through butter."

"Why put them there, then?" I asked with some concern.

He shrugged. "They have to go somewhere."

One of the big white animals lifted its head, liquid black eyes looking expressionlessly in our direction. I began backing away. Kyla on the other hand, jutted out her jaw and stared back at it.

"Hey, can you tell us where the hot dog stand is?" I asked.

This temporarily distracted Kyla from the bull, and the

cowboy from Kyla. The cowboy frowned for a moment, then answered, "There's a bunch of small buildings going up around the rodeo arena over there." He pointed, and added, "Maybe it's one of them."

"Thanks," I said, and grabbed Kyla's arm.

"What's your hurry?" she asked as we made our way through the pens and crossed the dusty field to the arena.

"Just not in the mood to be gored and trampled today."

"He was just yanking our chain. Those cows weren't going to break out and charge us."

I blinked. "Those aren't cows. They're bulls. Exceptionally large bulls."

"Cows, bulls, whatever."

I thought about trying to explain the difference, then figured the chances that Kyla would wander around the fairgrounds provoking animals in their pens were really low and decided to let it go.

As we approached the stands, we could see a half dozen ramshackle booths. A couple had been painted sometime recently, the rest remained weatherworn. All of them looked as though they had been slapped together from used lumber, and I found myself relaxing a little.

"Maybe Carl wasn't lying after all. Or at least not about the old wood," I said.

Kyla glanced at one of the signs, then stopped. "Fried Oreos. What the hell?"

I turned and read the freshly painted sign aloud, "'Fried Oreos, fried Twinkies, funnel cakes, sausage on a stick.'" I grinned. "On a stick! All food is better on a stick. Wish they were open now."

24

She looked appalled. "I'm judging you right now. Tell me you wouldn't actually eat any of that."

"Of course not," I lied, giving what I hoped was a convincing little laugh and thinking I would have to ditch her tonight when we came to watch the rodeo.

Kyla put her hands on her hips and looked around. "They're really going all out this year aren't they? I don't remember all this stuff when we were here last time."

"You haven't been here in at least five years. Plus the race-track is new," I reminded her. "But you're right, I don't remember them ever having a rodeo over Thanksgiving before. Looks like it's going to be fun."

She shot me a glance. "Fun. Yeah, right. Anyway, I'm starving. Let's go back."

We returned to the parking lot and stopped dead in our tracks.

A goat perched atop the mound of feed sacks in the bed of the red ranch truck and now appeared to be intent on chewing her way to the bottom.

I gave a shout and ran forward, waving my arms. The goat raised her head briefly, golden eyes with their odd horizontal pupils taking me in and then dismissing me. She raised a cloven hoof to liberate another few cubes from the torn sack and took one between delicate lips.

"How in the world did it get up there?" asked Kyla as she came up beside me. She looked around as though searching for a stepladder.

"Jumped. Goats can get into anything. I've seen them in trees. Besides, the tailgate is down."

I hoisted myself onto the pickup bed and then climbed

onto the mound of feed sacks. Face-to-face, the goat seemed larger and more solid than she had from the ground. She certainly was not at all bothered by my presence. I waved my arms again but got less response than she would have paid to a horsefly. I reached out and grabbed one of the curved horns and pulled gently at first, then as hard as I could. The goat shook me off with a nonchalant toss of her head and took another cube.

Kyla started to laugh. "Goat one, Jocelyn zero."

"Very helpful. Get up here and help me push."

"Yeah, right," she said, making no move. "Who do you think he belongs to?"

"She," I corrected.

"How can you tell? No, never mind, I don't want to know. What if we just get in the truck and start driving? Either it will hop down or Uncle Kel will be plus one goat."

"Or she'll fall out while we're driving, cause a traffic accident, and get squashed like a bug."

"Yeah, or that."

I climbed back off the truck and rejoined Kyla. "Maybe if we both got up there we could pull her off together."

"No way. I'm not climbing up there and tugging at some strange goat."

I gave her an exasperated glance. "Well, what do you suggest?"

A voice behind us spoke.

"Morning, ladies. Having trouble?"

We turned. Like many of the men working on the grounds, the man behind us wore jeans, a cowboy hat, and boots. Unlike most of them, his shirt was crisp and pressed, he was about our age, and he was, if not exactly handsome, then at least very nice looking. Kyla removed her hands from her hips, straightened visibly, and produced a dazzling smile.

"Yes, I'd like to register a complaint. This goat is bothering us," she answered.

He laughed and gave her a frankly admiring glance. "We can't have that."

He turned, put two fingers to his lips, and produced an ear-splitting whistle. At the sound, half a dozen assorted workmen and cowboys raised their heads. He beckoned to one of them and gestured to our pickup.

Within a few moments, a trio of men in boots arrived and slipped a rope around the goat's neck without any fuss. She made one bleat of protest, then accepted defeat with resignation and allowed herself to be led away.

Our new friend slapped the last cowboy on the shoulder as he passed and turned his attention back to us. Or rather, turned his attention back to Kyla. I might as well have been the goat.

"T. J. Knoller," he said, extending his hand to her.

She grasped it firmly and squeezed. His eyes widened in surprise, not quite watering, but close. Kyla didn't believe in limp, feminine handshakes.

"Kyla Shore," she said, smiling up at him through long lashes.

"I'm going to take a wild guess and say you are not a ranch-to-ranch feed salesman."

"You're a sharp one. I'm just visiting family."

"Shore," he repeated. "You a relative of Kel Shore over at the Smoke Quartz?"

"He's my uncle."

Not "our" uncle, I noticed. I also noticed that she had shifted her weight subtly to edge in front of me. Not that she needed to have bothered. T.J.'s eyes had not left her face.

"Then we're neighbors!" he said. "I own the Bar Double K. Our places meet up on the north side. Well, my north side. Kel's south."

"I've seen your gates," I said, remembering. "They're beautiful."

This was no more than the truth. The gates were enormous, made of ornately scrolled wrought iron hung between massive stone pillars and topped with two distinctive Ks under a single bar. I'd noticed them yesterday as I drove by.

He looked pleased. "I put those in myself a couple of months back. Cost a fortune, but they'll last a lifetime. Or three."

Kyla wasn't interested in gates or in my opinions. "What's your story? You're not in the rodeo, are you?"

His eyes crinkled. "I'm in everything around here, or I try to be. Today, it's horses. Come take a look."

He made an elaborate gesture and Kyla joined him instantly, leaving me to trail behind or not, as I chose. I glanced at my watch, then shrugged and followed. We recrossed the parking lot, this time in the direction of the racetrack rather than the rodeo stands. Beyond the oval track, the new grandstands gleamed in the sun: rows and rows of aluminum benches lined the concrete risers stretching up about three stories to end in a small glass-enclosed press box. Here, too, workmen were busy painting and hammering, giving an overall impression of frantic last-minute activity. I thought it was probably not a good sign to have this much construction occurring on the day before Thanksgiving, only two days before the big race.

Stopping at the fence, we could see the starting gates on the opposite side, where two horsemen were just loping across the finish line at an easy pace.

Raising fingers to lips, T.J. produced another painfully piercing whistle and one of the riders looked up. With a word to his companion, the two of them trotted to where we waited. I wondered if he always whistled to people as though they were dogs.

"You know them?" Kyla asked, glancing up at T.J. She was standing close enough to him that her long hair brushed his shoulder. Somehow, I didn't think he minded.

"Sure do. You're looking at the winner of Friday's big race."

Up close, the horses were larger and the men smaller than they'd looked from a distance. The rider of the first horse stopped inches from the fence, a lean man in his fifties riding a patient gelding with a dull yellow coat and black mane and tail. T.J. leaned over the railing and caressed the velvet black nose, running an affectionate hand around the jaw and ending in a pat on the neck.

Even my inexperienced eye could see the other horse was in a different class altogether. He danced to a stop beside his companion, a glossy rich bay with a single white forefoot and an aura of suppressed energy. His rider, too, was younger than the other man by twenty years, and at first glance seemed little more than a diminutive boy. Closer inspection, however, showed he was neither as young nor as fragile as he looked at a distance. The hands that gripped the reins were all sinew and muscle, and he had an intense, confident air.

"Like you ladies to meet Glen Blackman and Travis Arledge. Glen's my trainer and Travis here is the best jockey this side of . . . well, anywhere. Glen, Travis, want you to meet a couple of friends. Kyla Shore and . . ." T.J. frowned and turned to me, finally realizing he didn't yet know my name.

"Jocelyn Shore," I supplied.

"Her sister, Jocelyn," T.J. finished.

"We're not sisters," said Kyla quickly. "Cousins."

"You're kidding. Really?" T.J. looked from Kyla to me and back again.

I could see Kyla stiffening with irritation at being reminded of the resemblance between us.

"So these are your horses?" I changed the subject.

T.J. was easily diverted. "Yep. Well, Double is. Double Trouble, or rather Bar Double K Double Trouble, if you want to be formal." He gestured to the bay with his chin. "How's he doing today, Glen?"

The older man gave a considering nod. "He's ready. It was all Travis could do to hold him in."

The younger man nodded in agreement, but said nothing.

"You're racing Friday?" I asked.

He nodded again, but it was T.J. who answered. "Fourth race. The Cornucopia Stakes. Biggest purse in the state. Two hundred thousand dollars to the winner alone."

"Two hundred thousand? Wow." Kyla sounded impressed.

"Isn't that unusually large?" I asked. Not that I knew much about racing, but it sounded like a lot of money, especially in a tiny place like Sand Creek.

"Too large, if you ask me," said the older man on the buckskin.

30

T.J. shook his head. "There's no such thing as too large when it comes to diamonds or piles of cash. Back me up here, ladies."

"I like this guy," Kyla said with approval.

T.J. grinned and went on. "Glen's just got his panties in a twist because that kind of prize draws some out-of-state competition."

Glen managed to produce a weak smile at his boss's joke. Or at least he got the corners of his mouth to turn up a bit. It looked like it hurt. "I've seen the field. There's some good horses."

"I've seen the field, too. The only one that might come close is Big Bender, and he'll be lucky if he gets close enough to eat Double's dust."

The jockey Travis broke in. "It ain't the competition, it's the owners and jockeys." His voice was surprisingly deep coming from such a small chest. "That's enough money to make some folks think a risk or two might be worth it."

"You had any more phone calls?" asked T.J. sharply.

"No, sir," said Travis.

"Well, then, we just keep our eyes open and carry on." T.J. waved a dismissive hand at them, and they both nodded to us, then turned and loped away. Double Trouble's coat gleamed in the sun, his gait effortless and joyful as his hoofs threw up little puffs of dirt from the soft track.

T.J. frowned after them for a moment and then turned back to us. "Just like a couple of old women, worrying about every little thing. I tell you straight up, you want to make some money tomorrow, put a bet on Double."

"Has Travis really been getting threatening phone calls?"

31

I asked, as we began walking back to the parking lot. "That seems pretty serious."

"Not threats," said T.J. "Bribes. Some son of a . . . son of a gun called him up and offered him a thousand dollars to throw the race. Which was just ridiculous, because Travis gets ten percent of the prize money if he wins. Not to mention, a jockey is only as good as his reputation. A hint that he's bribable would end his career."

"What are you going to do about it?" asked Kyla. "Were you able to track the caller?"

"No. The number showed as 'unavailable.' I suppose we could have called someone, maybe the police, maybe the racing commission, but it didn't seem worth it. I trust Travis. He's ridden for me for a year now and before that he rode out of Ruidoso and Albuquerque. Has a sterling reputation."

"It must be a pretty limited pool of suspects, though. How many horses run in a race?"

"Eight in the Cornucopia Stakes."

"So seven possibilities?"

He laughed. "Hardly. Seven plus about seven hundred. The prize money in a race is only the teaser. The real money is in the private betting."

I spoke up. "You're kidding, right? Nobody really bets more than two hundred thousand dollars on races around here, do they?"

"You'd be surprised," T.J. answered. "And you have to understand that the prize money is only available to the eight owners. And even that's not all that much if you take into account the expense of keeping and training a horse, of paying the rider, of transport and entry fees. No, it's the side bets where everybody else gets in on the action. A thousand-dollar bribe? That's from some idiot who's bet the farm on an outsider and is panicking."

"So how about you? Are you betting on the side?" asked Kyla. "And how do you do that?"

"Of course not. That would be illegal," he said virtuously, then gave her a big wink. "No, I just meant for you all to put a twenty on Double in the pari-mutuel. They'll be taking bets at the windows under the stands Friday. He'll be the favorite, so you won't get much, but it makes watching the races exciting."

"Okay, but you better be right if I'm risking twenty big ones."

He grinned. "It's no risk. Just easy money. You'll probably make a dollar fifty. Hey, tell you what, I'm having a party at my place to celebrate the win on Friday evening. Why don't you come by? Both of you," he added as an afterthought.

"We'll be there. What time?" said Kyla instantly.

"What if you don't win?" I asked at the same time.

They both glared at me.

"Of course he'll win," said Kyla, who apparently based her betting strategy on the well-known if unproven horse-speed-to-owner-attractiveness correlation.

T.J. gave her an approving glance. "He'll win all right, but the party's on regardless, win or lose, rain or shine. Barbecue and beer, four o'clock," he said, then added generously, "All y'all are invited of course." By which I assumed he meant everyone in the family. Of course he couldn't have known this was a family reunion weekend. I pictured thirty of us descending on his home and devouring his supplies like locusts in a wheat field.

"We'll be there," Kyla repeated, and gave me a withering glance as though she could read my mind.

T.J. parted from us and took himself off to talk with some of his men. Kyla stared after his departing figure a little longer than necessary, and we returned to the truck and stopped abruptly. The goat was back, staring down at us from atop the pile of feed sacks with mocking yellow eyes, chewing as fast as she could. While Kyla bent double with laughter, I turned on my heel and went looking for either a cowboy or a gun, whichever came first. Fortunately for the goat, I found a cowboy, and in a remarkably short amount of time we were heading back toward town, minus the goat and half a sack of feed.

Kyla looked pleased with herself and the world in general.

"He seems really nice," she said thoughtfully.

"The goat?" I asked, to annoy her. "I told you it was a female."

"T.J., you idiot."

"You just liked his comment about money and diamonds."

"Yes, I did," she said, not at all put out.

"I hate to burst your bubble, but this is our family reunion weekend. I'm pretty sure we have stuff planned for Friday."

"Don't be stupid. I'm sure we can slip over to T.J.'s for a couple of hours. None of them will even miss us."

I tried another tack. "I thought you were dating Sherman the Vermin."

"So what? It's okay for you to have two boyfriends, but not me? Besides, we're just going for barbecue, and the last time I checked, eating ain't cheating."

I laughed out loud. "Where did you hear that? I know you don't listen to country music."

Her phone rang, and she pulled it out of her purse with a frown. "I don't recognize this number," she said, and started to put it back.

"Just answer it," I said. "It might be Kel wondering where we are with his truck."

It was Kel, but he wasn't calling about the truck.

Kyla said a few words, then hung up. "Ruby June is missing."

Chapter 2

RENDEZVOUS AND RODEOS

Ruby June had not returned by the time Kyla and I joined Kel and Elaine in the kitchen of the ranch house. Kel sat at the big scratched wooden table with his head in his hands, while Elaine busied herself baking pumpkin muffins. She had one batch in the oven already and the golden spicy smell filled the whole house. She looked up eagerly when we walked in, but then lowered her eyes in disappointment. We were not who she wanted to see walking through the door, but I hardly thought she needed to be worrying. Between Ruby June's well-meaning but overbearing father and her abusive but weak husband, who could blame her for refusing to answer her phone for a few hours? Like any woman, I was capable of envisioning the spectrum of possibilities, ranging from the mundane (she'd gone shopping) to the horrific (a serial killer had chopped her into little pieces and was planning to deep-fry and serve her on sticks at a food booth), but I figured it was probably something from the former end of the scale.

"She probably went to see one of her friends," I suggested to Uncle Kel, who gave me a baleful glance, then rose and began pacing, his heavy work boots stumping hollowly on the wood floor.

"What if she didn't? What if that inbred little weasel took her somewhere? I should have killed him when I had the chance." Kel bit the words off as though they tasted bitter.

"We saw Eddy at the feed store. He was heading somewhere with Carl. I don't think he'd have had time to go back and kidnap Ruby June."

Kel just gave me a jaded look and kept pacing. It was odd seeing him doing anything other than working. He'd been running the ranch ever since Uncle Herman, at the age of eighty-five, had fallen off the back of the pickup truck and broken his leg. Uncle Herman, having no children of his own and finally forced to slow down, had turned over the ranch to his nephew Kel. This could have caused hard feelings between Kel and his brothers, but neither my father nor Kyla's had any interest in the ranching life and approved the transition wholeheartedly. At the time, family rumor had it that the ranch was inches away from foreclosure, and no one wanted Herman to lose his land. Kel and Elaine had turned things around by sheer force of personality and the willingness to work sixteen-hour days. One of the first things they'd done was build a few small cabins complete with electricity and plumbing. In the spring and summer, they ran the place as a dude ranch. In the fall, they repurposed it into a hunting lease where they charged fairly steep weekly rates for access to the ranch's dove, deer, and quail populations. They were probably losing a considerable sum by opening the place up to relatives for Thanksgiving weekend, but I suppose it wasn't every day that the patriarch of the family turned ninety-five.

"We ran into a neighbor of yours out at the racetrack," I said, trying to take Kel's mind away from his daughter. "Seems like a nice guy."

The tactic worked, but not in the way I'd expected. Kel stopped in midstride, his head snapping up like wolf scenting blood on the wind.

"Which neighbor?" he asked. "Not that son of a bitch Knoller?"

I glanced at Kyla, who'd been fishing in the refrigerator for a beer. She straightened, looking puzzled.

"Yeah, why? He invited us to his place for a post-race party," she answered.

A muscle worked in Kel's jaw. Elaine put her mixing bowl down.

"Kel," she said as a warning. "Just take a breath. The girls don't know anything about all that, and there's no reason they should."

"There's every reason they should! That bastard is trying to steal my land. I won't have him trying to get at my family."

"What do you mean?" I asked.

Elaine sighed. "Fence wars. Our land touches the Bar Double K along Sand Creek. When T.J. took over and started putting up new fences, he crossed the creek and scooped up a long narrow strip of about two hundred acres. Kel tried to get him to reset his posts but he refused."

"He can't do that, can he?" I asked. "Aren't there records or deeds or something?"

"The ranches are both so old, the descriptions are a bit

vague. T.J. claims Sand Creek shifted in its banks since the original deeds were laid out and the land is his. We claim otherwise. We might have been able to settle it, but somehow some fences got cut." Here she threw Kel a glance. "And now he's suing."

"Suing? You're kidding me."

"Wish I was. The damages to the fence are the least of it. If we try to avoid the court costs by settling, it means admitting that the land was his to put the fence on in the first place."

"We're not settling!" Kel said. "Never. That son of a bitch can go—"

"Right," I cut him off. "We get it. But why does he want that land all of a sudden anyway? Haven't you been neighbors for years?"

Elaine pulled a tin of muffins out of the oven and set it on the stove top to cool. "Yes and no. Our families have been neighbors since the thirties, but old Tom Knoller passed away a couple of years ago, and T.J. inherited and started making changes."

"He's a thief and a liar, and his old man would be spinning in his grave if he knew," said Kel. "You girls stay away from him."

I saw Kyla's expression and decided it was time for another change of topic. The best way to guarantee that Kyla would do something was to forbid it. As I was casting around for a new subject though, the thump of rubber on wood heralded the arrival of Uncle Herman's cane, followed by the man himself.

Herman Shore was ninety-five years old. In his youth, he'd been a big man, taller even than Kel, but age had finally stooped his shoulders and the fall that had broken his leg had given him a permanent limp. The paper-thin skin on his hands reminded me of the transparent sheets of onionskin that people slip into wedding invitations, but the expression in his eyes was as alert as that of his nephew. He might have turned over the daily management of the ranch to Kel and Elaine, but he was still a force to be reckoned with and went to some pains to assert his authority at regular intervals. It was hardly his fault that between his thick glasses and his balding head, he looked like a stuffed frog.

"Uncle Herman!" I said with a smile, rising to give him a hug.

He grinned and patted my shoulder. "Well look at you. Little Annie Oakley and her faithful sidekick Grumpy, all grown up."

I could almost feel Kyla's quiver of indignation behind me and carefully did not turn around. "Jocelyn and Kyla," I reminded him gently. "I'm Keith's daughter, remember? And Kyla is Kyle's daughter."

He gave a snort. "Darlin', I know who you are. I'm not senile yet." He stumped forward a few steps and took a pumpkin muffin from the tin, then gave his nephew a sharp glance. "What's all the commotion about, son? I could hear you jabbering all the way across the yard."

"The girls ran into T. J. Knoller today, Uncle Herman," said Elaine quickly. "We were just explaining about the lawsuit to them."

Herman gave an odd cackle, reminiscent either of a psycho in a slasher flick or an extra large chicken. I said a quick prayer that certain genetic characteristics would not flow down to my twig on the branch of the family tree.

"You don't need to worry about that," he said. "I've taken care of it."

Kel's eyes widened in alarm. "What do you mean? What have you done?"

"Never you mind. After Friday, you won't have anything to worry about from that smart puppy. I've docked his tail for him—he just doesn't know it yet."

The mixture of anxiety and wary hope that rippled through both Kel and Elaine was painful to watch. For one thing, it made me realize just how bad this lawsuit must be, and I wondered if T. J. Knoller had any idea of the stress he was creating for his neighbors. He'd seemed so friendly, had never even flinched when he realized who we were, and had invited us to his party as persuasively as possible. Perhaps he considered the lawsuit just business, something unpleasant but necessary that need not interfere with relationships between friends and neighbors. If so, he was being woefully naïve, although it was not the first time I'd run across that attitude.

Kyla must have been thinking along the same lines. "Maybe he's trying to make a peace offering by inviting us over."

"Or maybe he's just trying to use you to get some inside information, feel you out, see if we're about to settle," snapped Kel.

"I don't think that's why he invited me," said Kyla with what I considered to be an offensive amount of smugness. "But if it is, he'll be disappointed. We can't tell him anything because we don't know anything."

"And because you won't be going," Kel reminded her.

"Yeah, about that," she began.

I quickly changed the subject. "Anyway, who else is coming this afternoon? I know Will and Sam are due in around four."

Will and Sam were my younger brothers who both lived in California. I hadn't seen either one of them in months and was looking forward to their arrival.

"Wonderful," answered Elaine. "It's just too bad your parents couldn't make it."

My parents both served in the diplomatic service, and as a result, I had spent my childhood growing up in a variety of cities in France, Italy, and Spain, before they'd moved to Austin to let the three of us have an American high school experience and spend a few years near our father's family. After I'd graduated, they'd returned to Europe and for the last two years they had been stationed in Paris, much to the delight of my very French mother, who did not quite understand why my brothers and I wanted to live anywhere else.

I shrugged. "They couldn't get away. The French have holidays every five minutes, but they don't celebrate Thanksgiving. Anyway, I think my folks are planning a trip to Austin over the Christmas break, and I'm sure they'll come out here to see you then."

"And my folks have gone over to the dark side," said Kyla.

Which meant they were visiting her mother's relatives in Phoenix. For reasons unknown to me, Kyla disliked her mother's side of the family with an intensity and passion she usually reserved for pedophiles and boy bands.

Elaine nodded, her mind obviously elsewhere. Kel seemed

equally distracted and tense. For whatever reason, they seemed excessively concerned about the whereabouts of Ruby June, who could hardly have been gone more than a couple of hours. Remembering how small she'd looked when we left her at her house, I felt a twinge of unease myself.

As the afternoon wore on, the Shores began streaming onto the ranch. The first to arrive were a set of second cousins from San Antonio who rolled up in an RV the size of a convenience store and strategically parked directly in front of the gate. Aunt Elaine took one look and gave a groan.

"They can't park there. They'll be blocking everyone."

"I'll go," I volunteered.

I hurried out to meet them as the side door opened and at least six kids under the age of ten poured out of the RV. They hit the dirt running and scattered like cockroaches as a heavy-set woman swung herself down from the cab with surprising agility and thumped to the ground like a jumbo-size gymnast sticking a landing.

"Aunt Gladys!" I said.

"Baby doll!" she boomed, enfolding me in a bear hug and squashing me into her massive bosom. I managed to turn my head to the side just in time to avoid being smothered. Death by boobage was always a risk when my relatives were around.

I returned the hug, then wriggled free with some difficulty. "Aunt Elaine wants you to park over on that side of the house," I said, pointing.

"Scotty! D'you hear that?" she shouted. Her voice had a resonance that James Earl Jones might have envied.

43

Her husband, just as hefty and good humored as herself, obediently returned to the RV and started the engine. The vehicle lurched forward as a slender girl appeared in the side door. She clutched at the doorjamb, flailed a little, and then more or less fell out onto the dirt. Gladys gave a little cry and rushed forward.

"Okra, honey, are you all right?"

I knew I had not heard that right. I watched as Gladys picked up the girl, set her on her feet, and brushed her off as though she'd been a toddler instead of a full-size teenager. If she didn't have any neck injuries from the fall, she probably had them by the time her mom was done with her. Gladys kept an arm around her shoulders and dragged her over to where I stood.

"Okra, you remember your cousin Jocelyn, right?"

There was that name again. What was she really saying? Although the girl was less than half Gladys's width, she was fully as tall, which meant she topped me by an inch or so. I guessed she was in her late teens, probably almost Ruby June's age. The resemblance ended there, though. This girl had obscured what I guessed was a very pretty face with purple eye shadow, heavy kohl eyeliner, and both an eyebrow and a nose piercing. She'd also cropped her hair short, dyed it raven black, and gelled it into spikes. Overall, she reminded me of a terminally depressed porcupine.

I smiled at her. "I know we've seen each other before, but I'm sorry—I'm just not catching your name."

Aunt Gladys laughed, another big booming sound. "Her name's Opal, but she said she didn't want to be called that anymore. So the kids started calling her Okra, and it sort of stuck."

A dull flush crept under the girl's pale skin. "Where's Ruby June?" she asked me, breaking free of her mother's grasp.

I hesitated, not quite sure how to respond. In that instant, we heard a shout, followed by a high-pitched squeal. Gladys snapped to attention like a bird dog scenting a quail.

She shouted, "Eric! Austin! You drop that right now!" and thundered away like a vengeful freight train, leaving me alone with my young relative.

We looked at each other.

"Where's Ruby June?" she repeated.

"We're not sure," I answered. "She and Eddy had a fight, and she left."

"But she promised . . . she said I could stay with her." The protest burst out, the underlying wail forced back at the last minute. Despite her appearance, this was a girl who had to work hard to maintain a façade of apathy. I looked at her with a little more interest.

"So what do you like to be called?" I asked her.

She shrugged, eyes down. "It doesn't matter," she muttered.

"It would matter to me. Unless you like being called Okra?"

The flash of her dark eyes was answer enough.

"So what do your friends call you?"

"I don't have any friends." This was said in a tone of bitter defiance.

I laughed at that, and she glanced up at me, startled. She'd probably expected the usual adult patronizing protests and fake encouragement.

"Not true. You've already told me you have at least one

45

friend—Ruby June. I bet you have a couple of others. But I'll call you Okra if that's what you want."

The desire to be dark and brooding warred with the deeper need not to appear ridiculous.

"Kris," she finally said.

"Is that your middle name?"

"Kristine is." Then she added with a sigh, "With a K."

Opal Kristine. O.K. One short step to Okra, especially for a girl with brothers. Parents could be so cruel.

"So who are all those kids?" I asked, staring across the yard to where Aunt Gladys was wagging a finger in the faces of four little boys.

"The oldest two are my brothers, who are bad enough. The rest are my nephews. Mom and Dad dragged them along so my sister and her husband could have a few days of peace. I'm supposed to help babysit." The tone in her voice was the one she would have used if she'd said, "I'm supposed to drive burning matchsticks under my fingernails."

"So you arranged to stay with Ruby June," I said, nodding. "Smart."

"You have no idea what they're like. And I don't know why I get punished for my sister's mistakes. I'm not the one who punched out four steaming little crotch droppings in less than six years."

I bit the inside of my cheek. Hard. After a moment, I managed to say, "Well, we're hoping that Ruby June will come back soon. But if not, there's a bed available in the bunkroom in the main house where I'm sleeping. You could always stay there."

She flashed a suspicious look at me and made a noncommittal grunt. As a teenager, and a Goth teenager at that, she was obligated not to appear either eager or grateful. And to be fair, she didn't know anything about me.

"Are you the one who shot that guy?" she asked.

Or maybe she did know something about me. We stared at each other. In a movie, crickets would have chirped.

"Yeah," I finally said.

I no longer felt like laughing. I also didn't know what else to add. Part of me wanted to explain I'd had no choice. Part of me wanted never to have to think about it again, although the shooting still haunted my nightmares. Less often than at first, it was true, but in my sleep I still regularly found myself back in that auditorium watching someone I thought I knew hold a knife to a student's throat. I'd never had a gun at the school either before or since, but I had one that night, and I'd shot him before he could kill her. I had no regrets, at least not about that. Death had not made me stop hating him. Even more, I hated that nothing had been the same for me since that night. I missed my friends, I missed not being "that teacher," and I missed working in a school where memories of violent death did not haunt the halls.

I'm not sure how long I stood there, but Kris was still watching me so it couldn't have been too long. I managed a smile. "Well, think about the bunkroom," I said, and turned away.

She might have said something else, but if so the noise of an approaching engine drowned it out. I looked up and saw a dark green Jeep, powdered white as a geisha's face by caliche dust, rumbling down the road. My heart skipped a little. I couldn't see the driver yet, but I knew who that Jeep belonged to.

Detective Colin Gallagher. We'd met when he'd come to investigate the first unexpected death at my school, which was hardly the most romantic way to begin a relationship. It also hadn't helped that I was dating Alan Stratton. At the time, I'd found the attraction between Colin and myself inexplicable and disturbing; now, I found it . . . what? Inconvenient and disquieting? I had no idea why I was incapable of just enjoying a great guy with headlong abandon, but a big part of me seemed to be waiting for the other shoe to drop. In a way it already had. For whatever reason, apparently I was attracted to men who were determined to uproot my life. Alan still wanted me to move to Dallas. Colin had mentioned in passing that he wouldn't mind returning to West Texas one day, to the small town in which he'd grown up or to one much like it. And now he wanted to join the Texas Rangers, and what would that mean? After a childhood spent moving not only from city to city, but from country to country, I didn't want to be uprooted. I loved Austin. I'd attended high school there, graduated from the University of Texas there, and now had a career, a set of friends, a house, and a fat poodle there. It was home. And although I loved to travel, I always wanted to return to Austin. Not Dallas and not some tiny town in West Texas. But there was no denying there was something pretty amazing between Colin and me.

Parking well away from the gate, Colin hopped out of the Jeep and lifted a hand in greeting. He wore jeans, well-worn cowboy boots, reflective sunglasses, and a black T-shirt. He reached into the Jeep and pulled out a black felt cowboy hat and his gun. I hadn't seen the hat before, but the rest was his normal off-duty wear, the gun as much a part of his clothing as his pants. I'd teased him once about the gun, asking him if he wore it to bed. He'd grinned and told me he'd let me find out for myself. I had to admit, I was sort of looking forward to that. I had never in my life met anyone else who could make my heart race just by standing next to me.

Now, Kris took a step forward and bumped my shoulder. "Who is that?" she asked in a low reverent tone. "Please tell me he's not a relative."

I gave her a stern look. "That is Detective Colin Gallagher of the Austin Police Department. And no, he's not a relative although I don't know why you'd care, since he's at least ten years too old for you. Besides, he's my . . . he's here to see me."

My acerbic tone made no impression, but my words did. Where kindness and generosity had earned me only grudging politeness, having a connection to an admittedly gorgeous man instantly gained me unmistakable . . . if unflatteringly astonished . . . admiration.

"I'm so moving to Austin," she said with a sigh and a faraway look in her eye.

If I'd had a hose, I would have sprayed her with it the same way I did my neighbor's cat when I found it burying its little presents in my garden. Instead I took her shoulders and turned her toward the house.

"Go ask Aunt Elaine about the bunkroom," I said, and gave her a little push.

Colin was just coming in the gate when I reached him. He caught me in his arms and lifted me up against his chest, giving me a gentle kiss before he set me back down again. It was unexpected and all too nice. I immediately forgot what I'd been about to say. He just smiled at me from behind his opaque sunglasses.

"Where's your luggage?" I finally managed, somehow selecting the most inane question from my arsenal.

"Change of plan," he said, glancing behind me. I didn't need to turn to know that there were half a dozen pairs of eyes trained on us. "I decided that it might be quieter if I stayed at a motel in town."

Disappointed, I did not say anything, trying to process what that meant. I could hardly blame him for not wanting to share one of the hunting cabins with a bunch of my male relatives, of course, but if he had to travel back and forth from his hotel, it would mean less time spent together.

"I thought that maybe you'd want to share it with me," he went on, but held up a hand before I could say anything. "That was, of course, before I checked in and saw the decor. The cardboard sign that says, 'Do Not Clean Your Birds in the Sink' is the nicest thing in the room. I'm pretty sure a black light would make that place glow like a jewelry shop in Vegas."

I laughed. "That's so gross. You can't stay there."

"I've been in worse places," he said, then added, "Not many, but a few. It'll be fine."

"No it won't. Look if you don't want to stay here, I know there's a brand-new Motel 6 on the west side of town. It hasn't been open long enough for anyone to have dressed a deer in the tub. Come on in, and we'll call to see if they have a room."

"Hmm. Well, maybe." He looked at me thoughtfully, the smile fading from his face. Taking my hand, he ran his thumb gently over the skin along my wrist, a tiny movement that had a disproportionately large effect on my heart rate. "If there's a vacancy, would you join me?"

I tensed, glancing up and inwardly cursing those reflective sunglasses. I couldn't tell how serious he was. I had not spent the night with him before, and not because I hadn't wanted to. In fact, sometimes it was all I could think about when he was anywhere within fifty yards of me.

"It depends on a couple of things," I said, carefully keeping my tone light. "One, if I sit down, will I stick to anything, and two, will I or won't I be able to clean my birds in the sink?"

He didn't smile. "Jocelyn . . ."

"You know I can't," I said, pulling my hand out of his.

"You're still seeing Stratton." It was not a question. "How'd he feel about me being here this weekend?"

"He didn't like it," I answered shortly.

"Good."

We stared at each other. Then I heard the sound of footsteps on gravel, and turned to see my aunt approaching, a look of welcome on her face. This conversation would have to wait until later.

At the fairgrounds that evening, the halfhearted warmth of the November day cooled from pleasant to frosty as the sun dipped behind the gently rolling hills. The breeze, though soft, stirred through the tree branches, lifted brown leaves from their tenuous grips, and swirled them into rustling piles in the corners. Wisps of chill air slipped through denim and probed beneath shirt collars like wicked little fingers looking for inconvenient places to pinch. Around the rodeo stands, banks of blinding halide stadium lights transformed dusk into noon and threw every clod of dirt in the arena into sharp relief. Beyond that, the fairgrounds twinkled like a vast horizontal Christmas tree, the thousands of multicolored twinkle lights on the vendor stalls and in the trees warring with the sputtering white of fluorescent bulbs pouring from the food booths. The dull bass thump of music played too loudly, and the noise and laughter of several hundred excited attendees filled the crisp air. The anticipation and good humor of the crowd was palpable.

Colin, Kyla, and I walked past the temporary animal pens and rodeo stands to the concession booths. After a few paces, Colin tentatively reached for my hand, a gesture that brought an odd lump to my throat along with the usual small jolt of pleasure. We hadn't had a chance to speak privately since his arrival, but I wasn't sure if it mattered. How much longer would we have moments like this if he got his new job? And did I even want to pursue it? After all, I thought I'd found love less than six months ago with another great guy, and that hadn't worked out very well. My so-called romance with Alan Stratton had faltered after just a few months, leaving me disillusioned and unhappy. Distance had seemed like the problem, but Alan was now making a big-time effort to make things work, and if I were honest, Colin was the real issue with my relationship with Alan. Part of me wanted to say to hell with the future and just savor the present with this amazing man. My inner voice simply asked whether I was in the mood to have my heart chewed up and spit out like a wad of chaw in the jaws of a minor league infielder. I hated that voice.

Colin gave me a curious glance, and I hurriedly squeezed back, then bumped his shoulder with mine. He smiled, reassured, and I shook the voices away.

"I want a sausage on a stick," I announced, catching sight

of a garish sign with a somewhat rude depiction of the food item in question.

Kyla wrinkled her nose. "We just ate," she protested.

"You don't have to eat one. You can get a fried Twinkie instead," I added, thinking that if she did, maybe I could have a bite.

"Yes, when hell freezes over." She was scanning the crowd as we spoke, then perked up. "Look, I see that T.J. guy. You two have fun." Then she was gone.

I glanced after her as she vanished into the crowd, but saw no sign of T.J. She must have her special hot-guy radar turned on. I did not think the situation boded well for Sherman, her current or should I say most recent interest. I made a mental note to quiz her about that later.

Colin blinked. "Not very subtle, but nice of her to give us some time to ourselves," he said.

I gave him a pitying glance. "She's not giving us time to ourselves. She and I met a racehorse owner at the track today. She's giving *him* time to herself."

"Racehorse owner, huh?" He craned his neck, trying to see the man in question.

"And rancher. I think the guy might be loaded." I tugged at his hand and maneuvered us into the short line in front of the food stand. The aroma of greasy sausage and vanilla funnel cakes wafted over us. I thought heaven might very possibly smell like that.

"Is that what Kyla's looking for?" Colin sounded both surprised and disapproving.

"No, I didn't mean it that way." I thought about it for a minute, trying to put it into words. "He's interesting and good-looking. Being well off is just a bonus. She told me a long time ago that just once she'd like to date someone that she wouldn't have to pay alimony to when they got divorced."

"Damn. And I thought cops were cynical."

I laughed at that. "The other thing he has going for him is the irresistible lure of being *verboten*."

"What do you mean?"

I explained about the lawsuit and my uncle's ultimatum. He digested that for a moment, then asked unexpectedly, "Is your uncle always like that?"

I paused, then answered, "More or less, I guess. He used to be a little more easygoing, or at least it seemed that way. Maybe that was just because we were kids, and we didn't see everything. But I do know that when he took over the ranch, he seemed to get a lot more serious and a lot less fun. Why do you ask?"

"I don't know," he said slowly. "It's probably nothing. But I've seen guys with that same look in their eye. They get burned out, overly stressed. And that's when accidents happen."

I glanced up at him, surprised by his tone. The brim of his hat cast a shadow over his eyes, and I couldn't read his expression. I did, however, notice the firm set of his lips, the clean line of his jaw, and the tiny pulse that beat in the hollow of his throat. For a moment, my attention wavered from the topic at hand.

His lips twitched into a smile, and he put his arm around my shoulders. I took the opportunity to slip my arm around his waist, feeling his warmth even through the layers of denim that separated us. He felt too damn good.

With an effort, I focused on his words. "What are you saying? You think Kel is headed for a breakdown?"

"I don't know him well enough to say, and I only saw him for a few minutes this afternoon. But from all you told me about the irritability, the shouting, the demands . . . I don't know. That doesn't seem like good sign. If I worked with him, I'd be telling him to take a vacation."

"He was pretty upset that the police wouldn't start looking for Ruby June. I have to say, it does worry me that she isn't back yet," I said. "There's just not that many places to go here, and Kel has called them all."

"She's an adult, there's no indication of trouble, and she hasn't even been gone a full day. There's not much the police can do. Besides, there's nothing that says she has to be in Sand Creek. She might have gone into Llano or even Austin."

"Except she doesn't have a car. How would she get there?"

He shrugged. "I'm guessing she has a few friends in town who'd either let her stay or who'd loan her a car. It wouldn't be that hard. She'll show up in a day or two when she's ready."

The line moved forward, and we finally reached the booth.

"You want a fried Twinkie, right?" I asked him hopefully.

He pulled out his wallet. "No, I don't. But I will buy you one if you promise not to throw up in my car. Sausage on a stick and a fried Twinkie," he told the kid behind the counter, who obligingly passed him the items wrapped in greasy white paper.

"This is why I like you so much," I said as Colin paid. "Hold my sausage for a minute, okay?"

The Twinkie was everything I could have hoped for. My

first bite sent a puff of powdered sugar into the air, and I closed my eyes in ecstasy.

Colin started laughing, and brushed sugar from my nose. "You look so happy."

"It's even better than I thought it would be. Why are all the good things so bad for you?" I asked. I thought about stuffing the rest of it in my mouth, but instead reluctantly offered it to him.

He shook his head. "Um, no thanks. I would hate to deprive you."

"You can have a bite of the sausage," I offered magnanimously.

"Gee, thanks."

We strolled through the motley assortment of booths, which were selling an odd mix of food, beer, and local crafts. In one, an elderly couple displayed an assortment of crocheted baby blankets and hand-carved wooden toys. In another, a wizened little man, fingers stained brown by years of leatherwork, proudly held up a hand-tooled belt to a portly customer. Even at a distance I could tell the belt in question would never go around that ample waist, but maybe it would end up under the Christmas tree. I tossed the greasy paper from my snacks into a rusting oil drum that served as a trash can and wiped the sugar from my fingers, then noticed Colin scanning the crowd with a wistful expression.

"What's up?" I asked. "You look almost . . . I don't know." I looked at him again. "Sad."

He turned to me and gave a patently fake smile. "It's nothing."

"Oh, come on."

"No, really. I was just thinking how happy and peaceful everything looks. This reminds me so much of my hometown, the way it was when I was a kid. You'd never know anything was wrong or ever would be wrong."

"And is something wrong?"

"When you're a cop, there's always something wrong. There's rumors one of the Mexican drug cartels is working this area. Maybe drugs, almost certainly money laundering."

I looked around incredulously. "You're kidding me, right? Here in Sand Creek? This town is practically Mayberry. It's so small you'd miss it if you blinked."

"It's not that small. It does have both a Walmart and a Dairy Queen after all," he added with a grin, then seeing my expression went on more seriously: "More importantly, it has a racetrack and a sheriff's department stretched too thin. There's some serious money in this county."

I looked at the denim-clad crowd milling past us. "It's well hidden then."

He laughed. "Look, never mind. Forget I said anything. We're here to have a good time."

He extended his hand like a peace offering, and I took it. I wasn't sure he was wrong about Sand Creek, but I still wished he hadn't said anything. When you spend long summer weeks in a place when you're a kid, it takes on magical properties, and I liked my illusions untarnished.

We walked around to the rodeo stands, where a group of cowboys had just backed a stock trailer full of sheep to the gates. Half a dozen children wearing crash helmets and ranging in age from about five to seven stood in a straggling line to one side of the gate as the announcer began his patter.

"What are they doing?" I asked, puzzled.

"Mutton bustin'," said Colin with a grin. "They put a kid on a sheep and let it run until the kid falls off."

"Seriously? They put those little kids on sheep? You're kidding, right?"

"Nope, not kidding. And if you haven't seen it before, you have to watch. It's pretty funny."

"Do I sense more nostalgia?" I looked from the eager kids to the less-than-eager sheep, then back to Colin. "Wait, don't tell me you're a former mutton buster?" I added with sudden delight.

He gave me a sideways glance. "Maybe. Maybe not. Depends on how long I'd have to get teased about it."

"I'll take that as a yes," I said, thinking I would have to pursue this hitherto unknown aspect of his past. I knew he'd been raised in a small town in West Texas, but I'd never envisioned just what that meant. I tried to picture this six-foot-tall broad-shouldered man as a grubby sheep-riding boy and failed completely.

We climbed into the stands and took our seats on hard metal bleachers. One of the rodeo clowns wearing saggy overalls and high-top sneakers hopped on top of a barrel and began imitating the announcer's gestures, while a cowboy slipped a lasso around one woolly neck, and began pulling a fat sheep to the center of the ring. The sheep balked, black legs stiff and resisting, reminding me very much of my earlier goat encounter. The cowboy pulled, the sheep dug in harder. Eventually, the clown hopped down and began pushing on her rear end, pretending that she was both immovable and flatulent to the delight of the crowd.

"What are they doing with that one?" I asked.

"They always put the lead sheep to the center so that the others will run toward her when they're set loose."

The lead sheep was finally in position, and two cowboys led a second sheep from the trailer. They held it still while a third man lifted a skinny seven-year-old wearing pink cowboy boots and matching helmet onto its back. The girl lay flat, clutching with arms and legs like a spindly spider clinging to an overinflated woolly beach ball. The whistle blew, the cowboys let loose, and the sheep bolted across the arena. Within seconds, the girl on top began listing to one side, but she hung on gamely until she slipped almost underneath the round belly. A blast of a horn marked eight seconds, and the girl released her death grip and fell, tumbling through the dirt like Wile E. Coyote falling from an Acme rocket.

We couldn't help laughing. Kid followed kid with varying levels of success. Not very many made it to the eight-second mark, but each hit the dirt with spectacular panache. At the end, the winner was presented with a shiny gold trophy almost as tall as herself, and the disgruntled sheep were led away.

This was the signal for the crowd to reshuffle itself, and at least a third of the spectators rose. A rodeo audience is in constant motion. Before, during, and after events, people walk back and forth carrying drinks and snacks, stopping to talk with friends. Sometimes it seemed as though the fast-paced and often dangerous events taking place in the ring were merely coincidental.

"I need a break, and I'll get us a couple of beers on the way back," I said. "Save our seats?"

"Sure thing," he agreed.

I stood in a long line to get our beers and spent the time looking up and down the row of booths for a sight of Kyla. I'd half expected to see her in the bleachers, although I was not really surprised that she hadn't caught up with us. Eventually, I reached the front of the line, paid and walked off carrying two cans of Shiner Bock, and on impulse decided to go the long way around the stands to look for her. Away from the lights of the arena and the commotion around the animal pens, the darkness seemed darker, and the shouts from the crowd and the amplified voice of the rodeo announcer seemed louder. I passed a drunken couple returning from what I guessed was a rendezvous behind the porta-potties. They were staggering and giggling, holding on to each other to keep upright. Ah, young love, I thought, somewhat revolted. How desperate—or horny—would you have to be to make out behind toilets? Beyond them, I could see no one and suddenly walking the long way around didn't seem very smart. I hesitated beside one of the supports, trying to tell myself that this was Sand Creek, Texas, and I was perfectly safe on the fairgrounds. Somehow, though, my feet didn't want to walk any farther.

I had just decided to go back, when I saw a movement.

Twenty feet away, someone else stood in the darkness beneath the bleachers. The sudden flare of a lighter was followed by a puff of smoke rising into the air, a wisp that floated against the lights streaming through the benches and then was gone. Probably some kid sneaking a cigarette away from the eyes of his parents, I thought, relaxing a little. But at that moment, another figure appeared around the corner. This time, I could see the silhouette of a cowboy hat and see the

60

vague outline of a pale shirt. The second figure joined the first in the shadows.

My teacher instincts kicked into high gear and without thinking, I slipped a little closer, just to the empty space beside the next set of supports. Now I was near enough to see the newcomer pass something to the first man and receive something else in return. I stiffened in indignation. Not a kid sneaking a smoke after all but a drug deal. In Sand Creek. Colin had been right, and I felt outraged. As I watched, the second man looked over his shoulder furtively, then hurried away, leaving the first man to slip back into the shadows like the slimy little snake he was. I decided I would go and find Colin, who was going to be very interested in drug deals going on literally under his . . . well, under his nose.

However, as I was turning back, Carl Cress and his massive belly hove into view like an Exxon tanker on a rolling sea. I hesitated, then stepped behind the pillar again, partly because I didn't want to talk to Carl and partly because I thought the drug dealer might take fright and set up elsewhere. I wanted to see where he would go before I tattled on him for all I was worth.

To my surprise, Carl walked purposely toward the dealer and made a demanding gesture. After a brief hesitation, the dealer reluctantly stepped forward into the light, and I gave a gasp. I couldn't see his face clearly but I recognized the skinny shoulders and the slouch. Eddy Cranny, wife beater and drug dealer. That son of a . . .

I wasn't the only one who was furious at Eddy. Carl pounced on him like a dog owner who'd caught his least favorite mutt killing a chicken. I wished I could hear what they were saying but the crowd and the announcer were sufficient to drown out even a shouting match. Deciding to inch a little closer, I moved from one pillar to the next until I was close enough to see the light reflecting off Carl's belt buckle. Which wasn't as close as it sounds since, on a clear night, that buckle was large enough to be visible from space. Still, I was close enough to know that Carl and Eddy were having a major argument. Eddy crossed his arms over his chest, shaking his head, refusing something or other. Carl puffed up like an angry rooster and threw his arms wide, then waved one long finger in front of Eddy's nose. Eddy shook his head stubbornly, and without warning Carl punched him in the face.

Eddy's head snapped back, and he went over backward, falling heavily onto the turf, both hands clutching his nose. Even from my hiding place, I could see blood running between his fingers. Carl reached after him, grabbed the front of his shirt, and hauled him to his feet. He slapped Eddy twice, the second time hard enough to knock the smaller man off his feet again. Eddy moved his arms protectively over his head while Carl shook him like a terrier shaking a rat.

All this happened in a matter of seconds, leaving me frozen and unable to process what I was seeing. In the next instant, I found myself running forward, a beer can clutched in each hand, and not at all sure what I thought I was going to do. There was no way I was big enough or stupid enough to try to break up a fight, but on the other hand I could hardly let Carl beat Eddy to a pulp, whether he deserved it or not.

"Hey! Stop!" I shouted, always eloquent under pressure.

Between the roar of the crowd and the amplified patter from the announcers, my voice was hardly audible. Nevertheless, Carl froze in mid-slap, head whipping from side to side looking for but not seeing where my voice had come from. As I drew closer, he spotted me and visibly relaxed. He also did not let go of Eddy, who was more or less hanging limply between his giant meaty hands. It was not exactly flattering.

"This is none of your business," he informed me. "It's between me and Eddy. Now git!"

I held my ground. "It's between you, Eddy, and Eddy's attorney if Eddy decides to press assault charges. I'd be called as a witness, and as far as I can tell, not only did you hit him first, Eddy hasn't even defended himself. I think you're looking at jail time, Carl."

I didn't know if this was true or not, but I was pretty sure Carl's already florid face was turning the color of Rudolph's nose. He released Eddy's shirtfront, but kept an iron grip on Eddy's shoulder, sausage-size fingers digging into the meager muscle. Eddy winced under the pressure, eyes darting from Carl to me as though not sure who posed the biggest threat, an attitude that puzzled me. I'd broken up fights between testosterone poisoned boys at school before and had encountered something similar. Usually the smaller boy was worried that the bully would wreak vengeance on him later for any official punishment, a fear that outweighed the pain of whatever abuse he was getting at the moment. Seeing the same thing in supposedly grown men was disturbing and kind of pathetic. And a little scary. I'm tall, which I use to great advantage when dealing with the undesirable element at school, but Carl Cress topped me by at least six inches and probably a hundred pounds. There was no way I was going to be able to intimidate him.

Nevertheless, I lifted my eyebrow and used my best teacher voice, the voice that had once quelled a dozen cheerleaders in a full-out Justin Bieber frenzy. "Let him go, Carl, or I'll call the police."

I saw his lips curl into a cruel sneer and remembered too late that he was pals with Sheriff Bob. So I added, "And I'll scream."

He dropped Eddy like a used tissue. "This is none of your business," he repeated.

I stared coldly at Carl, reminded strongly of the black malevolent stares of the Brahman bulls Kyla and I had seen earlier in the day. "For better or worse, Eddy's a Shore now, which makes it my business. And I'm telling you to leave him alone."

Hopefully Eddy wouldn't be a Shore for long, I thought to myself, but as long as he was married to Ruby June we could hardly let someone like Carl Cress beat the snot out of him.

The three of us stared at one another for a long moment. Above us, the stands had grown relatively quiet, the rodeo obviously between events, patrons moving about more than usual to stock up on beer and peanuts and fried things on sticks. Eddy met my eyes with a look I would be unable to forget, an odd pathetic gaze, half grateful, half pleading. Then he darted off, leaving me alone with a very large and very angry Carl Cress.

I lifted the beer cans I still clutched in a death grip and announced, "I'll be getting back to my friends."

I walked forward, moving within a couple of feet of the belly with its gleaming buckle and feeling Carl's angry eyes on the back of my neck as I passed. I suppressed a shiver and managed to keep a sedate and hopefully nonchalant pace until I rounded the corner. Then, I allowed myself to bolt back to the stands where Colin waited. I'd never been so glad to see anyone, I thought, taking in his broad shoulders and lean hard muscles. Even Carl Cress would hesitate before taking on Colin. I slid very close to him on the bench, feeling much safer.

Colin took the beer I handed him with a word of thanks and a questioning look.

"Long line?" he asked, popping the top.

Beer spewed like a geyser at Yellowstone, catching him in the chin and frothing over his hand in an icy golden flow. With a yelp, he leaped to his feet trying to stop it from drenching his clothes.

I jumped up, too, clapping a hand over my mouth. It hadn't occurred to me that breaking up a fight while holding a can of beer was likely to shake it up a bit. My mind worked quickly and decided there was no way for him to know it was my fault. After all, the vendor might have handed it to me like that. I went for a look of appalled innocence, although I wasn't entirely successful at preventing my shoulders from shaking.

Colin just stared at me and then shook his head. "I know you're laughing, and I know this is somehow your fault, so you might as well tell," he said.

It was hell dating a detective.

"You know, the smell of beer is really sexy," I said in my best sultry voice.

"And trust me, I'll be reminding you that you said that a little later on. Now, what did you do?" He was trying to look stern but not pulling it off very well. His lips kept wanting to twitch into a grin.

"I'll tell you later," I said, snuggling up to his dry side. Actually, on him the smell of beer-soaked denim wasn't at all bad, I thought. I held out my can. "Would you open my beer for me?" I asked.

The low rumble in his throat would have made a Doberman proud. In the ring below, another bull exploded from the pen and hurled its rider through the air in one graceful arc. The rodeo clowns ran to distract it before it could complete its mission of stomping the prone figure to death, and the cowboy leaped to safety with an impressive burst of speed. The portion of the crowd that was actually watching erupted into wild cheers, and Colin put his damp arm around my shoulders. Without thinking, I lifted my face for a kiss and instantly forgot about Eddy and Carl. And Alan.

We returned alone to the ranch house after the last bull riding event, having seen no sign of Kyla. My phone, which showed a single flickering signal bar, contained a text message from her saying she had gone dancing. I did not need to ask with whom, although I wondered what effect it would have on Uncle Kel's blood pressure if and when he found out.

As we walked in the door, shouts of "About time!" and "It's Stinkalyn!" greeted us, a dead giveaway that my brothers had arrived while we were gone.

Two years younger than I and apparently incapable of maturing beyond the age of fourteen, Sam and Will were fraternal twins, their only identical feature being the ability to yank my chain. Sam, the older by about six minutes, had the Shore looks through and through—tall, rangy, and dark haired. Will, on the other hand, most unfairly took after our petite French mother, from his short compact frame to his auburn hair, cropped close to hide the curls. If there was any justice in the world, those looks should have been mine. Both brothers had grown up to be surprisingly successful, something I would never have predicted for them when we were kids. In fact, back then I would have said that their reaching adulthood was something of a long shot. However, Sam was now an architect living in San Jose, married to his high school sweetheart who was expecting their first child, and earning recognition and awards in his field. Will was some sort of international investment banker who spent part of his time traveling back and forth to Europe and the other part raking up the enormous piles of cash his employers heaved at him.

Now, Sam gave me a hug while Will slapped me lightly on the back of my head. With a sigh, I introduced them to Colin, watching with some concern while they did the manly handshaking thing, everybody squeezing just a little too hard. I also took note of the narrowed glances they gave Colin, looking him over with suspicion. Neither of my brothers had liked my ex-husband, and being right about that made them insufferable. I hadn't told them that I had started dating again, and no one except Aunt Elaine had known in advance that I was bringing Colin to the reunion. Now Will sniffed a little too audibly to make sure I knew he could smell beer on my boyfriend, while Sam began asking the kind of questions usually uttered by overprotective Victorian fathers or particularly zealous members of the paparazzi. I glared at them from behind Colin's shoulder.

Some of my relatives gathered to watch, Aunt Gladys joining us with a bowl of popcorn and holding it out so the idle bystanders could grab a handful. And why not? As entertainment, it didn't get much better than this. Hardened criminals wanted for heinous acts of violence hardly got this type of grilling. What did Colin do for a living? Where did he grow up? Where did he go to school? Colin, however, just smiled pleasantly and answered in a light amused tone.

Uncle Kel stiffened. "Detective? I didn't hear that earlier. Maybe you can answer this, then. Why aren't the cops interested in helping me find my daughter?"

Colin blinked. "I was under the impression that she's only been gone a few hours, sir, and that she's an adult."

"What difference does that make? You think giving a kidnapper a head start is a good idea?"

We all looked at Kel with some concern. Color was already rising in his face, a deep anger obvious just below the barely controlled words. What in the world was going on with him?

Colin chose to address the issue with logic. "Do you have any reason to think that she's been kidnapped?"

"Goddamn it, I know she has! That son of a bitch she's married to has taken her somewhere."

"But Kel," I protested. "I saw Eddy at the rodeo. Ruby June wasn't with him."

He whipped around on me, eyes wild. "Where? Where was he? Why the hell didn't you call me?"

At the sound of her husband's rising voice, Aunt Elaine materialized from somewhere in the back of the house. She laid a hand on his arm. "Honey, the rodeo is over, Eddy's not there anymore, and Ruby June is going to walk back in here tomorrow for Thanksgiving supper and wonder what you were fussing about. Now, come on. You said you'd play Hearts with Scotty and Gladys and me. Let's go and let the kids have a chance to catch up with each other."

We watched as she herded him into the kitchen, followed closely and somewhat reluctantly by Gladys and Scotty.

Scotty was already protesting. "Hearts? I can't even remember how to play that. What about poker?"

"Hearts," answered Gladys firmly.

The rest of us stood silent, processing what had just happened. My mind raced. Why in the world was Kel so worried about Ruby June, and what else was going on to make him so volatile? This was not the steady, reasonable, and almost placid man that I remembered from my teenage summers on this ranch. Maybe Colin was right to be concerned about his mental state.

After a moment, Will turned to Colin and asked, "So you're a cop, huh? You ever shoot anyone?"

"Not yet," answered Colin with a pointed look at him.

This produced a burst of appreciative laughter, and I gave a sigh of relief. The mysterious man-grilling was over, and Colin had passed.

Sam grinned. "It's still early. Who wants to go varmint hunting?"

Twenty minutes later, the red ranch truck bounced over uneven roads, outraged shock absorbers squeaking in protest, wheels throwing a plume of white dust into the darkness behind us. Overhead, the stars were brilliant crystals in the vast black pool of the sky, and the moon, almost full, cast its silvery light over the rolling fields, so bright that the single live oak in the center of a field cast a perfect shadow onto the surrounding grass. The white caliche turned the road into a pale ribbon undulating through mysterious turns and twists, appearing on hillcrest, then vanishing over a ridge. The breeze in our faces was cold and smelled of dry grass, cattle, and cedar. Standing in the bed of the truck, I clung to the metal bars of the rear window guard, alternately laughing and pounding on the roof of the cab for the driver, my brother Sam, to slow down. Beside me, Colin gripped the guard with one hand, but gamely held a spotlight high with the other, sweeping the brilliant light back and forth in front of the truck. From inside the truck, Sam, his wife Christy, and my other brother Will shouted conflicting suggestions about where to shine the beam.

Colin swept the light along the left side of the truck, and the eyes of some animal flashed like two bright white sparks.

"There!" Colin shouted, and held the beam steady.

I pounded on the roof again, and my brother turned into the field, bumping through the long grass and over invisible bumps and ridges with bone-jarring speed. As we drew closer, the white sparks blinked off briefly, then appeared again.

"Oh, man!" came a disappointed shout from the cab. "It's just a goat."

And sure enough, we pulled up beside a brown and white mottled goat, blinking sleepily at us from a nest in the long grass. She could have been the twin of the pushy beast who'd invaded our pickup truck earlier, but this one just eyed us suspiciously without bothering to get up.

"Wonder what she's doing out here by herself," I said. "I thought they stuck together."

Colin grinned and swung the beam of the light into the

stand of trees just behind her. Instantly, the spaces between the dark branches were filled with dozens of matching white sparks. Most were near the ground, but a couple peered out from the low sprawling branches of a mesquite tree. I wished Kyla had been there to see, because I knew she hadn't believed me about goats in trees.

"Where to now?" asked Sam over the thrumming of the engine.

"Let's go through the Evil," I shouted back.

"The what?" asked Colin, turning to me as my brother swung the truck wide of the goats and bumped back toward the road.

"The Forest Primeval," I explained. "It's about a hundred acres on the south side of the ranch that Kel leaves untouched for the deer. I don't know who started calling it the Forest Primeval, but when we were kids, all we heard was the 'evil' part. It made it seem very mysterious and creepy."

"And is it?"

"Well, there used to be an old house that's pretty much a ruin now. You can still see part of the chimney and a bit of the foundation. And there's an old concrete root cellar that's full of broken bottles and junk. It's a snake's paradise." I thought about this, then added, "Yeah, it's pretty creepy."

"So are we looking for anything special out here?" he asked, still diligently sweeping the spotlight beam from side to side.

"Coyotes," I answered. "Well, that's the pretext anyway. Kel's had a couple of goats turn up without their kids, and a few of the neighbors say they've seen a couple of big males."

"And if we see one?"

71

"Then we shall shine the light of vengeance upon it," I answered in my best wrath-of-God announcer voice.

"What?"

I dropped back to my normal tone. "Seriously. We don't do anything. In the unlikely event that we come across one, we'll shine the spotlight in its eyes and maybe shout some insults."

"Then what's the deal with the rifle?" Here he tapped the back windshield with one finger where a gun hung on a rack.

"Oh, Kel always makes us take that, but none of us is going to shoot anything. We just like looking for nocturnal critters. Our dad used to take us out at least one night every time we visited the ranch when we were kids—it made a big change from Paris, that's for sure, and we absolutely loved it. You can see some cool animals out here at night that you can't see any other time—owls, armadillos, ringtails, possums—well, you know that. You grew up out this way. Anyway, coyote spotting is just tonight's excuse."

The truck bumped into a serious pothole, and I staggered. Colin moved closer, briefly releasing his grip on the guard to steady me. Another bump made him rethink that plan, but it was nice to be standing shoulder to shoulder. Two gates and a cattle guard later, we came to a narrow lane leading through the heart of the Evil. Sam did not bother to slow down. A branch scraped along the side of the truck like a long fingernail against a chalkboard.

"You two better sit down!" Will shouted, somewhat unnecessarily, because we had both dropped into the bed of the truck at the first shriek of branch against paint.

Colin snapped the light off, and I let him pull me against

him, unashamedly deciding that using him as a cushion out-weighed my concerns about too much physical intimacy. He didn't seem to mind. He wrapped his arms around me and rested his cheek against my hair. Under the essence of eau de beer, he smelled of soap and shaving cream, warm skin, and maybe just a little bit of dusty feed sack. It was intoxicating. The darkness wrapped around us like a protective blanket, trying to push away thoughts of a problematic future, or in fact any thoughts at all. Overhead, branches moved like shadows against a black sky, stars flickering on and off in between. His lips brushed against my forehead, sending a shiver southward in a very nice way. I was not sure I would ever understand the in-tense attraction between us, but then I probably didn't need to.

"Jocelyn," he said, voice low. "I . . ." He stopped.

I shifted my shoulders to try to look into his face, but it was impossible to see his expression in the dim light the moon provided. I waited, but he did not continue. The silence stretched between us like a rubber band waiting to snap, and I braced myself for something either overly romantic or heartbreak-ingly final. I wasn't quite sure which I feared most.

At last he said, "I'm glad you invited me here."

My sigh of relief wheezed out in a gasp, and I realized I'd been holding my breath. I'd been afraid he was going to try to talk about our relationship. I'd forgotten for a moment how unlikely that was, seeing that he was a man.

"Me, too," I answered a little more heartily than necessary.

"Are you?" he asked.

Apparently I'd experienced premature exhalation. Again, I strained unsuccessfully to see his expression in the darkness, but he didn't sound like he was teasing.

"Of course I am," I said automatically. Then reaching for something a little more genuine, I added, "I thought it might be awkward, but with the exception of that last little scene with my idiot brothers, it's been really fun. I'm glad you came."

And with mild surprise, I realized this was true. Colin fit in with my large and strange extended family. Even in the short time we'd had before the rodeo, he'd spoken ranch with Uncle Kel, football with Scotty, leaped to his feet to assist Aunt Elaine with groceries, and gently teased the younger cousins. He'd even handled the intrusive questions of both my brothers and my insane uncle without blinking. In fact, he seemed more at ease with most of them than I was. And best of all, he did it while keeping one eye on me, the connection between us constant and almost palpable. If this had been a boyfriend test, which it wasn't, he would have passed with flying colors.

I felt him relax at least a little. "I know it was Kyla's idea," he said.

"But it was a good one," I reassured him. I searched around for a change of topic, but he was too quick for me.

Reaching for my hand, he said, "We've been seeing each other for a couple of months now."

I sat up abruptly and pulled my hand away. Were we really going to have this conversation in the back of a moving truck? "One month," I countered.

Thank goodness just then the truck made a bone-jarring thump across something large and a shower of leaves and twigs sprinkled onto our heads like rain. We were bounced apart, and when he tried to steady me, his chin collided with my forehead hard enough to make us both yelp. Then the truck was out of the forest and both of us were left rubbing our bruises and feeling unhappy.

"What are you two doing back there? Spotlight!" Will shouted impatiently from the cab.

We hauled ourselves to our feet, and Colin fumbled with the switch. The brilliant white beam cut through the darkness far ahead of the headlights and almost instantly reflected off something large.

Sam braked, bringing the truck to a hard stop, and I gave a yip of protest, deciding right then that I was going to drive on the way back. I raised my eyes to follow the beam of light.

About twenty yards ahead of us stood an animal that had no business on a Texas ranch. In fact, I wasn't even sure what it was, although I could tell it was some type of antelope, and most likely the type of antelope that should have been grazing on an African savannah. Exceptionally tall and leggy, it had a gray-brown coat that was interrupted by a handful of narrow white streaks running vertically from spine to belly and long twisting horns that looked as though they belonged on some mythical beast in a medieval fairy tale. For one long moment, the creature stood frozen in the light, eyes reflecting like white stars, then whirled and leaped away. Colin kept the light trained on it. At the edge of the trees, it halted briefly, turning to gaze back at us with another flash of its eyes, then vanished into the undergrowth.

Switching off the engine, Sam got out, followed by Will and Christy.

"What the heck was that?" asked Will, still staring into the darkness where the antelope had disappeared.

"That," said Christy, "was a kudu."

She stretched, putting both arms above her head, and then moving them to her lower back. She was eight months pregnant, her belly round and hard as a large melon. My first niece or nephew to be.

We all turned to look at her.

"How do you know that?" asked Will.

She shrugged. "Everyone knows that. Haven't you ever been to a zoo?"

"Yeah, but not to look at boring stuff like that," he answered. "I'm strictly a lions, tigers, and bears sort of guy. You know, the manly animals."

"I would have said you were more of a monkey man," Sam said, but he wasn't really paying attention to his brother. He stared off into the darkness.

"What are you looking at?" I asked.

"I don't know. I thought I saw something move." He reached into the cab and turned the key enough to start the electrical system. "Hey, Gallagher, shine that light over there, will you?"

The brilliant white beam sliced through the night air, panning first left then right, following a line of trees and at last dipping down into a depression. Two pairs of green eyes reflected back, weird and alien in the darkness.

"Coyotes," said Sam, sounding pleased. "Big ones, too."

I stood on tiptoes so I could get a better view. Sure enough, two large coyotes, looking very much like lean and somewhat flea-bitten dogs stared back at us, confused by the light. The ground under their feet was powdery and white, and I realized they were standing in an old caliche pit. The ranch was dotted with pits of this type, depressions made when ranchers, both past and present, dug up the soft caliche clay to repair their roads. When the clay played out, the pits were used as garbage dumps.

This particular pit was large, one side sloping gently downward like the shallow end of a swimming pool and ending at the deepest some twelve feet below the surface. The deep end was now filled with the refuse of fifty years of ranch life. Anything that couldn't be repurposed or burned was dumped into the pit. Sometimes it was dumped into the pit and then burned. The moonlight illuminated rusting old barrels, rotten pieces of wood from a decrepit shed, tires, and even the shredded remains of a stained mattress, now probably the home for untold hordes of rats. Trash pits were a haven for rodents of all descriptions, which also made them a favorite hunting ground for snakes, who dug their tunnels in the soft soil. Fortunately, at this time of year, the snakes were hibernating.

Colin, however, was interested in neither the coyotes nor the contents of the caliche pit. He swung the light a few paces to the right and asked, "What do they have there?"

I looked again. The coyotes were standing near a dark lump. The beam moved over the shape, and I saw what looked like the bottom of a boot. A few inches more, and an unmistakable white shape materialized out of the shadows. A human hand.

Colin pushed the spotlight into my hands and vaulted over the side of the truck, a move I'd always envied. How did men do that?

"Flashlight!" he shouted, and Will dove for the glove compartment. The two of them set off at a run, shouting at the coyotes who bolted into the darkness.

I dropped the light, ignoring Colin's immediate cry of protest, and clambered over the back of the truck, half falling in my haste. Sam hurried to join me.

"They need the light!" he said.

I grabbed the power cord and hauled the spotlight over the side and thrust it into his hands, then raced after them. Behind me, the beam sparked to life, throwing my own shadow into the scrubby grass before me, elongated and black.

"Stay back!" shouted Colin, throwing up a hand.

I skidded to a stop at the edge of the pit next to Will, looking down the incline to where Colin was inching forward, sweeping the flashlight over the ground at his own feet.

"Who is it?" I called. "Is he . . . she . . . Are they all right?"

Colin raised his head briefly, but didn't answer. He reached the still form and squatted beside it.

Will swallowed. "I don't think coyotes would come that close to a human if he was alive," he said in a low tone.

My thoughts flashed with sudden horror to Ruby June, still missing.

"Colin, who is it?" I asked sharply.

Colin stood and began retracing his own steps, careful not to disturb the scene more than necessary.

"I don't know," he answered as he drew near. "It's a man, though. Young, maybe early twenties. We need to call the police."

I relaxed slightly and heard Will blow out his breath. He must have been thinking about Ruby June as well.

"Either of you have a phone?" asked Colin, holding a hand up to shade his eyes against the beam of the spotlight, which either Christy or Sam was now training directly on us.

We both shook out heads. "Left mine in my purse," I said.

Will said, "Mine gets zero reception out here. I don't even bother to take it out of my car."

We started back to the truck. The spotlight was absolutely blinding. No wonder the animals always froze. You couldn't see six inches in front of your own nose.

"Hey! Point that thing somewhere else," Will shouted, and the beam abruptly jerked to the side.

"Your eyes are bright red," came Sam's voice. "Kinda creepy. So what's going on down there."

"Dead guy," said Will, always succinct if not exactly sensitive. "Either of you got a cell phone?"

They hadn't. Sam now pointed the spotlight at the ground, the light reflecting back up from the ground so we could see each other in an eerie campfire storytelling sort of way.

"What happened to him?" asked Christy in an anxious tone.

"You think it was a hunting accident? There's a lot of guys with guns and beer out here this weekend," asked Sam, his eyes on Colin.

"There's no way to tell right now," said Colin, shaking his head. "You four go back to the house and call the sheriff. When he arrives, one of you can show him the way."

"What are you going to do?" I asked.

"I'll wait here, keep an eye on things."

Christy nodded and climbed into the truck without protest, looking sick and shaken. Sam joined her and started the engine.

"I'll wait with you," I said to Colin.

Will glanced around uneasily. "I'm not sure sticking around is a good idea. Why don't you both come back? You don't know who or what else might be out here. Besides, it's not like that guy's going to get any deader."

"I need to secure the scene," said Colin. "But you should go back with them, Jocelyn."

I felt a flicker of alarm. "You don't really think it's dangerous, do you?"

"No, not at all," he said, tone bright and reassuring like that of a doctor telling a toddler the shot wasn't going to hurt a bit. "The only thing that might come back are those coyotes, and they aren't any danger to a man."

"Then I'm staying, too."

He frowned at me. "I'd feel better if you left."

"I'd feel better if we hadn't found a dead guy," I said, then turned to Will. "Hurry back. Tell Sheriff Bob it's an emergency."

He took me at my word and moved quickly to the passenger door, hopping in as Sam shifted into first gear with a grinding noise. Like a barge on choppy water, the red truck turned a huge slow circle and then bumped off into the forest. As the headlights vanished, the night closed in around us, moon and stars brighter, shadows behind every blade of grass darker. The breeze played over my skin like a breath from a graveyard. I sneezed and then, with a glance toward the pit, gave a little shiver.

"You're so stubborn," said Colin. "There wasn't any reason we both had to stay."

"I couldn't leave you alone," I protested. "Don't killers sometimes return to the scene of the crime? What if whoever did this comes back?"

He snorted. "That's ridiculous. He's already dumped the body—there's no other reason to come here. And anyway, if he does, what are you going to do about it?"

"Probably wet my pants and hide behind you. Or," I added brightly, "you could use me as a human shield."

He started laughing. "As long as you know you have only yourself to blame. It's cold and it'll be close to two hours before anyone can get here."

"Sheriff Bob will take two hours, but someone will be back in forty minutes tops, probably with snacks and beer."

"What? You're not serious."

"You met my family, right? At least half of them are basically rabid hillbillies hopped up on *Judge Judy* and reruns of *CSI*. You'd need riot gear to keep them away from their very own crime scene."

"Maybe Will and Sam will have the sense to keep it quiet."

I laughed at that. Scornfully.

He sighed, shining the flashlight around us. "We might as well sit down while we wait," he said, leading the way to a couple of low rocks.

I stamped my feet against the cold, my breath a puff of smoke in the frosty air, and decided to remain standing. It was too cold for snakes to be moving about, but I still didn't care for the look of the crevasses and deep grass.

"This is a crime scene, right? No chance it's just an accident?" Even I could hear the forlorn note in my voice.

"The guy was shot in the chest at close range and dumped here."

"Are you sure? Maybe it was a hunting accident. Bullets travel pretty far you know," I said, realizing how stupid it sounded even as I spoke.

"Some bullets do, but this one stopped pretty damn quick." He saw me wince, and added, "Yeah. Well, I suppose it's possible that the gun went off by mistake, and then the shooter panicked instead of calling the police."

"Now you're just patronizing me."

"Look, we won't know anything for sure until we can check things out. And we probably won't be able to do that properly until daylight. Try not to think about it." He reached for my hand. "I wish you'd gone back," he said for the third time.

"You know, if you're not careful, you're going to make me think you wish I'd gone back." I could feel his eyes roll even if I couldn't see them clearly, and added, "Besides, you do this kind of thing all the time."

"You don't though. And there's no reason you should."

"It's just that I know so many people in this part of the world. The thought that it could be one of them . . . well, it's scary."

He nodded. "Sometimes the uncertainty is worse than knowing, and it would speed things up to have a name when the sheriff gets here. Do you want to take a look, see if you recognize him?"

I hesitated. No, I didn't. I didn't want to see another dead man as long as I lived. But what if it was someone in my family? Half my relatives had stayed in town after the rodeo to listen to the country band scheduled to follow the bull riding or to go to one of the bars for some post-rodeo celebrating. What if this dead guy were one of them? Or even someone like Carl Cress. That wasn't quite as disturbing. Not that I wanted him dead, of course, but it wasn't much of a stretch to picture someone wanting to shoot him. And where was Ruby June?

"You're sure it wasn't a girl, right?" I asked nervously. I didn't think I could take seeing my cousin's dead face in the moonlight.

"I'm positive," Colin answered. "It's not Ruby June."

I wondered how he did that. He had a true gift for remembering people's names, even people he had not met. Just something else I admired about him.

I thought of something else and felt a little sick. "And the coyotes?"

"They didn't do anything to him, at least not that I could see. I'm guessing they found him just a couple of minutes before we did. He can't have been here very long," he added thoughtfully. I could see his detective's mind was already beginning to process the scene.

I said, "Okay then. I'll take a look."

He rose, leading the way up the slope of the hill rather than straight toward the body. "We can see from over here without disturbing the scene," he explained as we walked.

I swallowed and followed in his steps, stumbling a little

over the uneven ground in spite of the light provided by the flashlight. We walked along the edge of the pit, careful not to step too close to the crumbling edges, until we stood almost directly over the body. From that vantage, I could see the outline of the still form against the pale ground, a shapeless collection of shadow and substance, as lifeless as the refuse that surrounded it. A faint but nasty odor rose from the pit, and I felt my stomach flip-flop. It was a bad place to die.

"Okay, here we are. Just a quick look at the face, see if you recognize him, and then we'll go back."

I nodded, although I knew he couldn't see me. I was finding it unexpectedly difficult to speak.

Colin aimed the beam of the flashlight onto the body, and I drew in a sharp breath. A young man's face, eyes half open, lips parted as though in surprise, nose swollen and bruised. In death, he looked even younger than he had in life, dishwater hair stirring in the breeze, caressing a white forehead that could no longer feel it. The plaid of his shirt, the same plaid that Kyla had poked just a few hours ago, was now soaked in a dark fluid. Eddy Cranny would never hit or be hit by anyone ever again.

"Jocelyn, are you okay?" Colin asked sharply.

The beam wavered, then dipped away from the body as he turned to grab my arm. A kind gesture, I thought, but unnecessary. I was completely fine. It was true that the scene had taken on an odd sort of unreality, as if I were watching it on a black-and-white television on the far side of a very large room, and it was strangely hard to focus, but I was fine. Just fine.

"Jocelyn?" Colin slipped his arm around my waist and pulled me against his side. "Come on, let's sit down," he said, and we returned to the suspect rocks. This time I sat and let him pull me into his arms. After a moment, my head felt clearer.

I drew a shaky breath. "It's Eddy Cranny. You know, Ruby June's husband." I enunciated carefully, feeling a little like a drunk trying hard to appear sober.

"The one who hit her?" he asked. "The same guy you saw dealing at the rodeo?"

I'd told him about that on the way home. One more instance of a name he'd remembered. I nodded, feeling the fabric of his shirt and the beat of his heart against my cheek, steady and reassuring. I wished now that I hadn't looked.

My thoughts were racing. Who would want poor, stupid Eddy Cranny dead? Or maybe it was easier to ask who didn't. Carl Cress had punched him in the face, Uncle Kel had held him at gunpoint, and Ruby June had been planning to throw him out. Even Kyla had threatened him. But surely none of them would have wanted Eddy dead. Not dead. Not really. I said as much to Colin, who shrugged.

"Then maybe it was the drugs after all instead of something personal. You know, from your description, I was picturing a small-time pot dealer, but we've heard rumors about some pretty large scale drug gangs moving into Texas. Los Zetas, for one. Once they get a foothold somewhere, violence and murder are never far behind."

This was even harder to believe. "A drug gang in Sand Creek? And one so desperate they would hire Eddy?"

"You're right, it doesn't seem all that likely." Colin clicked the flashlight off to save the battery. "Well, there's one bit of good news anyway."

"What?" I asked.

"The police will definitely start looking for Ruby June now."

Chapter 3

CRIME AND CRITTERS

The next morning, Kyla flopped down beside me on the porch swing, making the rickety wood creak and sway alarmingly. As usual, she looked crisp and fresh, wearing a turquoise jacket and matching flats. I had no idea why she thought those shoes were appropriate for a ranch and was already hoping she'd step in something nasty, which made me simultaneously ashamed of myself and unrepentantly defiant. It was Thanksgiving morning, the sky was sunny, the light breeze was no more than a whisper, and the air was warming nicely. It should have been such a glorious day, but nothing was turning out as planned. I was in a foul mood and didn't care who knew it.

"I was just talking to Aunt Elaine. I can't believe all the excitement you had here last night," Kyla said.

"Yes, very exciting. Next time I'll go out with the hot rich guy, and you can find the corpse," I said sourly.

She lifted one perfectly arched eyebrow. "Touchy. You

know I didn't mean it that way. Besides, I seem to recall that you were with your own personal hot guy."

I didn't answer. As I'd predicted, Will had returned last night with a truckload of my relatives who'd done their very best to invade the crime scene. At one point, I'd thought Colin was going to have to draw his gun on them, which would at least have been fun to watch. However, they finally saw reason and settled down, then began reminiscing about Eddy and the things he'd done as a kid, which eventually made me start crying. Fortunately, about that time Sheriff Bob had arrived and insisted that we go back to the house. Sheriff Bob had followed us within half an hour to ask questions, but Colin had not returned at all. I waited until well after midnight, but eventually gave up and went to bed myself. Now it was morning, his Jeep was missing, and I had no idea where he was. Had he eventually returned to his wretched motel room in town or was he still out at the caliche pit?

After a long moment, I noticed that Kyla was staring at me as though waiting for an answer to something.

"So how was your evening with T.J.?" I asked, knowing that no matter what else was on her mind, she'd be willing to talk about herself.

She gave a smile that I uncharitably thought of as smug. "Better than average. He is really very charming."

"Charming?" I asked.

"Very."

"Meaning he wanted to talk about you?"

"Meaning he wanted to talk about many subjects. Me, of course, but also about himself and his ranch. I had no idea that running a ranch was so complicated. You can't begin to imagine what he has to do just to keep his head above water."

"So all these years of watching Kel and Elaine run cattle and goats and a summer dude camp and a winter hunting camp and growing every possible kind of cash crop didn't give you an inkling?"

"Oh yeah," she said wonderingly. "Yeah, I guess you're right. I never really thought about why they were going to all that trouble. I just figured they liked it. Anyway, T.J.'s basically doing the same things, only instead of running a dude outfit during the summer, he keeps the hunting camp going all the time."

"Hunting season's only in the fall and what, a couple of weeks in the spring?" I pointed out. "He can't keep it going all the time."

"That's where you're wrong. He imports exotics. They're always in season."

"What do you mean, exotics?"

"Animals that aren't native. Different types of deer and other animals. You know, like from Africa."

"Africa? Wait, you mean like kudu?" For the first time, I recalled the strange animal we'd seen just before we'd found Eddy.

She looked at me blankly. "I have no idea what that is. I mean like big deer with funny looking antlers. Things like that."

"And what, these hunters come and shoot the animals in their pens?" I asked.

"No, don't be an idiot. T.J. says he gets a lot of flack from people who don't understand. The animals are loose and wild.

He says it's no different than it would be hunting them in Africa. People just don't have to travel so far."

"How does he keep them from running away then?"

"I asked that same thing. Eight-foot-high fences," she answered.

"So just a bigger pen," I said.

She shrugged, refusing to be provoked. "He's got four thousand acres. That's a damn big pen."

"Still, even if he can get hunters all year 'round, I'm surprised that he makes enough for it to be worth all the costs," I said. "I mean, importing animals, putting up the extra-tall fences, and all that must be pretty expensive."

She nodded. "It is. But do you know how much hunters pay for some of the animals?"

"No."

"Guess."

I just sighed. "How am I supposed to guess? I don't even know what a regular hunting weekend costs."

"Fifteen thousand dollars."

"What?"

"Yup. He's got three different kinds of antelope that are worth fifteen thousand. He has a bunch more in the three to eight thousand dollar range."

I looked at her with disbelief. "You can buy a car for that. Who would pay that much for a dead deer?"

"They don't pay for the dead deer. They pay to make the deer dead. There's a difference."

"A nice distinction," I said. "Honestly, does that sound like fifteen thousand dollars worth of fun to you?"

"Well, maybe not, but then I don't care about trophy hunting. I do like shooting, though. I'd definitely go on a hunt to see what it was like."

I just looked at her. Not once in all the years that we'd visited the ranch had she risen at dawn to join the deer hunters, and the one time she'd gone dove hunting, she'd moaned about the heat and ragweed until Kel, with admirable self-control, had driven her back to the house instead of slapping duct tape across her lips. On the other hand, she did like shooting and was more than skilled at most of the weaponry you could find on a ranch.

Now I said, "You mean you'd go on a hunt to see what T.J. was like."

She just laughed. "Now there's a trophy I could get into. You have to admit he's gorgeous."

"He wouldn't break mirrors, but he's not exactly Hugh Jackman."

Her blue eyes flashed with irritation, and she looked away. "Well, I guess that means you won't be trying to steal him away from me."

I was not the one with a history of stealing boyfriends, I thought, remembering a certain incident from our high school days that had almost destroyed our friendship before it began. Still, that was a long time ago, and I decided to let it go. Maybe Kyla really did have more of the hunter in her than I'd realized.

With an effort, I changed the subject. "Exotic hunting, horse racing . . . what else does T.J. do?"

She relaxed and smiled a little too brightly, obviously not in the mood to fight and glad I hadn't taken up the gauntlet.

"Real estate investments. He's one of the major investors in the racetrack. And by the way, we're invited to come watch the race in his box."

"Seriously?"

Kyla said, "Yup. I told him we would, of course, although I admit that was before I'd heard about Eddy getting killed and all. Still, you don't think all that should keep us from going to the race, do you?"

In spite of my worries about the murder and Ruby June, the thought of seeing the race from a box sounded intriguing, like something from the Kentucky Derby or the Grand National. Then with a pang, I remembered the pending lawsuit.

"Well if the murder doesn't, then Kel sure will. Remember the archenemy thing? We can't watch from T.J.'s box—Kel would have a fit."

"Kel isn't the boss of me," she said with a grin. "Besides, I don't see how he'll find out if you don't tell him."

"I won't need to tell him. Everyone knows everything about everybody in Sand Creek. You can bet someone will be telling him that you were with T.J. at the dance before the day is out. There's no way you can sit in his box at the races without the whole town knowing."

She looked outraged. "Why would anyone care? What business is it of theirs anyway?"

I just shrugged. "They care. For goodness sakes, they're sending someone from the newspaper to interview Uncle Herman about turning ninety-five. They know their neighbors. They're interested. In a way it's kind of nice."

She sat for a moment, looking disgruntled. "Well, I still don't see why we shouldn't go to the races tomorrow, do you?"

"I don't know," I answered. "I don't even know what's going on today. I mean, we're supposed to be having Thanksgiving dinner, but nobody seems to be in the mood. I asked Aunt Elaine if she'd like us to leave altogether, but she doesn't. In fact, she begged us to stay and help out."

"Help out with what? You know I can't cook."

"Not cook. Help with *your* relatives," I said, stressing the possessive and making a gesture with my chin.

She followed my gaze to where a group of boys ranging in ages from about four to ten were swarming around the pecan trees looking for late pecans. Every few seconds, one of them would pounce on something, examine it, and then chuck it at another kid.

"Oh hell, no!" Kyla said. "No, no, no! You know how I feel about kids."

"You were quite good with that class you taught at my school," I said slyly.

Her eye twitched. "Those were high school girls interested in technology, not monkeys wearing pants. Even you can't possibly want to take care of those little monsters."

"For once, we are in agreement." I thought for a moment, then added, "What would you think about going back to the Evil? I want to know if Colin is still there."

"I'll get my boots," she said instantly.

I slipped inside to get the truck keys, all the while thinking what a terrible person I was to sneak away just when Aunt Elaine needed help. The house was filled with the scent of pumpkin pie spice courtesy of a pair of jar candles burning on the mantel and the heavenly aroma of roasting turkey, courtesy of the twenty-pound bird that my aunt had trussed and shoehorned into her oven. My stomach rumbled a little in anticipation. Sure, Eddy was dead, but the living needed to keep their strength up.

I snuck past three assorted male relatives stretched out in recliners in front of the pre-pre-football show. How anyone could listen to burly former players droning on about some burly current player's passing record was beyond me, although I had to admit it was mildly amusing to see necks the size of my thighs squeezing out of tight collars like links of sausage. I carefully lifted the key ring off the rack by the side door, then noticed my cousin Kris staring forlornly out the window at the little pack of rabid kids. Her raven hair was spikier than ever, her lips halfheartedly smeared with black lipstick, her clothing an assortment of tattered black rags. She glanced at me with an expression of complete hopelessness, then returned her eyes to the carnage outside. Even over the sound of the television, faint squeals of outrage and the pounding of running feet were clearly audible.

On impulse I said, "Want to go for a ride?"

"Where?" she asked suspiciously.

"Does it matter?"

"Nope," she said and was at my side in a flash.

We slipped through the side door so the kids wouldn't see us. Kyla met us at the truck. She had changed into a glossy pair of boots with three-inch heels, which if worn by a real cowboy would make even the cows snicker quietly into their cud. She took one look at Kris, and rolled her eyes at me.

"Kris is coming with us," I said, opening the driver's door.

Kyla pressed her lips together, but opened the passenger door and gestured for Kris to proceed her. The girl scrambled over the back of the seat with impressive agility and crouched down on the narrow backseat as if afraid someone would drag her back. As I started the engine, Kyla settled herself in the front seat and turned to look at the girl.

"I thought your name was Kale or Arugula or something like that," she said, demonstrating her full range of empathy and mad people skills in a single sentence.

Kris opened her mouth as though to explain, but I interrupted, "Nope, it's Kris. Aunt Gladys's daughter."

Seeing us pull away, the pack of boys raised a shout and ran after us. I stepped on the accelerator and left them in a cloud of caliche dust. Kyla looked out the rear window with the same expression she'd use when seeing an unflushed gas station toilet.

"What do they think they're doing? Are they going to run behind us all the way?"

"They've been begging for a ride in the back of the truck since we got here, and my mom promised them they could go the next time someone went out," said Kris, raising her head to look at the receding boys. She gave them the finger, and then turned around with a sigh of relief. "So where are we going anyway? And do we have to go back?"

"We're returning to the scene of the crime," Kyla answered. "See if any more dead bodies are lying around."

I flinched. Kris was just a kid. What if such casual talk of death upset her? Having a relative, however distant, murdered might be traumatic for a teenager.

I needn't have concerned myself.

"Cool," she said instantly. "Do you think the body's still there?"

I glanced at her in the rearview mirror and wondered just how many genes she shared with Kyla.

"We can only hope," returned my cousin. "Hey, are there any bullets back there? We could take turns with the rifle on the way back. I haven't shot anything in a long time."

Kris vanished for a moment behind the seat and we heard rustling sounds as she poked around. She popped back up like a prairie dog a minute later. "Two boxes, but one's half empty," she announced. "Can I shoot too?"

"Sure," said Kyla magnanimously.

"We're not shooting," I said at the same time, with a frown for Kyla. "We're just looking around."

"She wants to see if she can find her boyfriend," Kyla explained to Kris in a knowing tone.

"I don't blame her," said Kris fervently. "Have you seen that guy?"

"I know, right? And she didn't even want to invite him."

I could feel Kris's incredulous stare burning into the back of my head as we approached the gate to the next field. "What's wrong with her?"

"You know, I'm right here," I protested before Kyla could spill my secrets to this teenage pest. "I can hear you. Anyway, get out and open the gate."

"I hate opening gates," she grumbled, reluctantly opening her door.

"Then you should learn to drive a stick shift."

The caliche pit was deserted when we arrived—no body, no police tape, no Colin. I pulled close to the edge and we got out.

"Are you sure this is the place?" asked Kyla.

"I'm sure."

"Do you think we're allowed here?" asked Kris, looking around nervously.

"It's our land," answered Kyla. "Well, it's Uncle Herman's land. We can go where we want."

"They would have left a guard or at least some tape if they needed to preserve the scene," I added.

"Where was the body?" they asked in unison, and then laughed.

I stared hard at Kris, trying to see through the makeup and the piercings.

"What?" she asked nervously.

"I'm trying to determine if you two are actually evil twins separated at birth."

From behind Kris's back, Kyla glared at me, but I thought Kris looked pleased, and I caught her throwing surreptitious glances at Kyla from then on. I know her posture improved significantly by the time we returned to the truck.

Despite their morbid interest, it took a few moments before we found the nerve to walk down into the pit. In the daylight and without the presence of the dead man, it did not seem as sinister and creepy as it had in cold moonlight. The refuse pile along the back wall of the pit no longer hid menacing shadows and looked like what it was—completely worthless junk. The remains of a dead cow, rotted away to little more than a skeleton covered in ragged strips of hide, explained the horrible odor from the night before. The white powdery caliche was scuffed with dozens of boot prints made by the police and whoever came to remove the body. I wondered who did that out in the country. It seemed unlikely that an ambulance or hearse could make it over this rough ground, but I really hoped they hadn't tossed Eddy into the back of a pickup truck.

Shoulder to shoulder, Kyla and Kris hurried to the epicenter of the footprints and stood staring at a dark spot on the ground the size of a quarter. Reluctantly, I joined them, feeling like a ghoul.

"Wow. Well, not much to see is there?" said Kyla, sounding disappointed.

I frowned. "You're right. He can't have been shot here. There's not nearly enough blood."

"Isn't there? How do you know?"

"I guess I don't. But I went deer hunting once with Dad and Uncle Kel a long time ago and there seemed to be a lot more blood than this."

"So what does that mean?" asked Kris.

"That I think he was dumped. Actually, Colin thought that, too," I added, suddenly remembering something he had said.

"That's stupid. Who would shoot someone and then drag them all the way out here? It's not that easy moving a grown man. Even that little bastard Eddy must have weighed at least a hundred and fifty pounds," said Kyla.

I looked around. We really were in the middle of nowhere. The empty sky stretched over us, clear and bright. The light breeze rustled through the branches of the trees, tugging at the dead leaves, rattling the dry branches in a halfhearted way. In the distance, the dull sound of the highway a mile away was barely audible in the silence. A single overgrown track led through the trees, but otherwise this place was barely accessible. It certainly couldn't be seen from the road.

"If you had to hide a body, this isn't a bad place," I said slowly.

"It wasn't hidden though, was it? It was right out in the open," protested Kyla.

"But what if the killer was interrupted before he could finish? Say he brought the body here intending to bury it. Everywhere else on the ranch is basically solid rock, except for the wheat fields, and you wouldn't want to bury a body where it could get plowed back up. But it wouldn't be too hard to dig in caliche. You dig a hole, cover up the body, then pull old junk over the top. No one would ever find it."

"I know who I'm coming to if I ever need to kill someone," said Kyla. "You've spent way too much time thinking about this."

I couldn't tell if she was appalled or impressed.

"But how would anyone know this was here?" asked Kris. "The caliche pit, I mean."

Kyla met my eyes, and I knew what she was thinking. Everyone in our family knew about it. I could still see Kel pointing the shotgun at Eddy in the kitchen, trembling with rage. I determinedly shied away from the thought.

I said, "Lots of people might know about this place. Anyone who ever hunted here could have seen it. In the summer, they lead trail rides out this way because it's fun going through the trees. Plus someone got a bulldozer back here to dig the pit in the first place."

"Yeah, fifty years ago," said Kyla. "Look at all the junk. This pit has been here a long time."

"Well, it hasn't been that long since someone dumped that cow carcass," I pointed out. "It still reeks. And it would have taken a truck to pull it here."

"I suppose."

We spent a few more minutes looking around, but other than the dark smudge of Eddy's blood, there was nothing to see, or at least nothing to give us any insight into what had happened. The elaborate pattern of footprints and tire marks were almost certainly those of the authorities, although even if the killer's tracks were present, they would have needed to be marked with neon lights and tap-dancing raccoons to mean anything to the three of us.

On the way back to the truck, I saw a movement in the trees and stopped. Kyla bumped into me.

"What the hell?" she asked.

"One, you rear-ended me, so it's clearly your fault, and two, shut up. I thought I saw something."

Kyla and Kris both stopped and followed my gaze to the scrubby line of mesquite and cedar to our right. The feathery leaves of the mesquite had turned bright yellow in the autumn air, dark branches splaying out every which way, wicked thorns exposed to the light. The cedars grew thick, providing dense green cover, and beyond them, the real trees began— oak, hackberry, sumac, and elm, all reluctantly fading into brown, gold, and rust. Tiny brown birds flitted in the branches, and from hidden depths a mockingbird sent out a single liquid trill, but otherwise I could identify no living thing. Nevertheless, the small hairs on the back of my neck rose.

Fear grows quicker than a virus in a petri dish and is twice as contagious. It raced through me like an electric charge, then leaped to Kyla and Kris in the next heartbeat.

"Get into the truck," I said quietly.

"What do you see?" demanded Kyla.

"Nothing. Just get into the truck."

I should have known better. If I'd told her to run over to the trees to find out who or what was watching us, then she might have returned to the truck. As it was, she gave me a withering look and started forward, her ridiculous boots wobbling ever so slightly on the uneven ground.

"Grab the vests from the backseat, will you?" I called to Kris over my shoulder as I hurried after Kyla. During hunting season, Kel and Elaine made a point of keeping bright orange vests in all the ranch vehicles. No one was supposed to be hunting on the Smoke Quartz this morning, but there was always the chance that poachers might have sneaked through the gates.

I caught up to Kyla. "What are you doing?"

"No one has the right to be out here spying on us. I want to know who the bastard is. Besides, we have every right to walk wherever we want."

"Yeah, well Eddy had the right to be out here last night, too, and it didn't help him."

She grabbed my arm and pointed. "Look!"

I followed the line of her finger. "I don't see anything."

"Come on," she urged. "I saw something."

Kris ran to catch up with us holding the bright orange vests. "Here," she said breathlessly. "There were only two."

"Put one on," I told her and took the other, proffering it to Kyla, who just rolled her eyes. I slipped it on myself.

"What did you see?" asked Kris.

We ignored her and moved forward. I took comfort in knowing that we were certainly not going to surprise whoever it was. Ahead of us a twig snapped, and we froze.

"It's probably just a deer," I said in a low tone. "We should go back."

Kyla stooped for a stone the size of a grapefruit and hurled it with surprising force into the middle of the densest growth.

Something erupted from the bramble, leaped skyward in a soaring graceful arc, and was gone. With a cry Kyla started forward, but I grabbed her arm.

"Don't!" I said.

"What was it?" asked Kris, so close her shoulder bumped mine. "I couldn't see!"

"That," I said, "was a mountain lion. And trust me, we do not want to get any closer. Let him run."

"Mountain lion?" asked Kyla, and stopped trying to pull away from me. "Seriously? I didn't think we had any of those here."

I nodded. "Technically, this is part of their natural territory, although they're rare. I just can't believe we haven't heard about it before now. Every rancher in the county should be talking about it."

We turned and started back to the truck, glancing uneasily over our shoulders as we went.

"They don't attack people, do they?" asked Kyla.

"It's highly unusual, but they can," I answered. I wasn't really worried about being attacked by the animal, especially since it had seemed intent on getting away from us, but something else was bothering me. "Don't you think it's weird seeing two different animals out here that don't really belong? That kudu isn't even from this continent, and now a mountain lion."

Kyla shrugged. "T.J. runs an exotic animal ranch, remember, and his place isn't very far. I bet you anything the ku-whatever got out of its pen. We'll have to ask him."

"And the mountain lion? I seriously doubt exotic ranches deal with predators. They could never control them."

She shrugged. "Coincidence. He probably ranged outside his normal zone because of the drought, and all the activity got him stirred up."

This actually made sense and made me feel better. I could feel my pulse start to slow. "Maybe. I guess there have been a lot of hunters in the area in the past few weeks."

"Not to mention murderers and police and us. Anyway, I'm glad that's all it was. For a minute there, I thought . . ."

I glanced at her, then nodded. "Me, too."

I knew we'd both been afraid the killer had returned. Which was ridiculous, because who would come back to the scene of the crime? Unless, of course, the killer did not know the murder had been discovered and had returned to bury the body. After all, no one could have anticipated a truckload of out-of-towners coming across the body in this isolated place.

Kris looked puzzled. "What? You thought what?"

"Never mind. Let's go find Colin."

By the time we returned to the ranch house, three vehicles had arrived and were parked in a neat row beside the yard gate. The first, I was pleased to note, was Colin's Jeep. The second was a white Ford F-150 with the gold seal of the sheriff's department emblazoned on the doors and the word "police" stamped in two places on the tailgate. The third was a silver Ford Escape that I did not recognize. I pulled the ranch truck onto the grass beside the Jeep, and we got out.

Kris looked at the cars with an odd expression. "Think I'll head over to the RV," she said, and hurried away.

I watched her go with some concern. A man was dead, a girl was missing, and the police were in the house. When I'd been her age, nothing on earth could have kept me from finding out what was going on inside. The presence of an unknown car alone would have been enough to quicken my pace toward the house, not away. So was it just a desire to avoid strange adults or was she trying to avoid the police? Apart from her appearance, nothing about her suggested that she was anything other than an average teen with average teen angst and average teen rebelliousness. Now I paused to consider whether she might have something to hide. However, I decided there was no way she could conceal anything in her bunk in the RV without one of her brothers or nephews discovering it within microseconds, and followed Kyla inside.

In the big dining room, Uncle Herman was holding court at the head of the massive oak table. He sat stiffly upright on a wooden chair clutching his ornate cane, his walker beside him, his perfect posture making him look less like a frog and more like a great horned owl, all eyes and tufted hair. At the seat to his left sat Sheriff Bob Matthews, looking both tired and exasperated—a not uncommon combination when speaking to my relatives. Sheriff Bob was in his mid-fifties, tall, spare, and weathered, with a white mustache and hollow cheeks. His build was that of a high school boy who'd shot up to basketball player height before the rest of him could catch up. His fingers and teeth were stained yellow from years of coffee and cigarettes and his voice rasped like a hoarse crow's, but for all that he was well liked and respected in the town. The kids in particular loved him and called him Sheriff Bob, which is how I'd been introduced to him and how I always thought of him.

Across from Sheriff Bob, Uncle Kel and Aunt Elaine sat shoulder to shoulder. Elaine's hands were hidden below the table, but from the doorway I could see she was shredding a tissue, a sure sign of nervousness. When Kel's grandmother had first become ill and Elaine had started taking over chores, the old woman had hounded Elaine unmercifully. Sometimes after a family dinner, the floor around Elaine's chair would be littered with a miniature snow flurry of little white scraps of tissue fluff. I hadn't seen her resort to tissue shredding since the old lady had died.

On the other side of the room, Colin leaned casually against the door frame, one long leg crossed over the other, listening intently to the conversation. He looked up as Kyla and I walked in, and gave me a brief smile, warm enough to linger in his eyes even after his lips relaxed. I felt my heart give an extra soft beat. He returned his gaze to the conversation at the table, but I knew he was as aware of me as I was of him. I quietly crossed behind the table and went to his side, to find his hand waiting to take mine. The warmth of his fingers, the muscle of his arm against mine, the faintest scent of clean shirt and soap rising from his skin were completely mesmerizing. My only comfort was in knowing that I was having the same effect on him. He straightened subtly, and I felt his thumb move along my wrist in a caress.

Across the room, Herman was sounding annoyed. "I don't

understand what y'all are on about. Aren't you here about my birthday? Ninety-five today. That's the story here. What is all this other nonsense?"

Sheriff Bob was trying to maintain a patient tone, but I could hear the underlying edge to his words. "Now, Herman, everyone is just pleased as can be about your birthday, but this here is about Eddy Cranny and Kel. It's been going around that Kel pulled a gun on Eddy yesterday. Pointed a shotgun at him and threatened to blow him to kingdom come is how I heard it."

Herman laughed and turned a hazy eye on Kel. "Damn, boy, didn't know you had it in you. Wish I'd been around. And you, Bobby"—here he pointed a finger in the direction of Bob's chest—"so what if he did? That little sumbitch had it coming, and it ain't illegal to point a gun at vermin."

"Actually, it is illegal," Bob responded. "And Herman, I'm not talking to you right now. I'm talking to Kel." He turned back to my uncle. "So how about it?"

Kel sighed. "Yeah, I threatened him with a shotgun. I didn't kill him though. Did your informant happen to mention that?" Here he shot a cold look in Colin's direction, which took me by surprise. It also struck me as unfair. Even if Colin had mentioned the incident to the sheriff based on what I'd told him, he could hardly have been the only one, not with Carl Cress having been an eye witness. Carl would have lost no time in spreading that story over the entire tricounty area.

"He did," said Sheriff Bob. "He also told me how Eddy got on your bad side, but I'd like to hear it from you."

"He hit my girl. Guess that's reason enough."

"Reason enough to go after him later? Maybe threaten

106

him again, try to find out where Ruby June had gone?" Bob paused, then went on in a tone both reasonable and persuasive. "Maybe you didn't even mean to hurt him. Might be he grabbed the gun, and it went off, sort of an accident."

Kel's mouth opened, but no sound came out. Elaine was the one who spoke up. "You can't be serious, Bob."

Bob made no answer, his eyes on Kel's face.

At that instant, Herman's cane came down on the table with a bang, just inches from Bob's fingers. We all jumped, and Bob jerked his hand away.

"You accusing my nephew of murder, Bob Matthews?" Gone was the expression of an upright old owl, gone the petulant self-absorption in his birthday. This Herman Shore was the man who had earned a Silver Star on the muddy fields of Normandy and then returned to Texas to build a thriving cattle ranch from nothing. Now he glared at Bob Matthews like Patton staring down a thieving kitchen boy, and poor Sheriff Bob had nowhere to hide.

Sheriff Bob sputtered for a moment, then finally said, "No, of course not, Mr. Shore. But I got to ask these questions. It's my job."

"Then do your job somewhere else. Get off my property."

Uncle Kel added, "You ought to be looking for my daughter, not wasting your time with me."

Sheriff Bob looked from one to the other of them, then slowly rose to his feet. "If you have any ideas on where your daughter might have gone, I'd like to hear them. As far as we can tell, the last place she was seen was right here."

I said, "No, that's not true. Kyla and I dropped her off at her house yesterday morning."

He turned to me, eyes sharp. "What time was that?"

I looked at Kyla for assistance, but she just shrugged. "I don't know exactly. Maybe ten thirty or eleven."

"She say anything when you left her? Mention going out?"

Kyla and I both shook our heads.

"No, she was planning to wait for Eddy. She was going to kick his ass to the curb," said Kyla with some relish.

"Maybe," I corrected. "I'm not sure she was really planning anything like that, but she was going to talk with him."

"She seem agitated? Maybe even angry? After all, he'd hit her."

Kel made a strangled sound at the implication.

"No," I said quickly, thinking back. "No, in fact she stood up for him at first. Then when we dropped her off, she said something about Eddy not going to be surprised. She didn't seem angry at all. Maybe a little sad."

Bob shook his head, probably not sure how much he could believe. "All right then. Well, if any of you all think of anything else, give me a shout."

He made his way around the table, boots clumping on the hardwood floor. He paused beside Colin. "You coming?"

Colin nodded. "I'll be along in a few minutes."

Bob nodded, then left, pausing to catch the screen door so it wouldn't slam.

I threw Colin a questioning look, then followed him as he led the way to the front porch. I could feel my relatives staring after us.

We moved a few paces from the door so we couldn't be overheard.

Colin spoke first. "I told Sheriff Matthews that I'd be

glad to assist him. He's shorthanded, and this is a bad thing. I hope you understand, and that you don't . . . mind."

"Mind?" I turned the word over in my head. "I don't think I have the right to mind. I might be disappointed that you're going, or proud that you want to help, or guilty that I've dragged you into this, but no, I don't mind that you're going to help the sheriff."

"You didn't drag me into this," he said. "And I'm okay with you being disappointed I'm going," he added with a grin.

I felt worried. "Still, it's not much of a vacation for you."

He shrugged, then said, "I wanted to talk to you. This isn't looking good for your uncle."

"What does that mean?" I asked, surprised.

"We've been asking around. Yesterday wasn't the first time Kel and Eddy got into an argument. Kel went after him in one of the bars in town only a few weeks ago. Spotted him carrying on with another woman is the rumor. And there have been other incidents. Now this. Threatening Eddy with a shotgun, then Eddy being killed with a shotgun. It's not good."

"You're wrong. Kel wouldn't do anything like that," I said automatically, but I couldn't deny that the authorities had a reason to be suspicious. Worse, I couldn't deny that I'd felt the same suspicion, even if only for a moment.

He sighed. "I figured you'd say that."

I bit my lip. "Look, I'm not stupid. I realize that Sheriff Bob has to check him out. And I can even see why it looks bad for him. But I'm telling you, he didn't do it. You need to look for somebody else. I can think of half a dozen people who wanted to kill Eddy, and I don't even live here."

"Why? Why don't you think he shot Eddy?"

I thought about it, then answered, "Because if he had killed him, he wouldn't have dumped the body like that."

Colin blinked. "Didn't expect that. I thought you were going to say he wasn't capable of killing a family member."

I snorted. "I wish I could say that. I saw him that morning, and I'm still not sure he wouldn't have pulled the trigger if the rest of us hadn't been there. I don't know what's going on with him, and you were right, he's not acting like himself. But he's not a sneak, and he's not an idiot. I don't believe he would have tried to hide the body. But if he did? He would have done a better job than that. You need to look for someone else."

Colin gazed beyond me toward the barn on the hill, eyes unfocused, mulling over my words. I took the opportunity to study his face, the blue eyes beneath black brows, the shadow of his beard along the long firm jaw, the way his dark hair waved just a little at his temple.

After a moment, he nodded. "We'll look. But, I just want you to be prepared for the possibility that things aren't what you think."

I frowned, not happy. But if Colin said he would consider other possibilities, then he would, and I decided to let it go for now. In the yard, the branches of the pecan tree twitched and then rustled in an unexpected breath of wind. Looking up, I could see a bank of gray clouds, still hazy and distant, rolling along the horizon. A cold front was on its way from the north, and I gave a shiver. Colin noticed and put his arm around my shoulders.

Without thinking, I slid both arms around his waist under his jacket and lifted my face to say something undoubtedly profound about the weather. His change of expression stopped me. I heard his sharp intake of breath, and the next thing I knew his mouth was on mine, and he was pressing me against the length of his body. An unexpected wave of desire flooded through me, heedless and wild, the passion I'd been trying so hard to hold in check for the past few weeks flaring. Colin ran one hand through my hair, caressing the nape of my neck and slid the other down my back, hard fingers hot through my shirt. My breath caught against his lips, and I arched against him, wanting to be closer, wanting to feel his skin against mine.

Fortunately or unfortunately, a dry little voice interrupted us.

"Jeez, get a room. Or at least a show on pay-per-view."

Bemused, I broke away from Colin's embrace and turned to see Kris, spiky black hair teased upright and restiffened with blue hairspray. She was glaring at us like a particularly strict member of the Order of the Little Sisters of Chastity and Piercings, lips pursed and disapproving.

Pushing by us, she stalked into the house, slamming the door behind her for emphasis. It would have been a very nice display of 1950s prudishness if she hadn't ruined it by giving Colin's backside what could only be described as an appraising look as she passed.

He gave a wry laugh, then looked down into my face. "We have got to work on our timing," he said.

"Yeah." I pulled myself away from him with a sigh, feeling and matching the reluctance with which he let me go.

His smile was warm, filled with promise and something far more. A look that a woman dreams of seeing in a man's eyes. It was almost certainly my own fault that it was a look that scared me to death.

"Now I'm willing to believe that you're glad I'm here," he said, his voice low.

"You have your good points," I said lightly. "For one thing, I'm not cold anymore."

The hurt in his eyes was more than I could bear. "Colin . . ."

"It's all right," he said abruptly. "I'm rushing you. I know it, and I just don't seem to be able to stop myself. I'll back off."

"Not too far," I said quickly, feeling a sharp pang of fear. What if he decided all the mixed signals were the sign of a neurotic mind, and that I just wasn't worth the effort? What if he decided he didn't want me anymore? I could hardly blame him if he did.

He slipped on his sunglasses and gave me an imitation smile. "Not too far," he agreed.

The words were right at least, but I still felt like the world's biggest idiot as I watched him walk away. Had my divorce and then my unsuccessful attempt at a long-distance relationship made me a coward? Was I willing to give up before I'd even started, just to avoid possible future heartache? I hated myself, but I did not run after him.

Chapter 4

BARS AND BOYFRIENDS

Colin did not return that afternoon, not even for Thanksgiving dinner. Considering the circumstances, I thought he'd made a wise choice. Kel and Elaine had fallen into a grim silence that spread a pall over the company. Uncle Herman, on the other hand, seemed to be preparing for battle. He'd appeared at the table wearing a pressed shirt and dress pants with a crease that could be used to slice bread. It was true that the pants were held up by both a belt and suspenders, but he'd left his walker in his room, a fact that had caused Aunt Elaine some alarm. She'd hurried to his side, but he just glared from under bushy eyebrows and she backed off. I hadn't seen him so upright since the days when he'd still been running the ranch himself, and wasn't sure what to make of it. On the one hand, I liked seeing him so much like his younger self, but on the other, I suspected he was making plans that would almost certainly bite one or more of us in the butt.

However, as the afternoon wore away, my fears seemed

groundless. After we'd finished the turkey and all the fixings, Elaine produced an enormous birthday cake with enough candles to trigger a smoke detector. Uncle Herman ate his cake with pleasure, told an off-color story about his visit to Paris after the war, and then retired to his rooms for a rest. With a collective sigh of relief, Will, Sam, Christy, and Uncle Scotty returned to the living room for more football, and Gladys suggested a game of Monopoly for the rest of us. Kyla met my eyes with a look of panic. Both of us would rather chew broken glass than play Monopoly.

"We'll do dishes!" I announced, and urged Elaine to join the game.

Kyla gave me a sour look, then with a philosophical shrug joined me.

Half an hour later, the dishes were done, and I started thinking about Colin again.

"Where do you think he is?" I asked, rinsing off a plate and placing it in the dishwasher.

"Your boyfriend? Who knows. I don't know why he has to stick his nose in around here anyway."

"Sheriff Bob needed the help. Besides, it's probably better to have Colin keeping an eye on what's going on. I can just see Bob getting it into his head to arrest Kel."

"You could hardly blame him. But I still don't think it's any of Colin's business. He should be here making eyes at you."

"Yeah. Well."

"You did it again, didn't you? Told him to back off?"

I didn't answer. I did begin pacing.

Kyla, with her usual tact, said, "You've gone batshit crazy, and you're trying to take me with you. Let's go see what's happening in town."

"Nothing's happening in town. It's Thanksgiving and it's after six. Even on a weekend, the streets would already be rolled up. Today they're rolled up and watching football."

"We'll go for a drive then. Look, for all you know, Monkey Boy's been trying to call you. We can at least drive up to the top of the hill to see if we can get some bars on the phones."

"Monkey Boy? Why Monkey Boy?"

"He dances for you," she answered.

"No, he doesn't. I don't even know what you're talking about."

"Yes, you do. Come on, let's go for a drive."

I considered. I was so used to my cell phone being useless near the ranch house that I'd forgotten to check it, but there were several places on higher ground where reception was possible. Maybe Colin had been trying to call after all.

We slipped out of the house quietly as we could to avoid detection. Outside, the temperature had dropped noticeably. The sky was a black void and outside the warm glow of the house lights, the darkness seemed immense.

"It's a lot darker out here than it is in the city," observed Kyla, holding out her hand to me.

I looked at her. "No shit. And what do you want?"

"Keys. I'm driving."

"It's my car," I protested. "It could have been your car, but you insisted we take mine so yours wouldn't get dirty."

"Yeah, well I'm tired of opening gates. So gimme." When I didn't immediately hand them over, she added, "This way you can check your phone while I drive."

I dropped the key ring in her hand and went to the passenger side. She slid in and immediately adjusted the seat position, the lumbar support, the rearview mirrors, the side-view mirrors, and the heater controls. I stared.

"What the hell are you doing? We're the same height. My settings would work perfectly for you."

"This is better. You'll probably thank me later."

At the top of the hill, I opened my phone. A single green reception bar flickered halfheartedly at the top of the display. Kyla glanced at it as we bumped up the uneven road.

"A flip phone? Are you kidding me?"

"Hey, it works. And it was free."

"I bet it was."

"It's a phone. It makes phone calls."

She shook her head, but decided to let it go. "So any message from Monkey Boy?"

"And no, I don't see a message, but I'm not convinced I've really got reception."

"Dig mine out of my purse. It was made in this century, so it might work better."

"Yeah, but he's not calling you."

"So seriously, what's up? You guys are crazy about each other. Why aren't you doing something about it?"

"We haven't been dating long enough to know if we're crazy about each other."

"Really? And how long do you have to date to know that? Is there a magic timer somewhere, and you're waiting for the big ding?"

She pulled up to a gate, and I took the opportunity to hop

out without answering. I glanced back the way we'd come, wondering just how long it would take me to walk back, but it was cold so I reluctantly abandoned that idea. Instead, I unlatched the chain and swung the metal gate wide enough to allow the car to pass through.

She appeared to still be waiting for an answer when I got back in.

I said, "So where are we going?"

"To town and don't try to change the subject. I've seen the way he looks at you, so I know the problem isn't him. What's up with you? Is it because he's a cop?"

"What? No."

She shrugged. "Scary job. You might have concerns about it."

"No, that's not it. Although thanks for putting that in my head."

"Then what?"

"Look, I don't know, all right? Leave it alone."

She drummed her fingers on the steering wheel. "He's not Mike. He's not going to transform into a giant douche and leave you for some blond bimbo."

Mike Karawski, lawyer, asshole, ex-husband. "Kyla, you're driving me crazy. I know he's not Mike."

"Then what? Is it the Ranger thing? Are you worried he's going to transform into Alan and get too busy to see you?"

Yes, I was, but I wasn't going to talk about it with her when I hadn't even discussed it with Colin. I gritted my teeth and stared out the windshield into the wedge-shaped glow cast by headlights into the inky blackness. Visibility to either side of the car was almost zero.

"Or is it that you're still wanting to make it work with Alan?"

"I'm dating, all right? Dating. That means you spend some time with someone so you can get to know them. I'm dating Colin because I don't know him yet."

"What about Alan? You know him by now, right? You're keeping him dangling, too."

Alan. That was far more complicated. I thought I'd loved him. No, if I were honest with myself, I was absolutely sure I had loved him. And then somehow we'd started drifting apart. I blamed the distance at first. Dallas was three and a half hours away, close enough to spend weekends together, but too far to be spontaneous. And over time, the daily or twice daily phone calls had dwindled to a couple a week. Every weekend had become every other weekend, then even less. It was as though the relationship had run out of fuel. But I still had feelings for him, didn't I? And now he was doing everything in his power to make things work between us. Should I discard a man like a used tissue because circumstances made seeing him inconvenient? Or because I'd met someone else who made me want to jump on him every time he walked into the room?

Kyla grew impatient. "Fine. Don't talk about it. But I'll tell you one more thing, and then I'll shut up."

"Good!" I interrupted.

She ignored this. "You're going to lose him. How long do you think he's going to hang around with all the mixed signals you're giving him?"

"You're the expert on successful relationships," I snapped. "Dating Sherman one minute, out with T. J. Knoller the next. My role model."

Her knuckles whitened on the steering wheel, but to my surprise she didn't bite my head off. "I've never dated anyone I wanted to keep. The guys I go out with are interesting or fun or nice, but never all three at the same time. And not one of them has ever looked at me like Colin looks at you. I'm not saying you won't get hurt, but if you drive him away without giving him a chance, then you're even dumber than I thought."

I swallowed hard. Hearing my own worst fears put into words made them all too real. I said, "Maybe I'll just dump them both and learn to like cats."

Kyla snorted. "Terrific. We can become the creepy spinsters living together in an old mansion on a hill with thirty cats and no litter box."

"Maybe in our spare time, we can take in boarders and kill them while they sleep," I suggested.

"Well, yeah. We'll need a hobby."

"Excellent."

We both grinned, then Kyla punched on the radio and hit scan. The radio eventually picked up a crackling San Saba station and started belting out a Brad Paisley song. Kyla's finger darted out to hit scan again, then froze an inch from the button.

"Did he really just say 'I'd like to check you for ticks'?" she whispered in horror.

"Romantic, huh?"

Then we were both laughing and trying to sing along, with me pretending I didn't know the words by heart and the awkward conversation behind us. At least for now.

As I'd predicted, Sand Creek was closed up tighter than an oyster. Most of the empty little shops twinkled with early Christmas lights, but the courthouse and the decorated hanging tree were dark, waiting for the official lighting to take place the next day. Kyla drove slowly around the square, then made a right onto the road that eventually connected to the highway to Austin.

"Where are you going?" I asked.

"Just looking around. Isn't Colin's hotel out this way? We could see if he's there."

"He said he'd back off. What's he going to think if I follow him to his room a few hours later?" I protested.

"He told you he'd back off, and you're letting him do it?" Her voice squeaked with indignation. "Anyway, it's Thanksgiving. Nobody should be sitting alone in a hotel room."

That made a pang of guilt shoot through my chest. It didn't help when I heard her mutter under her breath, "You really will be living with cats."

But when we drove into the parking lot of the seedy little motel wedged between a gas station and the John Deere franchise, we saw no sign of his Jeep.

"I wonder if he changed motels after all," I said.

Kyla wrinkled her nose. "Let's hope so. Otherwise you'll have to delouse him before you jump his bones."

She pulled back onto the road and drove slowly back toward town. A pickup truck, the only vehicle in sight, signaled right. Kyla followed him.

"What are you doing?"

"Just seeing what's what. Hey, look at that! Civilization," she said, then added, "Of a sort."

Just off the main square, lights streamed from R.T.'s BBQ and Sports Bar. The "and Sports Bar" had obviously been added as a marketing afterthought at least a decade after the original sign had been painted and which probably meant that someone had mounted a TV on the wall next to the dartboard. About a dozen vehicles, most of them pickups, parked on the gravel lot beside the building. Kyla guided my little Civic between a mud-spattered Suburban and a red extended-cab pickup and turned off the engine.

"We're going in?" I asked her. I actually liked R.T.'s, or at least I had before it had become a sports bar. The barbecue was excellent, and they had a decent selection of beer. The thought of Kyla voluntarily entering was another thing.

"Why not? It's the only game in town. Besides, we're still looking for Ruby June, right? This is somewhere she might be."

I thought it highly unlikely Ruby June would be sitting in R.T.'s. For one thing, by now everyone in town knew she was missing, and someone would have called Elaine if she'd been spotted in a public place. On the other hand, our only other choice was to return to the ranch and spend the rest of the evening playing Monopoly or watching football. I shrugged and followed her.

The restaurant was a long low building with a covered front porch stretching along the entire length of the building. The railing along the porch was wide enough to hold plates and was lined with wooden stools. At the far end, two plastic white tables and a stack of white plastic chairs were pushed into a corner where they would wait until the weather warmed enough for outside dining. Although no one manned the enormous black smoker, the cold air was filled with a faint lingering scent of mesquite smoke and brisket, rich and warm and tangy. In a halfhearted display of Christmas spirit, someone had tacked an uneven string of green twinkle lights along the gutter and wrapped the rough cedar support posts with fuzzy gold garlands.

Inside seemed overly warm after the outside chill. And smoky. Austin's strict smoking ordinances had not yet reached Sand Creek. The air inside was as murky as the bottom of a stagnant pond, and the haze produced a respectable halo around the neon glow of the Lone Star Beer sign above the bar. The television blared in the far corner, where a group of men and women sat in a circle of chairs pulled from the dining tables. A foursome circled the pool table while keeping one eye on the game, while another group did the same at the dartboard. It was loud enough and smoky enough that no one noticed our entrance except a harassed-looking waitress who hurried by with a pitcher of beer and a tray of bar snacks.

"Happy Thanksgiving. Sit anywhere," she called over her shoulder as she zoomed by.

Kyla immediately led the way to the bar. The bartender, a man in his late thirties with a gut that suggested he wasn't averse to sampling his own wares, was in the process of filling another pitcher. He briefly lifted his eyes from his task to glance our way and forgot to lower them. Kyla had that effect.

Now she held his gaze and gave him a dazzling smile. And waited.

Beer ran over the top of the pitcher, making him jump

and scramble for a bar rag. Red-faced, he spilled the excess into the drain and wiped the sides of the pitcher before setting it on a waiting tray.

"You're evil," I told her in a low tone.

"I love to do that," she whispered back, totally unrepentant.

The bartender joined us. Or rather, he joined Kyla. "Happy Thanksgiving. What can I get you?"

"Vodka martini," she said. "Extra olives, please."

He looked completely devastated. "Um, sorry. We're out. Of olives, I mean. Not vodka. We have that." His eyes darted back and forth as though he were watching a tennis game. Then a light dawned. "I could probably run next door, see if Alice has any in her fridge," he offered eagerly.

"Why, that is so nice of you," Kyla began. I kicked her foot. "But, no. I couldn't ask you to do that. How about a twist?"

"Absolutely!" he said eagerly and turned.

"I'll have a Shiner Bock," I called to the back of his head.

He waved a hand, probably to indicate he'd heard although possibly just to bat away an annoying distraction, and began pouring enough vodka into a silver shaker to make a Russian sailor say, "Whoa."

"How do you do that?" I asked Kyla.

She turned ingenuous blue eyes on me. "What? Order a drink?"

I turned away from her to survey the room. Now that my own eyes were accustomed to the dim light and had mostly stopped watering from the smoke, I could see the others in the room. One of the men playing darts was Manuel, Carl Cress's ranch hand. He was carefully not looking our way. I thought I could make out the massive shoulders and thick neck of Carl himself silhouetted in front of the glowing TV screen. Poor Manuel. If Carl didn't even cut him loose on Thanksgiving Day, he didn't stand much of a chance the rest of the year. I turned back to the bar in time to see the bartender handing Kyla both an overflowing cocktail glass and the shaker that contained the excess. He stood staring at her, and if his mouth wasn't hanging open, it might as well have been.

"Could I get a Shiner?" I asked for the second time.

"Make that two," said a voice behind me. A long arm reached around me with a debit card. "And these are on me."

I turned and saw T. J. Knoller, and felt my heart give a disappointed little drop. For one split second, I'd thought the deep voice might be Colin's, which was more an indication of my own thoughts than any similarity between the two men. It was the first time I'd seen T.J. indoors, and I thought that without his cowboy hat he looked both younger and less authoritative. On the other hand, I had to agree with Kyla's assessment that he was one fine-looking man.

Kyla greeted him with a brief flashing smile, then demurely lowered her eyes. He was at her side in an instant, bending over her, head cocked attentively to catch any word she might care to utter. I'm not sure his feet even moved—I think he might have been sucked directly into her orbit like a wayward satellite.

The bartender handed me my Shiner, set T.J.'s on the bar, and then turned with a disgruntled air to run the card. I suppressed a grin.

A thought occurred to me. "Hey T.J., are you missing any animals on your place?"

124

He turned, puzzled. "I don't think so. Why do you ask?"

"We saw a strange antelope, a kudu, on our place yesterday," I said.

Kyla added, "Yeah, right before they found the body."

T.J. frowned. "I heard about that. Terrible thing. Poor old Eddy. I'd known him since we were kids."

"I'm very sorry," I said, wishing I could kick Kyla again. I wanted to talk about kudu, not Eddy Cranny.

"Yeah, well. It's not like we were close. But still, when it's someone you know . . ." His voice trailed off, and Kyla put a comforting hand on his arm. He took the opportunity to draw her arm through his and cover her hand with his own. I suppressed an eye roll at such a touching display of grief.

"So no kudus missing?" I tried again.

"Nope, it's not one of mine. I've had them on my place before—hunters love 'em. But I've had a hard time getting them recently. They've gotten really expensive."

"Where the heck could it have come from then?" I wondered aloud.

T.J., who'd already turned back to Kyla, gave me a little smile. "There's another exotic ranch about thirty miles north, and there's not a fence between here and there that would even slow a kudu down. I'll give the owner a heads-up in the morning. Chances are it's one of his."

From the corner, a huge shout went up as concerned viewers expressed their displeasure at the outcome of a particular play and their opinions regarding the referee's eyesight, species, and head location. They also had many helpful suggestions about the types of personal actions that he could perform upon himself. In the general mayhem, Carl Cress stomped over, looking disgusted. And disgusting. He was somewhat worse for drink, his John Wayne walk unsteady and weaving. Above his gleaming belt buckle, his shirt was wet with what I hoped was just spilled beer. He caught sight of the three of us too late, and with only a slight hesitation joined us at the bar.

"Can you believe that bullshit?" he asked of no one in particular.

"Definitely not," answered Kyla, looking him up and down.

He reddened slightly. "'Nother pitcher, Joey!" he called to our bartender, who was already filling two at once at the taps.

T.J. gave him a cold glance. "Big Bender all set for the race tomorrow, Carl?"

Puzzled, I looked from T.J. to Carl and back. What in the world did Carl have to do with the race?

"What is a Big Bender?" asked Kyla, taking a sip of her martini.

For once, T.J. did not give her his full attention as he answered. "Carl's racehorse. My main competition tomorrow, not that I'm worried. Just looking for a good run." He kept his eyes on Carl.

Carl swayed again, looking slightly sick. Maybe he was even drunker than I'd thought at first.

"Yeah. Yeah, he's ready," he answered. Then he added, "I guess."

T.J. released Kyla's hand and straightened. "What's that supposed to mean?"

126

Carl shrugged. "Nothin'," he muttered. "Shouldn't have said anything."

T.J. took a step toward him. I stepped back. Whatever was going on had suddenly upped the tension to critical mass. We were one snotty remark away from a fistfight, and I wasn't sure how that had happened.

"What the hell do you mean?" T.J. repeated.

Carl held up both hands. "Hey, now. No need to get upset. I wasn't s'posed to say, but you'll know by tomorrow anyway. I don't own Big Bender anymore. Sold him."

A muscle worked in T.J.'s jaw. "Sold him to who?" he demanded.

Carl just shook his head. "That's private. But I'm out of it. Clean out of it. Washed my hands, you know what I mean?"

He held his hands up again, apparently to demonstrate how clean they were, then backed up a few steps before turning and rejoining his cronies around the football game.

T.J. stared after him blankly, fists clenched at his sides, fury almost palpable. I met Kyla's eyes and saw she was as puzzled as I was.

"What difference does it make who owns a damn horse?" Kyla asked.

T.J. slowly released a breath, drew another, and then turned back to us. He was in control again although it had taken some effort. "Honestly? It doesn't. Now, a different trainer, different rider—that might affect the race, but it doesn't matter who owns him." He sighed and took a long drag at his beer, then gave Kyla a rueful glance. "I was just really looking forward to beating that bastard," he confessed.

We both laughed at that, and after a second, T.J. joined in. Kyla rehooked her arm through his, and he looked down at her with an expression that sent a pang through my heart. They made a very pretty pair.

My phone rang, the faint sound so unexpected that it took me a moment to register what I was hearing above the sound of the noisy bar. I dug through my purse and pulled it out, flipping it open as fast as I could, expecting to hear Colin's deep voice full of apologies and explanations for where he'd been all day.

As I'd hoped, the voice on the other end was a man's. But it wasn't Colin.

"Hi, Jocelyn."

"Alan!" I tried to mask my surprise. "Hi. Oh, and happy Thanksgiving."

"Yeah, you, too." He sounded distracted. "Where are you?"

He must be wondering about the noise in the bar.

"Hang on," I told them, then slipped between two couples who had just come in the door and stepped out onto the quiet, if somewhat chilly, front porch. The twinkle lights cast a greenish glow across the picnic tables. I leaned against the wooden railing.

"That's better. I can hear you now. Kyla and I decided we needed to escape the football madness, so we drove into town and found a really happening place."

"I bet," he laughed, then became serious. "With Kyla, huh? What about what's-his-face?"

"He's not here at the moment, but . . ." I trailed off, my throat feeling like it was being squeezed. This was so awk-

128

ward. Hearing a burst of laughter in the background over the phone, I quickly asked, "So where are you? Watching the game with your friends?"

"Sort of. Well, no. Actually, I'm here. At your aunt's house."

Chapter 5

RACEHORSES AND RIVALRIES

Kyla could not stop laughing on the drive back to the ranch. I was not nearly as amused.

"What am I going to do?" I asked her.

"Did you notice that T.J. did not offer to give me a lift back?"

"Who cares? Maybe he had plans," I snapped. "Can't you think about someone besides yourself for five minutes? Seriously, what am I going to do? And what am I going to say to Aunt Elaine? What's she going to think about a second guy showing up to visit me?"

"Oh, she probably won't be that surprised."

"What do you mean? Of course, she'll . . ." I stopped, suspicion flooding into my thoughts.

I looked at Kyla sharply. She suddenly seemed extremely interested in the short strip of road illuminated by the Honda's headlights.

"You didn't," I said to her profile. "Tell me you didn't arrange this."

"Well, make up your mind. Do you want me to tell you I didn't arrange it, or do you want me to tell you the truth? I simply suggested to Alan that it might be smart for him to pop down to spend the holiday with his sweetie. It didn't seem fair that Colin was getting all this special attention."

"Colin's only here because you invited him."

"Well, one of us had to. Besides, you're having trouble making up your mind, and holidays can be an important differentiator. After all, you need to know how they're going to handle your relatives."

"I can't believe you," I said. "This is a nightmare."

"I don't see why. I think I've already accomplished my objective."

"What do you mean? If your objective was to drive me completely insane, then yeah, I guess mission accomplished."

"No, not that mission."

"I should make you walk home," I said, taking my foot off the accelerator.

She ignored this. "Look, what was your first reaction when you heard Alan was here?"

"It was a toss-up between 'oh, hell' and 'I'm going to kill Kyla,'" I snapped.

"No, that second one came later. The point is you're not happy Alan is here."

"No shit, Sherlock."

"Say it slowly. You . . . don't . . . want . . . Alan . . . here," she said.

131

I ground my teeth together. "I don't want you here, either. That doesn't mean I don't like you. Oh, wait. It does!"

She just laughed.

To my relief, the scene at the ranch house was less horrific than it might have been. I burst through the front door half-expecting poor Alan to be tied to a chair under a naked lightbulb while my relatives grilled him. Instead, he was holding a beer and sitting on the sofa between Uncle Scotty and my brother Sam watching the football game. The rest of the men were clustered around on various chairs and stools. All three of them were leaning forward in excitement, Uncle Scotty shouting something exceptionally uncomplimentary about the eyesight of one of the refs. At the sound of the door, Alan jumped up to greet me. The others didn't even turn their heads.

At the opposite end of the spectrum, the Monopoly players in the corner could not have been more riveted. Aunt Elaine gave me an encouraging, if worried, smile, Aunt Gladys and my sister-in-law Christy greeted me with patently fake cheeriness, and Kris just stared with open-mouthed curiosity. I let Alan give me a quick hug, then dragged him into the kitchen, which was blessedly empty. I closed the door and leaned against it.

I had last seen Alan less than two weeks ago, and he had not changed. Everything that I found attractive about him was the same, from his softly curling brown hair, to the fascinating gray-green of his eyes, to his broad shoulders. He was still fun, intelligent, and sexy. He had not changed. But I had.

He set his beer down, took a look at the way I was braced against the door, then rested a hip on the table. "I guess you weren't expecting me, huh?"

132

"No. Sorry, I had no idea you were coming. I would have been here . . ." I started, then faltered.

He nodded thoughtfully. "Not your fault. I guess I figured that Kyla would have mentioned it to you, but I knew I should have talked to you myself." He gave a twisted half smile. "I was afraid you'd tell me not to come."

I could not think what to say. The rules of hospitality demanded that I reassure him, that I make him feel welcome and comfortable, that I soothe everyone's feelings except my own. But I also didn't want to lie to someone I truly cared about. Through the door, the football gang gave another shout and then burst into a wild cheer.

"Why did you come?" I heard myself ask, then almost clapped a hand over my mouth. "I mean . . . oh, I didn't mean it that way. I mean, I'm really glad to see you, but you knew that . . ."

"That your cop was here?" he asked. "Yes, you told me."

I waited.

He finally said, "I just plain wanted to see you. And I guess I wanted to see for myself how things were between the two of you. I have to admit I'm not sure that this was such a good idea."

I had to laugh at that. "That might qualify as an understatement."

"Possibly, although I learned two fairly positive things. One, your cop isn't staying here. And two, he's not here now. Where is he, by the way?"

"He's in town somewhere," I answered, hoping my voice sounded positive and unconcerned. "I'm sure you've heard by now that my cousin's husband was killed. He's been helping the sheriff."

Alan glanced at his watch. "At eight o'clock on Thanksgiving? Pretty dedicated."

I nodded. I was starting to feel very warm and suddenly realized I hadn't taken off my coat. I unbuttoned it and threw it on a kitchen chair, glad to have something else to look at, if only temporarily. Having Alan here, seeing him again, feeling this awkward finally made everything clear. Painful, but clear.

"I . . . Alan, I just think . . . ," I began.

He gave a long sigh and then saved me from having to say the words out loud. "Yeah. And that's the less positive thing I was afraid I might learn if I came. And the one thing I had to know."

"I feel like an idiot. I don't know what I'm doing," I confessed. "And I've treated you terribly."

"Now you are being an idiot," he said, but gently. "We were in it together, and I've known exactly what was going on since . . . well, for the past few weeks. You've been completely honest with me. If anyone was an idiot, it was me. My fault for letting things slide between us."

This was true actually, although it would not be kind to agree. Moreover, I wasn't sure that meeting Colin wouldn't have torn us apart even if we'd been rock solid. And that certainly wouldn't be a good thing to admit, either.

Instead I settled for the inane and obvious. "You are the nicest guy I know."

He gave a snort. "Great. Now you get to ask me if we can be friends."

I swallowed and felt my eyes fill with tears. It was the first bitter statement I'd ever heard from him, and it cut hard. I struggled to think of something to say, but he saved me the effort again.

"Look Jocelyn," he said, "give me a few months, then ask me. Seriously. Because I really do hope we'll be able to be friends. Also because I don't think that cop is going to be able to make you happy. When things go south, you call me. You and I had something pretty special."

"I'm just so sorry," I whispered.

"Me, too," he said. He shrugged, then went to the sink to pour the rest of his beer down the drain.

"You want another one? Or some food? I didn't even ask if you'd had any dinner tonight," I said, suddenly realizing he'd been on the road for a good portion of the afternoon.

"Thanks, no. I think I'm going to head on home."

"To Dallas? You can't, it's too late," I protested.

"There's no traffic. I'll be home before midnight. Don't look so worried," he added with a smile. "I've made longer drives in a day. This is nothing."

He folded me in his arms one last time, and I clutched him back, breathing in the scent of him, feeling his warmth and strength, full of regret and relief. He squeezed hard for an instant, placed a kiss on the top of my head, then released me.

"I'll go say good-bye to your family. Do me a favor and wait here 'til I'm gone?"

I nodded, and he slipped through the door.

I sank into a kitchen chair, feeling numb, trying not to listen to the sounds on the other side of the door. Kyla walked in a few moments later, carrying a tumbler-sized martini full of olives the size of golf balls. She plunked it down in front of me.

I eyed it listlessly. "You know I don't drink that shit."

She went to the refrigerator, returned with a carton of orange juice, and topped up the glass to the brim. "There."

I took a sip and choked a little. "He's such a great guy. I don't know why it stopped working."

"Too little, too late," she shrugged. "He didn't really start trying until someone else was interested."

"Yeah. But what if that doesn't work either?" I felt an enormous wave of sadness. "I just met Colin. I don't know how I feel about him. Or actually, I do, but what if he's not who I think he is?"

"At least now you have a chance to find out. You would never have let yourself really try if Alan was lurking in the background."

She was probably right, but that did not make her less insufferable. "You know I hate you," I said.

"Yeah, I know. You're welcome."

Friday morning was chaos in the overcrowded ranch house. Even after drinking about a quart of vodka, I'd lain awake most of the night, and it felt like I'd barely drifted off when I was jolted awake by a cacophony of alarm clocks, fumbling steps, and the not-so-hushed voices of the little group who'd decided to go deer hunting. In the bunk next to me, Kyla groaned and pulled her pillow over her head. A couple of the cousins did likewise, the rest didn't even twitch.

"I'm going to kill them. What the hell are they doing?" came her muffled voice.

"At least we can be sure the deer population is in no danger. With that much racket, anything with four legs has already sprinted into the next county," I groaned.

Yesterday's nonstop schedule of cook, eat, clean, and repeat had somehow produced a burst of energy within the Shore clan. A couple of hours after the hunters departed, the rest of the house sprang into action, and shortly after breakfast a shopping expedition to Austin was organized. My head was pounding, but I gave up and wandered downstairs in search of coffee and aspirin.

In the kitchen, Aunt Elaine tried to interest Kel in accompanying her. "Why don't you go with us, hon?" she asked him. "Scotty and Sam are dropping the ladies at the mall, then driving down to Cabela's," she added as though trying to bribe a sulky toddler.

Cabela's was a sporting goods store almost bigger than the small town just south of Austin in which it was located. It specialized in hunting, fishing, and camping equipment and boasted among other things an indoor archery range and parking for semis. Without exception, my male relatives got a misty far-off expression at the mere mention of Cabela's.

Kel's eyes misted for an instant, but then he pulled himself together. "I'm staying right here. I haven't forgotten our daughter is missing, even if you have."

"Your staying here isn't going to bring her back any faster," Elaine retorted. "You know she's likely in Austin staying with Katy Ferrera and that young man of hers. Jocelyn's boyfriend is checking on her right now."

Kel looked from her to me with a sour expression. "Boyfriend One or Boyfriend Two? Or are there others we don't know about yet?"

I glared at him, remembering just in time that it wasn't good manners to flip off my elders. Instead, I turned to Elaine.

"Is he? Is Colin"—I stressed the name—"checking on Ruby June? How do you know?"

"Sheriff Bob called last night," answered Elaine absently, not taking her eyes off her husband. "He and Colin were canvassing the town, asking after all her high school buddies. Turns out that her friend Katy left for Austin Wednesday morning, and we figure Ruby June went with her. Katy's folks are mad—they've never even met this so-called boyfriend of hers, but at least they had his name. He's a nice young man—your Colin, I mean," she added, "not Katy's boyfriend. Doing all this when he's meant to be spending the weekend with you."

"That's really good news," I said, feeling both relief and a new anxiety. So Colin had gone to Austin without saying anything to me. What did that mean? Was he planning to come back or was this his way of giving me the space I'd so foolishly requested?

She smiled. "It's wonderful news. And," she added, looking straight at Kel, "I'm going to shop the sales with everyone else. You can stay here and stew by yourself. You want to come, Jocelyn?"

I shook my head. "I can shop in Austin any time. Kyla and I are going to the races."

"Well, good. Maybe you can take Uncle Herman with you. He wants to go, and I can tell already that Kel won't take him."

Kel said nothing, jaw set, looking mutinous.

Elaine added, "Guess that means you'll be in charge of the kids while we're gone," she said to him, and walked outside.

The look on Kel's face was such a mixture of defiance and horror that I actually felt a little sorry for him.

In record time, two Suburbans full of eager shoppers trundled down the ranch road heading toward Austin. Through the window, I noticed Kris wearing an oversize black leather jacket stalking up the hill toward the barns. The first Suburban slowed, the driver stopping to say something, but then the two cars continued on, leaving her alone again. A little way off, a pack of kids went running toward the pond. I went looking for Kyla to tell her the latest.

I found her in the bathroom running a straightener through her dark waves. Half her hair already lay sleek and shining on her shoulders. Today, she wore jeans and a pink cardigan with pintucks, ruffles, and what I believed was called a sweetheart neckline. Gold gleamed at her throat and her ears, and I could smell her perfume from the doorway. I frowned, wondering what this careful preparation might mean for T. J. Knoller. The phrase "dead man walking" sprang to mind.

I dropped my bombshell about Uncle Herman.

"Oh good. That won't cramp our plans at all." She glared at my reflection in the mirror as through it were my fault. "What are we supposed to do with him when we go sit in T.J.'s box? Not to mention the party after. There's no way I'm missing either."

Oh yeah, T.J.'s party. Well, that explained the primping at least.

"We'll take him with us. If he refuses to sit with T.J., I'll stay with him and you can go to the box. And then we can drop him off here after the races."

Somewhat mollified by my sacrifice, she nodded agreement. "So Colin went to Austin, did he? Did he tell you he was going?"

"No."

"Is he coming back?"

"I don't know. And if you say I told you so, I'll kick your ass."

She clicked her tongue. "I wouldn't be so cruel. Besides, give Monkey Boy some credit. He's not the type to pull any of that passive-aggressive shit. If he was dumping you, he'd just say so."

"I wish you'd quit calling him Monkey Boy," I said absently.

However, she was right about Colin. I'd let my own insecurities give me a scare.

From the mirror, Kyla's blue eyes swept over my clothing. "You should get dressed," she said. "We don't want to miss the first race."

I looked down at my worn jeans and bulky cotton sweater, which I'd thought was pretty cute until about two seconds ago.

"I *am* dressed," I protested. "And it's not like we're going to Ascot, if you know what I mean."

She rolled her eyes heavenward as if asking for strength, but then with a sigh returned to her hair straightening. Which was just as well, because a front had blown through and it was chilly outside. I wasn't going to freeze so she could have a stylish companion. I also couldn't wait to see her reaction to my puffy goose-down coat.

I wandered back downstairs, figuring that with Kyla's state of preparation I had time for another cup of coffee if the pot was still on. In the kitchen, Uncle Kel sat at the head of the wooden table, staring down at his hands. Behind him, the coffeemaker sputtered a little and let off a puff of steam. Elaine must have started it before she left.

I walked past him to get a coffee cup. He didn't even raise his head.

"You want some coffee?" I asked.

His shoulders lifted a half inch or so, which I interpreted to mean yes. Filling two mugs, I sat beside him and slid one in front him. After a moment, he listlessly cupped his hands around it, but made no move to drink.

"It's good news about Ruby June. Being in Austin, I mean," I ventured.

This did produce a reaction, although not the one I expected.

"That's bull! There's no way she went to Austin. She's in trouble, and no one is doing anything about it."

I frowned at him. "She was pretty upset that day you threatened Eddy. Why don't you think she might have gone off with one of her friends?"

"She just wouldn't," he said, as though saying it made it true.

I tried another approach. "You've seemed a little on edge since we got here," I said, which was a candidate for understatement of the year. "I mean, even before Ruby June left. Is there something going on?"

He shook his head. I looked at him, exasperated. It was like talking to a post, only less rewarding. I tried one more time.

"You know the police are investigating . . . the family," I sidestepped saying "you" at the last minute. "In connection with Eddy."

At this, he did raise his head, and I was surprised by the flash of amusement in his eyes. "You can say it. They think I killed the miserable little bastard. I know it, and I can't even blame them," he said, then added with some bitterness, "Much. I admit, I wanted to kill him that morning."

"You almost did kill him. I've never seen you like that."

He looked ashamed. "Well, now. I might've lost my temper, but I hardly almost killed him." At my doubtful expression, he gave an exasperated sigh. "The gun wasn't loaded. I just wanted him to think it was."

I stared at him, then rose and went to the back door. Picking up the shotgun, I broke it open. Sure enough, the two long barrels were empty.

"Shells are on top of the fridge," he said with a chuckle. "You don't honestly think we'd keep a loaded gun where all those kids could get at it, do you?"

I slowly put the gun back in its place, feeling both relieved and puzzled. "Why didn't you tell Sheriff Bob?"

His eyes narrowed. "I don't waste my time arguing with fools. And he wasn't exactly in the listening mood. Seemed hellbent on disbelieving everything I said. Suspicious cuss."

I thought it probable that Kel's surly attitude might have something to do with Bob's suspicions, but I thought diplomacy might be in order. "You think Bob is looking for a scapegoat?"

He shrugged. "I think Bob is in over his head and feeling panicky. He'd like to catch the murderer fast—it'd look good come next election. But mostly he'd like to be able to sit back and have himself a merry Christmas. Not that I can blame him for that."

"Colin says that there are rumors about some Mexican drug cartel operating around here."

Somewhat to my surprise, he didn't immediately deny it. "What kind of rumors?"

"I'm not sure. Something about drugs and money laundering."

Taking another sip of coffee, he said, "There's a lot of money in town these days. That racetrack . . . I have no idea how they raised the funds for that thing. I'll grant you it's pretty rinky-dink compared to someplace like Ruidoso, but it still cost plenty."

"So who started it?"

"No idea. But Carl Cress is one of the contractors, if you can believe that shit. And Sheriff Bob is on the board of directors. So's one of our county judges, a few ranchers, some big lawyer from Dallas. It's almost like they went out of their way to get the most respectable people possible. 'Cept for Carl, a' course."

"On the other hand," I said, "even the most legitimate enterprise would want respectable people on the board."

"Yeah, I suppose."

"And I thought you liked Carl," I said. Which admittedly was something I'd never understood.

He grinned. "Sure I like him. Don't trust him farther than I can throw him, but I like him fine. He's useful, gets things done. He'll skim off the top if he can get away with it, and I have to add his bills up myself because he tends to make 'mistakes,' but he's usually worth it."

How you could like someone you didn't trust was beyond

me, but I let it go and instead said, "So, do you think Eddy could have been involved with the cartel?"

He took his time answering. "I wouldn't have put much past the little rat except making it to the big time in drug dealing or anything else. But getting himself shot like that? Could be."

He picked up the coffee cup and took another sip. "You know, two days ago I couldn't imagine anything much worse than losing this place."

I followed his gaze. Through the window, the pecan trees framed a wide expanse of grass field sloping down to the wide pond, its surface mirroring the steel gray of the sky. Beyond that, mottled brown cattle grazed in a field dotted with mesquite and prickly pear. The desire for land ran strong in Shore blood. Even I, despite a childhood spent in cities across Europe, felt a tug when I looked out over these rolling hills.

"Are you really in danger of that?" I asked.

He shrugged. "We've had a few bad years. The drought is hurting the cattle and crops. Economy means we haven't had the hunters or vacationers like we've had in the past. We're scraping by like we've done before. We figured another year or two would set us right again, but this lawsuit . . ."

"Does T. J. Knoller know what he's doing to you?" I had a hard time reconciling my impression of a man whose focus seemed to be solely on pretty girls and racehorses with this portrayal of a ruthless land robber.

"How could he not? He's not the man his father was, but he surely knows how tight a ranch runs." He rose abruptly, coffee slopping out of his cup and onto the table. He patted my shoulder as he walked by. "I guess it's time for me to do something about it."

"Do what?" I asked, but he just shook his head, grabbed his hat from the rack, and headed for the door.

I jumped to my feet. "Seriously, where are you going? You're not going to do something stupid are you?"

He half turned, looking amused again. "It's time to feed the cattle."

I watched him go with a feeling of deep uneasiness. Too many of my family members seemed to have hidden plans and secret agendas. It made me very nervous.

Half an hour later, the race-going contingent was ready to go. I held the door for Uncle Herman, and Kyla stared at me as she passed.

"Are you really wearing that coat? You look like the Michelin man."

"It's warm," I protested. "You'll be wishing you had a better coat within ten minutes. And I'm not leaving early because you're cold," I added.

Kyla just rolled her eyes and took the opportunity to slip behind the steering wheel while I was helping Uncle Herman into the front seat of my little car. She'd do anything not to have to open gates.

I handed Herman his cane and pulled his seatbelt down for him. He was in rare form, griping about the quality, size, and discomfort of goddamn sumbitch foreign cracker boxes passing themselves off as automobiles and what was the world coming to? I closed the door in midstream.

The door of Aunt Gladys and Uncle Scotty's trailer opened, and Kris drifted into the yard along with a swirl of fallen pecan leaves carried by the brisk breeze. She looked like the mournful ghost of piercings past, spiky hair blown flat, nose rapidly reddening with the cold.

"So where are you going?" she asked. Her tone was carefully indifferent, but her expression seemed wistful.

"The races," I answered. "Want to come?"

She glanced dubiously through the rear window at the back of Herman's head and met my eyes.

"I know," I agreed. "But think of the material you'll have when you're back home and bitching to your friends about all of us."

She brightened at this and went to the rear passenger door.

"Don't you want a bigger coat?" I asked as I opened my own door. "There's a few spares hanging in the hall closet."

Her scornful expression encompassed both my suggestion and my own choice of heavy outerwear. Really, her resemblance to Kyla was almost unnerving at times.

With a fickle change of heart, the gray sky lightened and the heavy clouds parted to reveal patches of blue by the time we reached the racecourse. A respectable-size crowd had already gathered, a few people sitting in the stands, but most still milling about the betting windows under the bleachers. Although it wasn't yet noon, the air smelled of popcorn and funnel cakes, lending to the festive atmosphere.

T. J. Knoller met us near the front gates, and I couldn't help but suspect he'd been waiting for Kyla. If he was taken aback by her little entourage, he was far too polite to show it and immediately extended the invitation to sit in his box to all of us.

"Good morning, boy," said Uncle Herman, shaking hands. "Can't imagine what your grandpappy would be thinking if he could see you now."

This was such an odd way of putting it that T.J. blinked before saying, "Thank you, sir. I hope he'd be pleased at some of the improvements I've been making."

Herman ignored this. "I'm going to take a look at the horses, but I'll join you before the race starts. The fourth, isn't it?"

"That's right," said T.J.

Uncle Herman turned to me and extended his arm in a courtly gesture that I could not refuse. I took it and glanced back at Kyla, who shot me a smug grin.

"We'll meet you in the box then. Top tier, right in front of the finish line," called T.J. as we walked away.

Kris hesitated, then drifted along behind Uncle Herman and me. Herman carried his cane over his right arm, shoulders square and proud until we rounded a corner, then he lowered it to the ground and began thumping along at a respectable clip that forced me to lengthen my stride to keep up. I heard the tap of Kris's boots quicken behind us.

"In a hurry, Uncle Herman?" I asked.

"We shoulda been here an hour ago. I want to have a word with a trainer."

"Don't you think the trainers are probably a little busy right now?" I asked, thinking that even if they weren't, they were hardly going to welcome advice from this particular member of the race-going public.

Herman just gave me a knowing smile and hobbled forward, generating enough breeze to make his eyebrows flutter.

When we reached the stables, a sheriff's deputy holding a clipboard stopped up.

"Sorry, folks. Only authorized personnel can enter," he said formally.

Herman didn't even slow. "I am authorized, you damn fool. And why aren't you out looking for my granddaughter?"

"But I'm off duty . . . ," the deputy began as we breezed by him.

I could hear him flipping through the lists attached to his clipboard, but to my surprise, he did not call us back and we made it safely into the cool dim interior, filled with the scent of straw and cedar chips, horse sweat and leather. We stood aside as a stable hand led a glossy gelding from one of the stalls toward the door. Animal and boy both gazed at us in the same patient incurious way.

"Son, can you tell me where Wes Carstairs is?" asked Uncle Herman.

The boy paused briefly. "Next aisle over, 'bout halfway down. Sir," he added belatedly. There was something about Uncle Herman that prompted long ago learned tokens of respect from even the most recalcitrant youths.

"Thank you," said Herman, then took my arm and led the way to the next aisle.

"Who's Wes Carstairs?" asked Kris.

"Yeah, and why are you authorized to be here?" I added.

Herman just gave a secretive smile.

In the next aisle, a diminutive man held open a stall door as another stable hand led a tall chestnut horse from within. It danced and sidestepped on its lead, muscles rippling under a coat so glossy it almost shone. This display of energy made no impression on either of its handlers, but I figured keeping a healthy distance was good policy. Uncle Herman, however, seemingly had no such qualms. He walked right up to the trio.

"How's he looking, Wes?"

The smaller man looked up. I guessed him to be in his forties and even in boots, the top of his head barely reached my chin. I wondered if he was or had been a jockey.

"Mr. Shore. Good to see you, sir." He turned to the stable hand. "Take him out and walk him 'round a minute. I'll join you directly."

He and Herman shook hands, then Herman nodded to the departing animal.

"Looking good. Frisky. I like that."

"He's in great shape. I have every confidence he'll have a good run."

"But will he win?"

"He's got a better chance than most," said Wes carefully.

Herman chuckled. "I've got a feeling. We're winning today, and that sumbitch T. J. Knoller will be history."

I looked from Herman to Wes and back again, a terrible suspicion filling my mind.

Wes looked pained. "He's the best horse I've ever worked with, but I'll tell you what I tell all my owners. Nothing in racing is a sure thing, and never bet more than you can afford to lose with a smile."

Herman made a noise that I could only describe as mouth flatulence. One of the nearby horses lifted a startled head.

Wes sighed. "Well, I better go supervise the saddling."

"See you in the winner's circle," said Herman.

Herman turned and almost ran into me. I stood with hands on hips, my best teacher stare in place. It was the same look I used when confronting a pack of boys who had just duct taped one of their own to a flagpole.

Herman paled a little, but met my eyes defiantly. "Let's get back, missy."

"Not so fast. Why are you authorized personnel here, Uncle Herman? And what do you care about racehorses?"

"Not racehorses. One racehorse. That's Big Bender, the favorite in the Cornucopia Stakes. Biggest purse in the state."

"Uh-huh. That's not an answer to the question I asked."

"He's mine. And he's going to beat Knoller's chunk of walking dog food, and I'm going to be there to watch him do it. Now come on." He tried to hobble around me, but I blocked his way again.

"What do you mean he's yours? I thought he belonged to Carl Cress," I said, thinking that the conversation I'd heard at R.T.'s BBQ and Sports Bar was starting to make more sense.

"Up until last week he did. And now he belongs to me."

"How can you could afford to buy the favorite in a big race? The last time I checked, Kel and Elaine were wringing their hands over getting sued, and I'm pretty sure they're not only worried about losing the suit, they're worried about losing the ranch. So where'd you get that kind of money?"

"Ever heard of horse tradin'? Mr. Cress and I came to an understanding. Cash wasn't a part of it."

I didn't like the sound of that. What in the world could he have traded Carl for a valuable racehorse?

"But why? Why would you want a horse?"

"T. J. Knoller is messing with the wrong family. He might

have had a little understanding with Carl about the outcome of this race, but he doesn't have it with me. We'll see how he feels about suing his neighbors when he doesn't have a pot to piss in or a window to throw it out of. And this is none of your business, little lady."

And with that, the old man actually whacked my legs with his cane until I stepped aside and then stomped back toward the racetrack without looking back.

I stared after him. My mouth might even have been hanging open a little. I finally remembered to shut it and turned to Kris. "I guess we better stop and put a bet on Big Bender," I said.

Kris and I made our way to T. J. Knoller's box about fifteen minutes later, corn dogs and Cokes in our hands, pari-mutuel tickets hidden in our pockets. After all, T.J. didn't need to know we were betting against him. Herman had found the box on his own and was sitting in the row below T.J., pointedly ignoring him and, after one sweeping owl-eyed glance, the rest of us. Kyla, who was sitting beside T.J. and wearing his padded jacket over her shoulders, took one look at my snack and wrinkled her nose.

"Do you know what hot dogs are made of?" she asked.

"Pig anuses, I believe," I said with my mouth full. "Want a bite?"

To my left, Kris lowered her corn dog and took a hurried sip of Coke. T.J. laughed out loud, probably to keep warm. His fingers were turning blue. If he stayed around Kyla much longer, he would have to learn to wear two coats. Kris also looked a little chilly, whereas I was toasty warm in my puffy coat. I tried not to feel smug. I also tried not to wonder how long I'd have to wait before asking Kris if she was going to finish her corn dog.

We watched the next two races with interest, running down to place small bets, then returning to cheer on the runners. T.J. had been right—betting made the event more exciting, and winning two dollars in the second gave both Kris and Kyla the opportunity not only to recoup their losses from the first, but to gloat. Kris had once again forgotten about maintaining her teenage angst, and practically skipped beside Kyla as they went to collect their winnings. When they returned, Kyla showed her how to fold the bills in half and then fan through them while holding them in my face.

"You see," she instructed a rapt Kris, "it doesn't matter how much you win as long as it's more than Jocelyn. Notice how flicking it this way makes just enough breeze to blow back her hair."

"Like this?" asked Kris.

I jerked my head back in annoyance. "No, you horrible little monster." I glared at Kyla and added, "Can't you teach her anything good?"

"It's a valuable lesson in savoring the small pleasures of life."

The two of them giggled.

After the third race, however, the atmosphere in our box changed dramatically as preparations began for the next race. T.J. absentmindedly tucked Kyla's arm through his, but he no longer continually glanced down at her with attentive adoration. Uncle Herman stopped throwing dirty looks over his shoulder at the rest of us and turned his complete attention to activity on the track.

Kris looked around. "Anyone going down to make a bet?" she asked hopefully.

Because she was under twenty-one, she needed one of us to place her bets for her.

I patted my pocket. "We already have our bets for this one," I reminded her.

"Oh, is this it? Go Big Bobo . . . Wait, what's his name again, Uncle Herman?"

"Big Bender," said Herman.

Kyla shook her head. "No, this is the race T.J.'s horse is running. You want to bet on Double Trouble."

The rest of us said nothing, and her smile faltered. She shot me a puzzled glance and mouthed, "What?"

I just shook my head. There was just no way to pantomime "your insane uncle bought a racehorse that he's hoping will beat the shoes off your boyfriend's horse."

Near the track railings, a small group gathered around a grizzled bent little man holding a lesson on racing forms and giving betting tips and strategies. Around our box, people trotted downstairs to place bets, then returned at a more leisurely pace with tickets and drinks. Despite the chill, everyone was having fun, getting into the excitement and novelty of the new track.

At last, a line of horses ridden by brightly clad jockeys began dancing their way to the starting gate. T.J. shifted forward, resting his elbows on his knees as a muscle tightened in his jaw. The first two horses walked into their gates with little fuss, but the third balked, skittered and had to be coaxed in. The fourth, recognizing a brilliant idea when it saw it, spun away until I wondered how his jockey managed to maintain his perch on a saddle the size of a coaster. Finally he, too, was subdued, and the last four pranced into their gates like pros. The announcer began his prerace patter.

No one in our box was saying a word. Uncle Herman sat rigidly upright, his blue-veined hands clenched atop the handle of his cane. Beside Kyla, T.J. rose and gripped the painted railing next to his seat as if afraid someone were going to wrestle it away from him. I did not like this. If betting a dollar produced mild excitement, I wondered how much it took to produce this type of white-knuckled terror. I felt sympathy sweat break out on my own hands and surreptitiously wiped a palm on my jeans, no longer sure I enjoyed racing after all. Kyla kept trying to catch my eye, but there was nothing I could tell her.

Down on the track, a buzzer sounded, the gates burst open and eight horses surged onto the open field, a blur of legs and power topped by a rainbow of fluttering silks. Within seconds two colts surged ahead of the rest, the sky-blue colors of T.J.'s Double Trouble and the yellow of Uncle Herman's Big Bender. From our vantage, they seemed to be only inches apart, as though one jockey could put out a hand and touch the other. The crop held by the inside rider rose and fell in a frenzied slash. I could almost hear the slap of leather on rump, although of course that was impossible above the roar of the crowd. What I was never sure afterward was whether I heard the rifle shot, the brief pop ripping through the sound of hooves, shouts, and cheers. It seemed as though I did, as though the sound itself knocked the man in sky blue from his perch on the glossy back. One moment, yellow silk and blue fluttered together like stripes on a flag, then blue listed to one side and vanished.

The nearest horse swerved violently and crashed into its neighbor, propelling both toward the fence. The jockey atop the second horse tipped sideways and began sliding down before the first jockey grabbed and yanked him back. Behind them, the rest of the horses scattered, parting around the startled pair like water through rocky narrows, then continued around the track. In the lead, the jockey in yellow looked over his shoulder in bewilderment, then urged his mount onward. Far behind, the riderless horse slowed first to a canter, then to a trot, and at last stopped near the railings. In the dust of the track, a crumpled form in sky blue lay motionless.

For only a moment, for the infinitesimal beat of a heart that nevertheless seemed to last an eternity, the crowd sat stunned and silent. Then, with a collective gasp, the race-goers leaped to their feet, pointing, questioning, hands to throats or mouths. Within seconds, paramedics ran out onto the field with a stretcher and someone else ran to catch the horse. One of the medics gave a shout, and a deputy joined them, then started talking into his radio. Two other deputies ran onto the track to confer with the first, then raced off again. Moments later a white police Bronco bumped across a nearby field toward a stand of trees.

T.J. stepped over Kyla, pushed past me, and pattered down the steps, his cowboy boots clicking on the concrete like hooves, leaving us without a word.

In our box, stunned silence prevailed, until finally Kyla said, "What just happened?"

As if in answer to her question, the announcer's voice came on over the intercom system. "Ladies and gentlemen. There is no need to panic, but we ask that you proceed in an orderly fashion to your vehicles."

The resulting stampede began at the word "panic." I glanced at the open field beyond the track to the stand of trees where a gunman lay concealed, then back to the race-goers running and pushing their way down the steps. I quickly blocked the way out of the box.

"Just wait!" I ordered. "Wait until the aisles clear. We don't want to get trampled."

"What the hell is going on?" asked Kyla again.

All around, terrified spectators streamed down the aisles, mothers clutching children by the arms, husbands and fathers protectively guarding their families. As the last family from the rows above us clattered down the stairs, I offered Uncle Herman my arm.

Uncle Herman reluctantly allowed me to assist him down the steps and the others followed.

"Has everyone here gone insane?" Kyla asked.

I had no answer for this. I glanced over my shoulder to the track. The paramedics were still bending over the motionless figure in the dirt. I thought back to our first visit to the racecourse, when T.J. had so proudly shown off his beautiful horse and introduced us to his trainer and jockey. Travis Arledge. The name came back to me, as did the worried line between his black brows when he'd spoken of bribery. Please, please, don't let him be dead, I thought.

We finally reached the ground floor where a good percentage of the crowd was still milling about in confusion, family members trying to find each other, fear thick as smoke in the chill breeze that whipped around concrete pillars. Someone in a hurry bumped into Uncle Herman, knocking the cane from his hand and almost sending him off balance. I gripped his arm to steady him while Kris hurriedly retrieved his cane.

"Come on, let's get out of here," I said.

I was just leading the way past the betting booths when we heard a shout.

"There! Stop him!"

It was loud enough that we turned, only to see T. J. Knoller and Sheriff Bob Matthews bearing down on us. I looked over my shoulder to see who they meant, but there was no one there. Puzzled, I turned back, realizing they were coming for us.

Realizing the same thing, Herman shook off my hand and stood straight. "What's this about?" he demanded.

T.J.'s face was white, and he carefully kept his eyes on the sheriff, avoiding Uncle Herman or Kyla. "Ask him. Ask Herman Shore what he knows about it."

Kyla and I flanked Uncle Herman like protective guards and Kris took her place by my side in a nice little display of family solidarity.

"What is this about?" I asked before Herman or Kyla could explode.

Sheriff Bob looked grim. "Someone shot that rider right off his horse."

Kyla threw me a wild glance, her lips forming a silent "oh."

"And Travis? Is he . . . is he going to be okay?" I asked.

"It's too soon to tell. He's still holding on, but it doesn't look good," said Bob.

"No, it doesn't," said T.J. "And the one responsible is right there." He pointed at Herman, who stared at him first in surprise and then with growing anger.

T.J. continued. "I know you bought Big Bender off Carl Cress, old man. What, you placed a bet and then decided you couldn't afford to lose?"

Herman gripped his cane and took a step toward the younger man. I put my hand on his arm. I probably wouldn't be able to stop him lashing out with it, but I might be able to deflect the first blow.

Kyla gave T.J. a startled glance, not even angry yet. "That's ridiculous. We've been with you this whole time."

"I said he was responsible, not that he pulled the trigger."

Sheriff Bob patted the air with his big hands. "Now let's stay calm."

"Calm?" said Herman with a certain amount of justifiable outrage. "With this little upstart accusing me of murder?"

Bob ran his hand through his white hair. "You're right," he admitted, then turned to T.J. "That's a serious charge. It ain't murder yet for one, and God willing it won't be. And two, you can't honestly think Herman here would do something like that."

"Why not? He bought a racehorse didn't he? Just to beat me."

"That don't mean he'd try to kill your jockey, Knoller. A shot like that? This ain't Hollywood. There's not a man in a thousand who could hit a rider on a galloping horse."

My heart sank. Even before T.J. spoke, I knew what he was going to say.

"No?" T.J.'s voice was ice. "I can think of one not twenty miles from here who could do it. Someone who won the Lion's Club rifle contest just last month. So tell me. Where is Kel Shore right now?"

Chapter 6

MUGGINGS AND MURDER

"Well, that was fun," said Kyla, pulling open the door of the barn and holding it for me.

After dragging Uncle Herman away by his scrawny arms to keep him from using his cane to pound T.J. into a quivering cowboy-shaped bruise, we'd managed to push him into the car and drive back to the ranch. Kel had returned to the ranch house a few moments after we arrived and he and Herman were still in the middle of a heated discussion. Kris vanished, and Kyla and I grabbed two beers and a sack of chips and headed for the barn on the hill. It was chilly, but at least it was quiet. I flopped down on a bench seat that had been scavenged from some old truck and opened the Doritos, trying not to think about the rodents that were probably using the seat as a nest.

"I wish I knew what was going on around here," I said, hoping my voice didn't sound too whiny.

"What do you mean? It's pretty obvious what's going on,"

answered Kyla, taking a swig of beer and looking around, as though wondering if there were some better place to sit.

There wasn't. The barn was a massive wooden structure topped by a tin roof, mostly empty except for a green John Deere tractor with tires as tall as a man crouching in the middle of the dirt floor like some prehistoric juggernaut. The truck bench was the only piece of furniture, a redneck version of a loveseat resting on the small concrete slab that formed the floor of a makeshift tool nook. The chill air smelled of old hay, dust, and gasoline, and our voices vanished into the vast space without even a hint of echo.

"It's not obvious to me," I said, feeling irritated by her knowing tone.

She rolled her eyes. "Someone didn't want T.J.'s horse to win that race. They made damn sure it didn't. What's to understand?"

"Okay, yeah, I guess that part is obvious. But why? And more importantly, who?"

Kyla shrugged. "Money. Wasn't it the biggest prize in the state or some such nonsense?"

She walked to the tool bench, gingerly pulled a pink rag from the little stack on top, and examined it. She returned and began flicking it against the seat beside me, which had the effect of puffing the dust onto me. I closed the sack of chips and glared at her.

"Do you mind?"

"These are my good jeans," she said, as though that made it okay. However, she stopped flicking, spread the rag on the seat, then perched on it gingerly.

I went on. "Anyway, shooting a jockey seems a little on

161

the extreme side, don't you think? Especially since Big Bender was already out in front."

"Maybe someone needed to make sure."

"Then we're back to who. The one who benefits most is Herman as the new owner, but we know he didn't do it and we know Kel didn't either," I said.

There was a pause, then Kyla said, "We don't actually know that. And don't give me that look," she added as I opened my mouth to protest. "Kel was here all by himself, driving the truck around doing chores all over this place. He could very easily have slipped away to the track, shot the jockey, and made it back without anyone knowing he was gone. You can't tell me any of the kids would have noticed anything."

"But—"

She held up a hand. "I'm not saying he did. I'm just saying he could have."

Since this was exactly what T.J., the police, and probably half the town were thinking, I could hardly argue. I took a swig of beer, crammed a few chips into my mouth, and looked around.

Although I'd visited the ranch a couple of times a year since my high school days, I hadn't been inside this barn in a long time. Not, in fact, since the year Kel and Elaine had decided to try their hand at raising sheep. I'd been delighted with the woolly newcomers, all curls and bleating, and I'd eagerly volunteered to help hold the lambs for their vaccinations. What I hadn't realized until after we'd started was that lambs have long plump tails, Texas ranchers believe that those tails need to be docked, and that the docking operation was going to occur simultaneously with the vaccinating. My brand-new pair of Red Wing work boots were splattered with blood by the time we were through, and I still had a vivid recollection of Carl Cress counting the pile of tails to tally the number of new lambs. Even as a teenager, I'd instinctively disliked him for no particular reason, but my feelings gelled into loathing on that day when he'd tossed a tail at me and laughed.

"Carl Cress," I said suddenly, sitting up straight.

"What about him?"

"Maybe he didn't want Double Trouble to win."

"Why would he care?"

I was excited by this idea. "Look, Carl owned Big Bender, right? I know he sold him, so he wouldn't be eligible for the prize money, but remember what T.J. said about the real money being in the side bets? What if Carl had made a huge bet on Big Bender? One that he couldn't afford to lose."

Kyla considered. "Why sell then? Why give up the prize money?"

"We need to ask Uncle Herman that. I don't know how he got Carl to sell, but I bet you anything Carl wasn't too happy about it. Remember what he said to T.J. in the bar about how he wasn't supposed to tell? Maybe Herman forced his hand somehow."

"Maybe," she said doubtfully. "But then what? Carl decides he can't take the chance that Big Bender will win fairly and decides to shoot T.J.'s jockey?"

When she put it that way, it seemed pretty thin. On the other hand, desperation could make even smart people do stupid things, and Carl, although endowed with a certain amount of feral cunning, was not exactly bright. I also knew he could handle a rifle. And more importantly, it was a theory that did not point directly to one of my family.

"I just don't think it would hurt to see what Carl was doing during the race." I pulled out my cell phone and checked for messages. Colin still had not returned my call, a fact I found unsettling. I could think of a dozen logical reasons for this, but "he's dumping me" ranked well in the upper third. Besides, it was annoying since I definitely could have used his help.

The crunch of tires sounded on the drive outside, and I leaped to my feet and rushed to the door, hoping to see Colin's Jeep. Instead, I saw the white Ford F-150 with gold sheriff's logo bumping its way down the uneven drive.

I turned to Kyla. "Looks like Sheriff Bob is here to talk to Kel."

"Well, great. I guess we better go down."

We'd made it halfway down the hill when Kel and Herman came out of the house, followed closely by Sheriff Bob. The three of them got into the truck and started up the hill toward us. I broke into a trot, then stopped in the middle of the road to block the way.

Sheriff Bob slowed and rolled down his window. "We're just going down to the station for a statement. Nothing for you to worry about."

"Are you arresting them?" I asked, voice squeaking a little.

"Nope. Just a little chat."

"Then why can't you do it here?"

He didn't answer, instead giving me an impatient look and growling, "Move."

From the backseat, Kel leaned forward, white-faced, and said, "I've called your aunt, and she's on her way. You stay here and look after the kids 'til the rest of 'em get back."

Reluctantly I stepped aside, and they drove on, leaving Kyla and me in a cloud of caliche dust and confusion. We stood for a moment, looking across the open fields of yellow grass that swept down toward the pond where a group of children had paused in their play. Kris came out of the house holding arms in front of her chest, her spiky raven hair whipped by the breeze.

"Come on," I said, making up my mind.

"Where are we going?"

"To talk to Carl Cress."

"On purpose?" she protested, but she followed me down the hill and into the house nonetheless.

It took me a few minutes of digging through kitchen drawers to find Aunt Elaine's battered Rolodex, but at last I unearthed it from beneath a pile of junk mail and thumbed through for Carl Cress's number.

"I can't believe anyone still uses those things," Kyla said, staring at the Rolodex in the same way she might have looked at an abacus. Kris nodded in agreement.

I took the house phone from its cradle on the wall.

"It's the same reason people still have landlines. They work when the power goes out, and you don't have to worry about reception," I said as I dialed.

Carl had three numbers listed on the card, and every one of them went to voicemail. I ground my teeth a little.

"We'll just have to go hunt him down. I think I remember where his ranch is."

"Really?" asked Kyla.

"Yeah, I think the turn's off the highway past the airport."

"No, not 'really, do you remember where his ranch is?' I mean 'really do we have to go talk to Carl?' He's such an ass, and what would be the point?"

"I want to know where he was during the race. None of us saw him—don't you think that's suspicious?"

"Not especially. It's not like he had a horse in a race after all, and it's certainly not like we were looking for him."

"Nothing goes on in the town that Carl doesn't try to control, and I want to know why he wasn't there."

"Oh, and you think he's going to tell you that if you ask?"

I hated when she used logic against me. I thought for a second, then said, "We'll ask Manuel. We don't even need to talk to Carl. And then when Manuel says that Carl took his rifle and drove to the racetrack, we'll go to the sheriff and get Kel and Herman out of there."

For one moment, I thought Kyla was going to refuse. But just then, we heard the pounding of feet on the front porch and the door burst open, revealing a rabid pack of kids. I don't think there were actually six hundred of them, but it seemed like it.

"We're hungry," shouted one shrill voice.

Kyla met my eyes, then turned to Kris. "Sorry, Arugula," she said. "Duty calls. It's your turn to take one for the team."

We fled, leaving Kris staring after us with an expression of horror-stricken betrayal. Kyla laughed all the way to the first set of gates.

◆   ◆   ◆

I had not been to Carl's ranch in years, and if it had not been for the double Cs on the gate, I would have thought I was in the wrong place. The house was probably the same modest 1940s long low rectangle, but someone had painted it pale green and tacked white gingerbread trim along the wide front porch. Curving beds of mostly leafless shrubs were dotted with concrete fawns, rabbits, and ornate birdbaths. A fat plaster gnome peered out from beside a fake weathered wishing well full of dead geraniums.

I parked.

Kyla spoke first. "Either Carl had a nervous breakdown or he married Snow White."

"I'm absolutely speechless," I said.

"I assume with envy." She pulled her phone from her purse and snapped a picture. "I'll send this to you to use as a model for your next landscaping project."

"Good. A few gnomes and a concrete mushroom would really spruce up my front porch." I looked more closely. "Those birdbaths are dry as a bone and the flowers have been dead for a while. Whoever put them here isn't taking care of them anymore. Wonder if Snow White left him."

I opened the door and got out. The faint sound of hammering reached us from the direction of a tin outbuilding a hundred yards away.

"Someone's home," Kyla said.

"And it sounds like that someone's working, which means it's definitely not Carl. Let's go see."

We found Manuel bent over what looked like an old feed trough, carefully replacing a splintered board with a new one. He straightened as we entered, his expressions changing from warm welcome to a certain wariness as he recognized us. I was not sure what to make of that.

"Hi, Manuel," I said. "We're looking for Carl. Any idea where he is?"

"No. I am sorry," he answered. Although heavily accented and seldom used, Manuel's English had always been quite good.

"Did he go to the races today?" asked Kyla.

So much for beating around the bush.

"I . . . I am not sure," he answered, his eyes sliding to one side.

"What do you mean you're not sure? Haven't you talked to him today?" she asked.

He responded with a stream of rapid Spanish and ended by holding both hands in the air as though to prove how empty they were.

Kyla stared at him blankly. "Well, okay then. Thanks anyway."

I gave him a half wave, and we returned to the car. Behind us, the sound of the hammer started again.

"I wonder what that was about," she said. "He speaks English perfectly well. That was just rude."

"He said that Carl comes and goes at all hours, and he, Manuel, has too much work to do to keep track of a . . . I think 'scoundrel,' although it might have been 'asshole.' He wishes that people would stop asking him where Carl is and that one day he will have enough money saved to be able to return to his family in Mexico and never see Carl again. That day cannot come soon enough, and he wishes that stupid girls would stop pestering him when he has better things to do."

Her eyes widened. "Shit, I forget you can do that. Why didn't you answer him? He would have died."

I laughed. "Yeah, that would have been fun, but he really doesn't know where Carl is and it never hurts for someone to think you can't understand what they're saying. You learn loads of stuff."

"So what now?"

"Let's go to the police station. I still don't like it that Sheriff Bob took Kel and Uncle Herman in like they were criminals."

"What, you think he's applying the thumb screws?" she asked.

I didn't smile. "Hey, I watch cop shows. What's the most important thing you learn?"

"How would I know? I don't watch that crap—I actually have a life," she protested.

"Never talk to the police. Never." I was sure about this, even though I knew if Colin were present, he'd be rolling his eyes.

"Why not?" she asked.

"Because they always twist your words and then end up arresting you."

"Aren't the people they arrest in those shows usually guilty?"

"Well, technically yes. But the advice is sound."

I started the engine, and we bumped back toward the main road. We'd driven about another mile toward town when I saw a truck parked by the side.

I slowed. "Wonder what they're doing. That's a weird place to stop."

Kyla looked up from her phone. "Who cares?"

"We do. I think that might be Carl's truck."

I thought that mostly because I was pretty sure I'd seen Carl in the front seat as we whizzed by. I applied the brakes. No one was coming in either direction, so I performed a skillful four-hundred-point turn—the road was that narrow—and pulled up behind the pickup.

"What the hell are you doing? Are you going to walk up and ask him if he's the one who shot the jockey?"

"That's what you would do. I'm the tactful one, remember?" I said, as I got out of the car.

I thought it was odd that Carl still hadn't turned to see who was walking up behind him, but maybe he was on his phone. I tapped softly on the glass, hoping I wouldn't startle him too much, then I froze.

The rifle between his knees had tipped a little to the left, but the barrel still pointed toward his face. Glazed and unfocused, his open eyes stared straight ahead, a thin trickle of blood streaming from one corner of his mouth above the red mess that had been his throat. I backed away slowly, fighting down a wail I could feel rising from somewhere in my chest.

Nothing would ever startle Carl Cress again.

I bumped into Kyla, who had her head down looking at her phone.

"Hey, watch it," she said automatically.

I gripped her arm and pulled.

She shrugged me off impatiently. "What are you doing? Let go."

"Don't go any farther," I urged. Of course, I might as well

have told her to hurry up and look in the window, because that's what she did.

To my surprise, she neither squealed nor threw up. Instead, she stared at the dead figure for a moment, then turned. Her face had lost all color but she seemed in control.

"Well, damn. That's really gross. I think that qualifies as one of those things that just can't be unseen."

She let out a shaky breath and suddenly sagged against the truck. I looked at her in concern. She did not look well.

I didn't feel very good myself. "We should call someone," I said. "Should we ask them to send an ambulance?"

"What for? He's not going to need medical attention. But the police will know what to do. Hey, at least they can let Uncle Herman and Kel go now."

"What do you mean? And get off that truck. It's a crime scene. Besides it's dirty," I added since she didn't seem interested in obeying me.

At that, she did straighten up, turning to check her backside for dust. "Crime scene my ass. Carl Cress killing himself is hardly a crime. You know, I wonder if this means he's the one who shot the jockey. And maybe Eddy, too. You said you saw them arguing, right? Maybe he figured he wasn't going to be able to get away with it."

"Yeah, but . . ."

"But what?"

"You think he killed himself?"

I could not bring myself to look inside the truck again. However, I didn't need to. The image of the rifle and the bloody throat was imprinted on my memory forever. I suppose it was possible to commit suicide with a rifle held between the knees, but it didn't matter. Carl Cress was not the type. He might beat up Eddy, he might cheat a neighbor or kick a puppy, but kill himself? No way.

"Hello?" Kyla was speaking into her phone. "Yes, I'd like to report a death."

I walked back to the car, feeling sick to my stomach. I opened the door and sat down in the driver's seat, trying to concentrate on the cool breeze on my face and not on Kyla in her pretty clothes standing beside a dead body as though it was just another mess that needed cleaning up. Still talking, she followed me.

"No, I don't know where we are. In the middle of no-where as far as I can tell. Hang on." She lowered the phone and glared at me. "Don't just sit there. Tell me where we are."

I realized I had no idea either. I wasn't sure the road even had a name, and I couldn't remember having seen a street sign, which in general had a short life expectancy in a county with a sizable population of teenage males and no shortage of guns.

"Tell them it's the road in front of Carl's place. They'll be able to figure it out."

She did so, then frowned. "No, no, I don't want to wait here. We're on our way into town. Well, yes. Yes. Okay, fine. But please hurry." She hung up looking annoyed.

"They want us to stay here until the police arrive. Like we don't have anything better to do. I tell you, no good deed goes unpunished. This is just one of the many reasons why caller ID is not always a good idea. No prank calls, no anonymous tips to the police. Shit."

I started laughing. Then I buried my face in my hands and stifled a sob.

She patted my shoulder a little awkwardly. "It's not that big a deal. I don't really mind waiting."

I raised my head in exasperation and wiped away a couple of hot tears.

"Yes, my problem is that you're inconvenienced!" I snapped. "He's dead, Kyla. Really dead."

"Oh. Yeah, I guess so. I mean, yes, I know he is. But it's not like we can do anything for him now. It's sad and all, but maybe it's the best thing for him. Better than a trial and going to prison for the rest of his life."

Maybe she was in shock, I thought. "He didn't kill himself."

"Of course he did. Maybe you didn't notice the gun, but it was right there. And his truck is locked."

"Yes, and no one could possibly lock a car door and then shut it. But let me rephrase this. Why would he kill himself?"

She rose, putting her hands on her hips, then walked around the car and got in, closing the door against the chilly breeze. Her cheeks were pink from the brisk air, and I caught a whiff of her perfume. A faint furrow appeared between her brows.

"You said you thought he might have been the one who shot the jockey. Now he shot himself, so I figure you were right."

"But why? Say we're right and he did shoot the jockey. Why kill himself? As far as I can tell, no one except us even suspects him. The sheriff is questioning Kel and Herman for goodness sakes. Why would Carl suddenly decide his only option is suicide?"

"Here's a better question," she countered. "Why would Carl suddenly decide to let someone else cram a rifle between his knees and pull the trigger? He was a big guy. You think he'd just sit there and let that happen?"

I had no answer for this. On the surface, she was absolutely right. It was ridiculous to think that anyone could have killed Carl in his own truck without a fight. But was it more ridiculous than thinking he'd committed suicide? I didn't believe it. I knew Kyla was right, but I still didn't believe it. Which didn't mean it wasn't true.

My own phone buzzed in my purse, and I jumped. Answering, I heard an unfamiliar voice on the other end.

"Yes, this is Sand Creek Medical Center calling for Jocelyn Shore."

I felt my stomach clench. "I'm Jocelyn Shore."

"Ma'am, I've been asked to notify you that a friend of yours has been admitted. His name is Colin Gallagher."

My Civic spewed gravel and caliche dust from beneath its tires as I whipped a U-turn and peeled past Carl's truck with the impressive high-pitched shriek of four underpowered cylinders. Still, it was enough to sling Kyla first against the window and then against my right shoulder as we fishtailed thirty yards before regaining traction.

She reached for her seatbelt and yelped a protest that I ignored. "What the hell? I thought we were supposed to stay with Carl!"

"Damn Carl Cress," I answered. "Colin's in the hospital. Find out where that is," I added, realizing that I had no idea where I was going.

One thing about Kyla, she keeps a cool head in an emergency. The same calm reaction—or lack thereof—that made me question her humanity when viewing Carl's corpse now served me very well as she looked up directions and read them to me. We arrived at the hospital in what must have been record time.

I pulled directly in front of the doors, left Kyla with the car, and raced inside. After I pounded on the counter for a few minutes, a wide-eyed young receptionist gave me Colin's room number and pointed the way.

Not wanting to wait for the elevator, I raced up the stairs, took a wrong turn, then finally got my bearings. The hospital halls seemed deserted except for the faint smell of stale lunch overlaid with antiseptic. Just outside Room 201, I hesitated. The door was open about six inches, and I could hear voices in addition to the low sound of a television. Tapping gently, I pushed it open. Directly to the left, another open door revealed a tiny bathroom. Beyond that, the room widened, and I could see the foot of the bed and a doctor in a white coat making notes on an electronic tablet. She looked up as I entered, but I scarcely glanced at her.

Colin lay in the bed, mint-green blanket pulled up to his chest, IV connected to his bandaged hand. One arm was in a cast, a large white bandage covered one cheek and eye, and a second one crossed the bridge of his nose. His lips were bruised and torn. The eye I could see was surrounded by a purple bruise, but it crinkled into a smile that looked like it hurt when he saw me.

"There you are," he said. His voice was hoarse.

I circled the bed to avoid the doctor and the machines, and took his hand in mine. It was cool to the touch, but he squeezed back hard.

"What happened to you?" I asked, then I turned to the doctor. "How is he?"

The doctor gave me an appraising look. "Are you a family member?" she asked.

"Yes," said Colin instantly.

I nodded in agreement, although I could feel my cheeks turning pink at the lie. I've been told never to play poker.

The doctor looked from Colin to me and back again, then shook her head. "Fine. I'm not even going to ask the relationship. I'll assume extremely distant cousins."

Colin grinned, and I gave a gasp.

"Your tooth!"

"Yeah."

His front tooth was broken almost in half. I swallowed hard, horrified.

"He's very lucky," said the doctor absently. "It could have been a lot worse. As it is, he'll be out of here in a day or two."

"I feel lucky," said Colin solemnly.

She glanced at him sharply, and I suppressed the urge to laugh.

"How is he really?" I asked again.

"Broken ulna, two cracked ribs, moderate concussion, lacerated cheek, minor contusions," she answered. "We'll keep him for observation, but he'll be fine. You can stay with him, but let him rest." And with that, she left.

I looked him over, trying to see past the bandages and bruises, then bent down and kissed the one small place on his forehead that was neither bandaged nor bruised. His hand tightened on mine, and he brushed my lips with his own, then dropped his head back to the pillow. I could tell every movement hurt.

"So, should I ask about the other guy?"

He snorted. "You can ask. Unfortunately, I believe he is just fine. Sucker punched me."

"What?" I squeaked, appalled. "Someone did this to you? On purpose? I thought you must have been in a wreck."

"It was a wreck all right. One man, no car." He sighed.

I pulled the mint leatherette visitor chair closer to the bed and sat down, taking his hand in both of mine.

"Who was it? I will hunt them down and make them sorry."

"Great, I feel so much better. If only you had been there to protect me when it happened." He released my hand long enough to squeeze my biceps.

"Well, fine. I'll have Kyla hunt them down."

"Now that might work," he said.

As if on cue, the door opened, and Kyla poked her head in. She took one look at Colin, and said, "Whoa, what happened to you? You look like shit."

Colin and I glanced at each other and started laughing.

"Colin was just about to tell."

"Yeah, well, it's embarrassing." He stopped, then shrugged. "Guess you'll have to know sooner or later. I'd been canvassing some of the ranches out near the racetrack asking after Ruby June when I saw a guy by the side of the road. Looked like he was changing a flat, so I stopped to help. I bent over to pick up the spare, and he hit me with the tire iron." Colin tapped the blue cast on his forearm. "I saw him out of the corner of my eye and threw up an arm for the first blow, but he got in a few more after that. I don't know what would have happened if another car hadn't come along just then. The guy heard the engine and ran for it."

I was horrified. "Why would he do that? What did he want?"

"Money. It was a straight-up mugging. He stole my wallet. I'm just glad he didn't take my gun."

"Out here where everyone knows everyone?" I asked, incredulous. "That was really risky. Do you know who it was?"

"No idea. Big guy in a white pickup, which I know hardly narrows it down. I'd recognize him again, but I've never seen him before. And it was bold, but maybe not that risky. There's a lot of strangers in town for the races. I'll bet he wasn't from around here and thought it was an easy way to get some cash."

"See?" asked Kyla. "What did I say? No good deed goes unpunished. You try to help someone, they try to kill you."

I asked, "How about the second guy? The one who came along just in time. Did he recognize him?"

Colin shook his head, then winced. "No, the guy drove away before he could get a good look."

"Did he recognize the truck?" I asked.

"No, but then he's not from around here, either. He's just in town because he's riding in the race today."

Kyla and I both stiffened.

"He's a jockey?" I asked carefully.

"Yeah. Travis Arledge. Hope he won. You don't know how the races went, do you? I can't remember the name of his horse."

Silence filled the room. If we'd been outside, crickets

would have chirped. As it was, I could hear the ticking of the clock on the wall and the sound of soft-soled shoes moving through the hall. My mind was churning. Travis Arledge had stopped to help Colin on the way to the races, and then he'd been shot. Was there a connection? What if the shooter had wanted to stop him from identifying Colin's attacker rather than from winning the race?

Colin looked from Kyla to me. "What am I missing?"

"Someone shot Travis Arledge during the race. I haven't heard how he's doing," I answered.

"I think we can safely say not well," said Kyla. "If the gunshot didn't kill him, the fall from a galloping horse probably did."

"What?" Colin struggled to sit up, and I hurriedly laid a hand on his shoulder.

Kyla went on before I could stop her. "While you were just lying around here, a lot's been going on. Let's see." She held up a hand and began ticking items off on her fingers. "Jockey shot, Carl Cress killed himself, Uncle Herman and Uncle Kel both arrested. You've really missed out."

"What is she talking about?"

"She's exaggerating," I said soothingly, shooting Kyla a glare that she ignored. "Herman and Kel haven't been arrested. Sheriff Bob has just taken them in for questioning."

"You don't know that. They could be behind bars this minute," she said, although she didn't sound too concerned about it.

"Back up," said Colin. "What do you mean Travis was shot?"

Kyla looked at him sharply. "Do you have a head injury?

179

Because we can talk slower, but we really can't say it any more simply. He was shot. They don't know who did it."

Normally Colin is fairly even tempered, even easygoing, but Kyla has a special way about her. His hand tightened on mine, and I watched him clench his jaws. So did Kyla.

"Hey, are you missing a tooth? You look like a hillbilly," she said.

Colin's one visible eye twitched. I quickly said, "Kyla, why don't you see if you can find us a Coke or something. I'm dying of thirst."

"You just want to get rid of me," she protested.

"Exactly. But I'm also thirsty."

"Fine. But get your own Coke. I'll drive over to the jail and check on Kel and Herman. I'll swing back by for you in a bit." She glanced at us, made a point of staring at our clasped hands, and then gave me a smug little smile. "Feel better, Monkey Boy," she said, and then left.

I turned back to Colin propped against the pillows, looking not only annoyed, but somewhat pale. He looked like he was hurting.

"When do you get your next pain meds?"

"I'm fine," he said.

"That is not an answer. Are you refusing to take your pills?"

"They make me groggy."

I gave an exasperated sigh. "That's half the point. They're supposed to help you sleep so you can heal and get out of here. Let me go find a nurse."

His hand tightened on mine. "Leave it. Someone will be in soon anyway. I want to know what's been going on."

180

I sighed. "I wish I knew."

I told what I knew about Travis, then described finding Carl Cress by the side of the road. "Kyla is positive he shot himself, and I admit it did look like it, but I'm just as positive he didn't. I don't know how to explain it, but Carl just wasn't the type."

"I don't think there is a type. Not that I'm saying you're wrong," he added as I opened my mouth to argue. "But I've seen more suicides than I care to remember that took the victim's family completely by surprise. And you didn't really know Carl very well, right?"

"No," I admitted.

"It's important to keep an open mind until we have all the facts. Still, I grant you that the timing is suspect." He grew quiet, thinking things over.

I took the opportunity to study his face. Now that I was over the initial shock, his injuries seemed both less horrific and more disturbing. The bruises would fade, the bandages would come off, the chipped tooth would be capped. But I knew from my own recent experience that the memory of the violence would linger, and I felt anger, deep and hot, flare in my stomach. I wanted to catch the bastard who did this. I envisioned a white pickup truck swerving off a cliff and bursting into flames on the way down. No, too quick. Better if the white pickup broke down in the desert, the driver staggering away into the wilderness, impaled on countless cactus spines. After endless days of burning sun and futile attempts to drink his own urine, he would drop to his knees, tongue black and swollen with thirst, blistered skin peeling from his face. Coyotes would begin eating him while he was still alive, but he would be too weak to do more than wheeze in fear and agony. At last, as buzzards began circling above, one of the coyotes would lift its leg on what was left of the pathetic torn remains.

"What are you thinking about?" asked Colin.

I came to myself with a small jolt.

"Nothing," I said quickly. "Well, I was just wondering if the police are looking for the guy who did this to you."

"I'm sure they are," he answered, looking at me suspiciously. "Why do I not believe that's what you were thinking about?"

"Probably pain is making you light-headed. You should let me call the nurse."

"Not yet." He ran his thumb along the back of my hand in a miniature caress, then said in a low tone, "I'm really glad to see you."

I gripped his fingers tightly. "I wish you'd called sooner. You must have been in here for hours, and I didn't know it."

"I wasn't thinking too clearly. Anyway, it took them a while to patch me up. You couldn't have seen me earlier."

"Then I would have waited in the hall."

He searched my face, the blue eye wary and hopeful.

My throat suddenly felt dry, but I said, "Perhaps I should mention that I spoke with Alan yesterday. In person, actually. He drove down here yesterday evening."

He drew in a sharp breath and waited.

"I, um. I sort of broke things off with him," I said. I was having a hard time meeting his gaze.

The eye widened and his grip tightened on my hand. "'Sort of' or 'really'?"

182

"Really." I swallowed. "I'm not seeing him anymore."

He closed his eyes and relaxed against the pillows. I hadn't realized how tense he'd been before.

"And are you still seeing me?" he asked, although the smile playing on his lips told me he already knew the answer.

"That depends on whether you'll be getting that tooth fixed. I'm not sure I'm okay dating a hillbilly."

"Come here," he said.

I leaned in. Releasing my hand, he lifted his fingers to caress my cheek and then gently pulled me closer for a kiss. Even bruised and smelling of antiseptic, he made my heart beat faster.

I brushed his lips very gently, then straightened. "I'm afraid to touch you. You're just one big bandage."

"I'll be out tomorrow. Maybe you could drive me home in my Jeep. Kyla could bring your car, couldn't she?"

"Yes," I answered slowly.

"But?"

"I hadn't thought of leaving so soon. My cousin's missing, her husband is dead, and half my family is in jail. But I suppose there's absolutely nothing I can do about it, so going home is probably a good idea. I can bring you tea and chicken soup," I offered, not wanting to add that those represented the full extent of my nursing abilities.

"Make it beer and nachos, and you have a deal. But I meant home as in somewhere other than this hospital. I don't plan to leave town until I have a chance to find the guy who did this."

"I'll help you," I said with a little more vigilante rasp in my voice than I'd intended.

He smiled, but his eye shut briefly, then flickered open reluctantly.

I said, "You should get some sleep. I'll just slip out and get something to drink, then be right back. Do you want anything?"

"No, thanks. You don't have to hang around, you know. You should go check on things with your uncle. And I'd like to know about Travis, if they'll tell you anything."

"I'll see what I can find out." I rose, then turned back, struck by a sudden thought at the mention of Travis. "Colin, what were you doing canvassing houses this morning? I thought you were going to Austin to ask about Ruby June."

"Now why would you think that?"

"Elaine said that one of Ruby June's friends went to Austin for the weekend and that you were going to find her to see if Ruby June was with her."

"No, I didn't know they'd found a friend of hers. Besides, I wouldn't have needed to drive in myself—I would have called the APD and had them send out an on-duty officer," he answered sleepily.

"Elaine must have misunderstood," I said. "Get some rest. I'll be back in just a few minutes."

I slipped out of the room, closing the door quietly behind me, then stood motionless, thinking hard. Why would Sheriff Bob say that Colin was going to Austin? Either he had misunderstood Colin's plans or he had lied to Elaine, and it didn't seem like the kind of thing you'd misunderstand.

The more I thought about Sheriff Bob, the more worried I became. If Colin had been going to the ranches near the track asking after Ruby June, surely he would have coordinated that with Sheriff Bob. And if so, that meant that Bob had known where Colin would be. What if the attack had not been a random mugging after all? Did that mean that the subsequent attack on Travis had not been about the race, but instead about protecting the identity of Colin's attacker? And if the attacker was that worried about not being discovered, did that mean Colin might still be in danger? It couldn't have been Bob himself, but what if he'd sent someone?

I struggled for a moment with a deep and nameless fear, glancing up and down the hall as though for signs of a lurking attacker. However, a moment later I was kicking myself for having an overactive imagination. Sheriff Bob was a decent man, a popular sheriff, an active member of the community, and a longtime friend of my uncle's. He wasn't trying to kill my boyfriend or the jockey who saved my boyfriend. I would go to the station as soon as Kyla returned with my car and just ask him why he'd thought Colin had gone to Austin.

I walked to the nursing station halfway down the hallway. A young redheaded nurse in flowered scrubs perched on a stool in front of a computer monitor. A little gold cross on a thin chain gleamed in the hollow of her throat. I smiled at her.

She looked up with a smile. "Can I help you?"

"I was just wondering if you knew how the jockey who was shot today is doing?"

Her eyes widened. "Isn't that something else? That poor little guy. Just riding along, doing his best, and shot right out of the saddle. In front of everyone."

"Yes, it was terrible," I agreed.

"And they say that no one saw the guy who did it. But I heard they arrested someone just a little bit ago. A real sharpshooter. They say it would have taken a crack shot to do something like that."

"Someone's been arrested?" I squeaked, hoping Kyla hadn't been right after all. "Who?"

She shrugged. "Someone from around here is all I know. I wouldn't have thought a local would do something like that but I guess you never know about people, do you?"

"Maybe he didn't do it," I said faintly.

"They wouldn't have arrested him if he hadn't done it. Nope, sounds like he's guilty, and I hope he gets the death penalty. My cousin and her kids were there and saw the whole thing. They'll probably be scarred for life." She sounded a little envious.

More likely they'd have something to talk about at bingo tournaments and Lion's Club socials for life, I thought, but arguing would have been pointless. Instead, I returned to my original question.

"So, do you know how he's doing? The jockey, I mean."

"We're really not supposed to discuss the patients," she said, apparently remembering that she was on duty.

"I don't want to discuss him. I just want to know if he's still alive."

"Oh." She pondered this, then decided to answer. "Well, yes, he is. Or he was the last I heard. I know he's out of surgery anyway, and the nurses on that floor said they thought he was going to make it."

I breathed a sigh. "Well, thank goodness for that."

She nodded.

I asked, "Where's a Coke machine?"

"We don't have one, but there's a cafeteria on the first floor. You can get one there."

I took the elevator this time and was just passing through the waiting area when Kyla entered, and for once she looked flustered.

"They've arrested Kel and stuck me with Uncle Herman. He's in the car and so angry he's just about ready to chew through the dashboard. You have to come save me."

"They can't have arrested Kel," I protested. "You can't arrest somebody just because they're a good shot."

"It's not that," she said. "You were right about Carl Cress—he didn't kill himself. And the gun that did belonged to Kel."

Chapter 7

HUSTLERS AND HUNTERS

I stayed at the hospital all afternoon with Colin. Although Kyla had not been happy about it, she eventually agreed to take Uncle Herman home by herself and to come back for me after dinner. The nurse and I somehow managed to persuade Colin to take his pain medication, and he slept while I sat in the mint-green chair. He urged me to go home, but it had not been very many weeks since I'd awakened in a similar bed to find him by my side. I did take a few minutes to buy a magazine from the gift shop, but I flipped through the glossy perfumed pages only briefly before closing it and letting it lie on my lap. I needed time to think, and the hospital room of a sleeping man was an almost ideal location.

Or so you'd think. I'd barely settled myself in when the door opened, and Sheriff Bob poked his head in. I sat bolt upright, and the movement made Colin stir.

Sheriff Bob approached the bed, holding his hat in his

hand. I glanced uneasily at the gun on his hip, remembering my earlier ridiculous suspicions, then immediately felt guilty.

"Hi, Bob," I said.

"Jocelyn," he answered. "How's he doing?"

"Pretty well, considering. They've got him on pain medicine. Do you need to wake him?"

He smoothed his white mustache with thumb and forefinger, then shrugged. "Nah, let him sleep. It can wait until morning. I mostly wanted to check up on him."

"Have you found out any more about who did this?" I asked.

He shook his head. "No. It's the damnedest thing, and the worst part is, it's not even at the top of my list. I think the whole goddamn town has gone batshit crazy. Pardon my French," he added.

"I'd have to agree with that," I said with a touch of acid, "since you've arrested Kel of all people."

He looked uncomfortable but stubborn. "I had no choice, not after we found his gun in Carl's truck. I don't like it any more than you, but there it is."

"You can't seriously think he'd shoot anyone."

He coughed a raspy smoker's cough that sounded like an attempt to eject a lung or two. "It don't matter what I think. The evidence says I have to hold him. It surely doesn't help that he threatened to kill a man in front of witnesses."

I said, "If you arrested everyone who ever threatened to kill Eddy, you'd have to build a new jail."

He barked a humorless laugh. "That's the truth. Goddamn it, this is a mess and a half." He looked down at Colin

189

then started moving to the door. "Will you tell him I'll be back in the morning?"

I nodded, then remembered my own question. "Elaine said you told her that Colin had gone to Austin today to look for Ruby June."

Sheriff Bob paused in midstride and turned back to me. "No, I don't believe I did. I told her that we'd probably send someone to Austin if we had to."

I watched him. "She seemed pretty sure."

He shrugged, his thin face impassive. "He didn't go, so what difference does it make?"

I didn't know the answer to that, so I sidestepped. "Did you find Ruby June's friend?"

"Called her. She says Ruby June's not there."

"Says? No one went to check it out?"

"Ruby June is over twenty-one. If she's kidnapped or in trouble, that's our business. But if she's just hiding, that's hers. Now, I've got to get back to the station. You have yourself a good evening."

I settled back into the chair, but popped up again after a moment, feeling edgy. I began pacing the tiny space at the foot of Colin's bed, thinking hard and getting nowhere. Sheriff Bob's answer had been reasonable. In fact, as Colin said, it would be unnecessary to send anyone to Austin when they could call the Austin police. But then why had Elaine been so sure? I remembered her happy relief when she'd told me, her gratitude to Colin for making the journey to Austin on her girl's behalf. It did not make sense, but as Bob said, why did it matter? I paced and thought.

190

"Are you trying to wear a path in that tile?" asked a sleepy voice.

I stopped. Colin had awoken and was watching me.

"How are you doing?" I asked. "Can I get you something?"

The afternoon light was fading in the small room as the weak November sun dipped into the west, making him look gray and drawn on the white pillow. I hoped he didn't feel as bad as he looked.

"I'm okay," he answered.

I recognized guy-speak when I heard it. "That good, huh? I'll go get the nurse."

"And maybe some water?" he asked.

I had a fresh pitcher of ice on the bed tray. I'd refilled it twice while he slept so it would be ready for him. "You get ice chips."

He wrinkled his nose, but didn't protest as I raised his bed and then handed him a small cup of ice.

"Sheriff Bob stopped by. He says he'll be back tomorrow."

"I heard. I just didn't want to talk to him."

"That was sneaky," I said, half shocked, half approving. "What if I'd said something I didn't want you to hear?"

"All the more reason to listen. I never know what you're thinking."

This was probably just as well. I bent down to kiss the one unbandaged place on his forehead, and he wrapped his free arm around my waist and pulled me onto his chest. Off balance, I mostly fell on him, which made him give a gasp, but he refused to let me up all the same.

"I've been trying to get you into bed for weeks," he said.

I struggled a little and at last managed to raise myself on my elbows to take some of the weight off his bruised ribs. I looked deeply into his eyes . . . well, into his eye. The left one was still covered.

"Is it everything you expected?" I asked in my most sultry voice.

He started laughing and let go, but only long enough to shift to one side to make room for me to cuddle against him. I looked at the good six inches of white mattress he seemingly expected me to occupy, and instead slid off, pulling my chair closer.

"Timing. It's always timing with us, isn't it?" he asked, giving me a wry look.

I nodded. "I think all that's about to change though. As soon as you don't look like the Mummy from Hillbilly Hollow, maybe we can start over."

"I don't want to start over," he protested. "I want credit for the dates we've already been on."

"You got it." I hunched forward to rest my head on his shoulder. He stroked my hair, and I listened to the steady thump of his heart through the thin hospital gown. It was the first time I'd held him feeling as though I had the right, without any pangs of guilt regarding other boyfriends to whom I should but did not want to be loyal. It felt wonderful. Not comfortable, but wonderful. I supposed I really should thank Kyla. Maybe. Sometime.

I was just starting to get a crick in my neck and thinking reluctantly about sitting up, when Kyla burst through the door. She took one look at us and stopped.

"Good God, get a room," she said.

"We're *in* a room," I pointed out, sitting up. "And you could learn to knock."

She ignored me. "You're never going to believe this."

She paused to give us time to think about what we weren't going to believe. Colin glared at her sourly.

"Could we not believe it some other time?" he asked.

She held our gaze a few seconds longer, letting the silence grow. I often thought she should have pursued an acting career, rather than waste her dramatic instincts on computers. At last she spoke.

"Ruby June is back."

We left the hospital a half hour later. I was silent as Kyla drove through town, partly because I was thinking, and partly because she continued to describe the chaos at the ranch house when Ruby June returned.

"Pull in there," I said suddenly, interrupting her.

"Where? Sonic?"

"Yup."

"You can't possibly . . . ," she started.

"Just do it!" I snapped.

She shot me an irritated look, but she slowed and pulled into one of the few empty parking spaces under a tin canopy. A carhop on skates whizzed in front of our bumper with a tray of Styrofoam cups on her way to another vehicle. The clouds had thickened and the temperature had dropped again, making the late afternoon seem even darker and later than it was. The fluorescent lights spilling from the kitchen already seemed brighter than the sky.

Kyla shut off the engine and waited.

"Number two combo with a cherry limeade," I instructed.

"We're eating in less than two hours. Gladys was already rolling out biscuits when I left."

"Fine. Cherry limeade, large tater tots with cheese."

She shook her head, but rolled down the window and spoke into the intercom anyway.

When she was finished, I turned in my seat so I could see her face. "Start over," I said. "What exactly did Ruby June say? And none of your dramatic bullshit."

I could tell she wanted to argue, but something in my face must have changed her mind. She drew a deep breath and thought, then produced a clear summary, minus the flare.

"Eddy had been working for Carl Cress for several months, mostly hauling equipment and livestock around the state. Every once in a while, Carl would have him pick up something that Eddy suspected was illegal, but he went along with it because he needed the money. Recently, Carl expanded into something else—and before you ask, Ruby June was not sure what—and Eddy tried to quit. However, Carl threatened Eddy and told him that he'd have him arrested if he didn't keep going."

"Drugs," I said, thinking of the encounter I'd witnessed beneath the rodeo stands. "It had to be drugs."

"What else?" agreed Kyla. "Anyway, apparently Eddy was really spooked. After we dropped Ruby June at the house, he returned and told her to lay low for a while."

"Why didn't she come to the ranch? There's no place on earth as safe as that."

"She was mad at Kel. She didn't say it, but I'm pretty sure she wasn't opposed to causing him a little grief."

I shook my head, but reminded myself that Ruby June wasn't much more than a kid and probably not a very bright one at that.

"At least this means that Kel isn't the only suspect in Eddy's murder," I said.

The sound of wheels on concrete made us look up. A blond carhop wearing the Sonic visor and black pants skated up with our tray. She wore a jeans jacket, but her nose and cheeks were pink with cold. Kyla took our drinks and handed me a hot foil pack containing my tots. I tore it open eagerly.

Kyla gave the girl a dollar as a tip, then quickly closed the window as she skated away. The temperature inside the car was already approaching uncomfortable.

"Can we go now?" she asked.

"In a minute," I answered. An unformed idea was flitting inside my head, and I was trying to let it get close enough to grab it. "So where did Ruby June go?" I asked idly, mostly to stall.

Kyla paused. "That's the interesting thing," she said finally. "She went to T.J.'s."

"T. J. Knoller? Your T.J.?" I asked with surprise.

"How many T.J.s do you know? And he's not mine. But yes, that one."

"But why?"

"I didn't ask. Elaine was pretty shocked, though. You know, I think you might have had a point when you said they'd pitch a fit if they found out I'd gone out with him. I swear she was madder at Ruby June for going to him than she was about Ruby June hiding from us."

"That doesn't surprise me. This is the beginning of a feud that has the potential to make the Hatfields and McCoys look like a sorority girl tiff if someone doesn't do something soon. But why would Ruby June think she could go there? Does she even know T.J.?"

"Like you said, everyone here knows everyone. And I guess Eddy'd been doing some work for T.J., too."

"Do you think she has a crush on him?"

One of Kyla's perfect eyebrows flicked upward. "Probably. He's a fine-looking man. And he's rich."

"Pretty much the opposite of Eddy in every possible way," I said. "And very unlikely to spill her secret location to her family."

"Exactly."

"You okay about it?" I asked her.

She did not take offense. "I doubt he feels the same about her. For one thing, he was out with me on Wednesday night. Seems like he would have been home with her if they had some kind of thing going. My guess is that he saw it as a chance to help Ruby June while sticking it to Kel. I have no idea why, but T.J. must really hate Kel."

"You don't believe the whole 'it's just business' argument?"

"I did at first. But after today at the track . . ." She took one of my cheese-covered tots. "I mean, why would he accuse Kel like that if he wasn't trying to get him for some other reason? It's like you said, half the men in the county are deer hunters. Why specifically go after Kel?"

We sat in silence for a few more minutes.

"Who knows about Ruby June?" I asked.

"Us and the sheriff. Elaine called him right away so they wouldn't be wasting any more time on the search. He was going to come out this evening to question her, for whatever reason. Guess she's in trouble for causing a manhunt."

"More likely it's because she's a person of interest in Eddy's murder. They always take a hard look at the spouse." I considered for a moment. "So Sheriff Bob is going out to our place. Good. Let's make a stop on the way back."

"A stop where?"

"I want to talk to Eddy's family before they hear that Ruby June is back."

"Good God, why? I remember them from Ruby June's wedding. Yes, they walked upright, but their resemblance to humans ended there."

"Look, I know they're horrible people, especially Mr. Cranny, but at least they kept their violence in the privacy of their own home. They were okay in public."

"But why would you want to talk with them?"

"Think about what has happened since we got here," I said, trying to get my own thoughts in line. "And think about where we are. This is a nice town."

At this, she snorted, but I went on.

"No, I mean it. You might not want to live here, and probably for all the reasons that it is a nice town, but a lot of people do. People know each other. This is the kind of place where your mechanic is married to your second cousin. The butcher knows your aunt and remembers how she likes her steaks cut. The ladies get together for luncheons and garden clubs and the men go hunting or to Kiwanis meetings or whatever it is men do. Sure, there's always a few stinkers like the Crannys and Carl Cress, but not many. So . . . in the space of one long weekend, what has happened?"

Now I had her attention. She took another of my tots and then a sip of my limeade. I suppressed the urge to slap her hand.

"A whole lot of really strange shit?" she asked.

"Exactly. Ruby June goes missing, Eddy gets into a fight with Carl then gets murdered. Colin gets mugged on the road, the jockey who helped him gets shot and almost killed, Carl Cress gets murdered . . ."

"So what's your point? Other than it's a whole lot of really bad things in this supposedly nice town, what do all those things have to do with each other?"

"That's what I can't figure out. There has to be a connection, but I can't see what it is."

"What if there isn't? What if these are all pretty much random and it's just coincidence that it all happened this weekend? Maybe Carl killed Eddy and then killed himself because he was afraid he'd get caught. After all, someone else killing him in his own pickup seems pretty farfetched. And maybe some big-time gambler decided that T.J.'s horse just could not be allowed to win that stupid race. And maybe . . . Wait, what else happened?"

"Colin," I reminded her.

"Oh yeah. And maybe that was just some random jerk who saw an easy way to get cash for drugs or gambling. The holidays make people go crazy." Kyla ate the last two tots. "Let's go back. It's getting cold here."

"No, I want to go to the Cranny's house," I said stubbornly. "They won't know Ruby June is back, and we can tell them we're still looking for her if we need an excuse. Eddy might have told them something, and I want to know what it is. Gimme my keys and switch with me. I'll drive, you can navigate."

The Cranny house was a double-wide trailer sitting in the middle of a half acre of mostly unmowed weeds and abandoned auto parts. However, someone was making a gallant if misguided effort nearer the front door. The grass around a walkway of broken concrete squares was carefully trimmed, and under the windows sat a few containers that would hold flowers when the weather warmed up again. Even now, purple pansies fluttered apathetically in the center of the largest, waiting for the first hard freeze to put them out of their misery. Beside the planters, a large plywood cutout resembling a very large woman's polka-dotted backside completed the picture. Someone had cunningly stapled a string of twinkle lights along her skirt in acknowledgment of the festive Christmas season.

The open doors of a tin portable at the back of the lot revealed a red car on blocks being tended by a weedy man in overalls. I glanced at Kyla, who shrugged, then led the way around the side of the house.

We stopped just outside the shed doors. The man looked up with a wary expression. He was younger than I'd thought, probably not even twenty-five, but he already wore an air of apathy and desperation like a seasoned pro. I scanned his face for any resemblance to Eddy and found it in the close set watery eyes and hollow cheeks. I guessed he was Eddy's brother, and I wondered if he was the one who'd been mean to Eddy, which wasn't hard to believe. Of all the words that could be used to describe this man—and they included a long list beginning with "weasel"—"nice" was not one that sprang to mind. I knew kids like him from my high school classes. My fellow teachers and I spent endless hours wracking our brains about how to, if not exactly educate them, then at least provide them with enough rudimentary reading skills to help while away the long hours in prison. Keeping them from making some other kid's life miserable was an ongoing challenge.

"Who are you?" he asked, running his eyes over us with deliberate slowness and flicking his cigarette onto the dirt. He probably imagined that he looked like an arrogant James Dean in *Rebel Without a Cause*, whereas he actually looked more like a horny and bad-tempered Barney Fife.

"Beautiful Mustang," I said, careful to keep my eyes on the vehicle and not on the man. "'Sixty-seven?"

He frowned and glanced at the car. "'Sixty-eight," he corrected.

"V-eight?"

"Damn straight," he answered, then produced a little bark of laughter at the unintentional rhyme.

I could feel Kyla's incredulous eyes boring into the back of my skull. While it was true I was fuzzy on most automotive topics—and by fuzzy I mean that I needed to look in the user manual to figure out where the spare tire was kept—my brother Will had been obsessed with classic cars, and the ultimate object of his obsession had been the Mustang. Short of duct taping his mouth closed, it had been impossible not to pick up some of his incessant ravings on the topic.

"I'm Ruby June's cousin, Jocelyn Shore." I didn't introduce Kyla, mostly because I didn't want him to say anything to her that might make her try to snap him like a twig. "I wanted to stop by for a couple of reasons. The first, of course, is to say how sorry I am for your loss."

A little furrow appeared between the close-set eyes, and he suddenly seemed very interested in something in the dirt at his feet. "Yeah."

"Eddy was a nice kid," I said, and who knew, it might even have been true. Well hidden, but true.

He nodded but said nothing. He studied the pile of empty beer cans that overflowed the top of a rusted oil drum that apparently acted as a recycle bin.

I waited. As a teacher, I'd learned early that the value of silence can't be overestimated. It drives most people crazy, and they'll do and say almost anything to fill the gap. It also gives the quiet types a chance to formulate their thoughts, and I could almost hear the rusty gears of this man's brain begin turning. I could also hear Kyla shifting from one foot to another behind me, and I silently willed her to keep quiet.

At last he said, "Most people didn't know Eddy. No one else has come by to say sorry. You should probably talk to our ma."

"I would be glad to. But actually, I'd like to talk to you. You're his brother, and I expect he talked to you about things he didn't tell your mother."

A faint smile flickered across his face. "Lucky for her," he said.

"Whoever killed him should get the death penalty," I said.

"Goddamn straight!" He was suddenly animated, eyes bright with anger and pain. "Eddy was . . . Eddy didn't deserve that. Getting shot like some goddamn animal. He was . . .

201

yeah, he was a good kid. Death penalty's too good for whoever did that."

"What's your name?" I asked.

The boy-man sniffed and ran a sleeve over his nose. "Billy. Billy Cranny, but you know that part."

"Has the sheriff been by to talk to you about Eddy's death?"

"He came around to tell us when it happened. Hasn't been back since."

"So he hasn't asked you anything about what Eddy had been doing recently? Nothing about who he'd been working for or who he'd been hanging out with?"

Billy shook his head. "Nothing. Nothing at all."

"That son of a bitch," I said, mostly because it needed to be said.

So what had Sheriff Bob been doing in the last couple of days? He hadn't been interested in finding Ruby June, and he hadn't been asking questions about Eddy. Was he simply the world's laziest sheriff or was he not asking because he already knew the answers?

Billy suddenly looked at me, really searching my face for the first time. "You're that one! The girl who stopped Carl Cress from hitting on Eddy."

Surprised, I gave a shrug and a nod.

"You told Carl that Eddy was a Shore now. That's about the last thing Eddy ever said to me. How he never expected no Shore to own him. Meant a lot to him."

To my astonishment, Billy held out an extremely grubby hand. I took it gingerly and let him pump my arm up and down. Then what he was saying finally registered.

"Wait, you spoke to Eddy that night?" I didn't tell him that I'd been thinking that was the last time anyone but his killer saw Eddy.

"Yeah, he stopped by," said Billy, eyes sliding away from me. He shifted uncomfortably, then sniffed and ran his hand under his nose. The same hand he'd just shaken mine with. "I owed him some money. Look, I ain't proud of it, and I'd do it differently if I could and that's a fact but I told him to fuck off."

He stared at his feet, and I saw not an evil-tempered bully but a kid whose last words to his younger brother had been unkind. Words that, in all honesty, had probably been spoken hundreds of times, but which now echoed in his memory like the whisper of dirt on a coffin lid. He could never take them back now, and to my horror I felt tears burn at the back of my eyes.

"So what?" asked Kyla, speaking for the first time.

Eddy and I both jumped. I turned and gave her an appalled glance, but she ignored me.

"I mean it. So what? I tell Jocelyn to fuck off all the time. If you're standing here feeling all sorry for yourself because your last conversation with your brother wasn't all rainbows and roses, then you're an idiot. If you cared about him, then he knew it, and if you didn't, then he knew that, too. The last thing you said to him doesn't mean squat."

Billy was staring at her, mouth hanging open ever so slightly. Definitely a mouth breather. But he didn't seem offended.

I pressed the advantage. "She's right. The last thing you said isn't important. But the last thing Eddy said to you might

203

be. Because it might help us find out who did this to him. Did he tell you anything?"

Billy's desire for justice for his brother warred with his innate reluctance to help another human being. However, after a not inconsiderable struggle he said, "Eddy wanted his money because he was clearing out of town. He said things had gotten out of hand, and he wanted out."

"Did he say what things?"

"Nah, not exactly. But he was always running around after that goddamn Carl Cress like a whipped pup. I told him once, I said 'Goddamn Eddy, you ain't his bitch,' but he always said the money was pretty good. Better'n what he could make at Walmart. And he liked hauling livestock. Cattle and goats going to market mostly, but Carl gave him a few gigs picking up weird shit for that T. J. Knoller guy."

"Weird shit?"

"Yeah, you know, funny-looking animals. Zebras and whatnot. Once he had to go get a lion from a rinky-dink zoo that was getting shut down. He didn't like that one. The lion scared him, and he said he felt sorry for it."

A lion? Something seemed wrong about that, but I shelved it for later.

"But why now?" I asked. "Did something specific happen?"

Billy shrugged. "Him and Carl had a fight. Well, you saw."

"He didn't say what it was about?" I pressed.

Billy's eyes shifted. "How the hell should I know? Why don't you ask Carl?"

I stared at him. For one thing, he was lying. He knew exactly what Eddy and Carl had fought about. For another, apparently the Crannys weren't on the main branch of the Sand

Creek grapevine. Kyla opened her mouth to correct this gap in Billy's education, but I gripped her arm hard enough to make her squeak. It was not a subtle move, but then Billy was in the process of hawking up a ball of phlegm and didn't seem to notice.

He spit, watched the arc of the loogie until it pinged against an empty beer can, then wiped the backsplash from his lips with his hand. The same hand he'd used to shake mine. I suppressed the urge to rub my fingers vigorously against Kyla's jacket.

"Are you thinking you might step in for Eddy and start working for Carl?" I asked.

"Don't see why not. Not that it's any of your business."

"Aren't you worried that Carl might have had something to do with Eddy's death?"

"I can take care of myself."

"Yeah. I'm sure Eddy thought that, too."

He was scornful now. "Eddy was in over his head. I won't be."

"And Carl? Was he in over his head, too?"

Billy did not understand this, but was not the type to admit it. "We're done here." He took a menacing step toward us.

Well, sort of menacing. Kyla and I both topped him by a couple of inches, and I was pretty sure my left thigh weighed more than he did. Still, I hardly wanted to engage in a backyard brawl with the scrawny brother of my dead cousin-in-law.

"Fine," I said, then turned to Kyla who was already in her fight stance. "You have something to write on? I want to give him my phone number."

She threw me a disapproving look but began digging in her purse. Billy unpuffed himself, looking at the two of us with some perplexity. It probably wasn't often that his imitation of a crazed terrier didn't produce instant results.

"Carl Cress is dead. Shot in the throat," I said as bluntly as I could.

"What?" he said, his voice squeaking a little.

I was watching him closely, and I was convinced that he hadn't known. But his shocked expression was swiftly followed by something else, something I couldn't quite identify. Whatever it was, he controlled himself and met my eyes defiantly.

I knew I'd lost. "You still won't tell me what he and Eddy fought about? Fine. Here's my phone number if you change your mind. Or you can call the police. But not Sheriff Bob," I added. "Call the county."

He reluctantly took the crumpled receipt on which Kyla had scrawled my name and phone number, and we returned to my car. He was still standing motionless where we left him as I reversed and drove away.

"I don't like how that turned out," I said. "He was planning something, and probably something not smart."

"Gee, there's a shocker. Billy 'the Drooling Idiot' Cranny doing something stupid? What a complete waste of time."

"Not quite," I answered. "We learned a couple of things. Eddy was planning to leave town because he was scared. That tells us he was involved in something pretty bad and almost certainly illegal."

"And he was working for Carl Cress," Kyla agreed. "You think Carl killed him?"

"I did until Carl turned up dead," I said.

"Maybe he killed himself out of remorse or because he figured he'd be caught," she suggested.

"I keep telling you, I don't think he killed himself."

"So there's someone else involved. Someone who wanted both Eddy and Carl dead? Besides every right-thinking person who ever met either of them, who do you have in mind?"

I didn't answer. I was replaying our conversation with Billy over in my head. I had the feeling that he'd said something important, but I just couldn't quite grasp the fleeting thought.

She continued, "Sheriff Bob thinks it's Kel, with or without Uncle Herman's support. I suppose you don't agree."

"No. But what about Sheriff Bob?"

"What about him?"

"No, I mean what about Sheriff Bob as the killer?"

She turned in her seat to stare at me. "Sheriff Bob. The Sheriff Bob who drives the lead tractor in the Miss Sand Creek pageant parade on the Fourth of July? The Sheriff Bob who sits in the dunking booth at the carnival? The Sheriff Bob who puts on a Santa suit and lets the kids climb all over him at the Lion's Club Christmas pancake breakfast? That Sheriff Bob?"

"For someone who hasn't been out here in years, you sure know a lot about Sheriff Bob."

She sniffed. "We both visited often enough when we were kids. And don't change the subject."

I sighed. "Fine. But think about it. He hasn't been exactly on top of things, has he? He didn't want to look for Ruby June. He hasn't been out to talk with Billy. He told Aunt Elaine that Colin was going to Austin, even though he knew otherwise."

"He says he didn't tell Elaine that. And the other stuff?

This is a man who spends most of his time dealing with cows breaking their fences and wandering onto the highway. He's not exactly Sherlock Holmes, now is he?"

"Maybe not, but he's hardly Inspector Clouseau, either," I said. For all his good-natured community participation, Bob had always struck me as being both bright and dedicated.

"I'm sure he's fine with what he usually has to do. But let's face it, there hasn't been a murder out here in this century. And being out of his depth hardly makes him a suspect."

"Why are you defending him?" I asked.

"I'm not. He might be the killer for all I know. I just think your reasoning is flawed."

She was right, of course. I had a handful of dubious facts and a bad feeling in my gut. Not enough to stand up in a court of law, but then again, I wasn't in court. And no matter what Kyla said, something was not adding up when it came to Sheriff Bob.

Kyla said, "I didn't know you supported the death penalty. Or was that just talk for Billy's sake?"

"I go back and forth. Life in prison means getting beaten by the other inmates on a regular basis, which I'm all for. But then I figure that some of that time they aren't being beaten and they might even be happy, so then I lean toward the death penalty. It's a hard call."

She stared. "You have thought about this way too much."

I shrugged. She might be right. But on the other hand her best friend had not been murdered.

We drove another few miles in silence, and we were just turning onto the road that led to the ranch when a thought occurred to me.

"Do you think T.J. is still having his barbecue?"

"Um . . . no. He doesn't have a lot to celebrate, now does he?" Kyla said. She had pulled a nail file from her purse and was busy rasping away at one of her nails.

"He said rain or shine, win or lose."

"Yes, but that was before his jockey got shot. Why do you care anyway?"

"I think we should go."

She stopped filing. "Are you kidding me? After he accused Kel of attempted murder? After he's been hiding Ruby June?"

"Yup."

"Why?"

I shrugged. "We were invited. I'd like to find out what kind of work Eddy and Carl were doing for him. Besides, he might know something about Carl's other activities, and if he doesn't, then maybe one of his people does."

"Even if he does, do you really think he's going to tell us?"

"No, but I think he might tell you." I grinned at her. "I think he'd tell you anything you asked."

She glanced down at her pink cardigan with its frills and pintucks. "Hmm."

"Don't you want to see him again? You were pretty interested this morning."

"Yeah, but I told you—I didn't like the way he tried to blame the whole racecourse shooting on Kel."

"No, that wasn't very smart if he was trying to impress you. On the other hand, he was upset. Did you get the feeling that an awful lot of money was on the line?"

"Now that you mention it, yes." She frowned. "I wonder what happened with the bets."

I hadn't thought about that. "Surely the race was declared null and void or . . . well, whatever you declare a race. They won't be able to award the prizes would they?"

She shrugged. "Uncle Herman's horse crossed the finish line. I have no idea what they'll do. But that's something else we could ask T.J."

I turned the car between two massive stone pillars that marked the entrance to T.J.'s ranch. The wrought-iron gate stood wide open, topped with two distinctive Ks under a single bar, and someone had tied a bouquet of red balloons to the bar.

"Looks like the party is still on."

Kyla didn't answer, and I felt a pang of remorse. "Look, if you don't want to see him again, I can take you back."

"And come back by yourself? No, that's silly. I went on one date with him, and it was fun. There's no reason not to go to his party. Besides, I have to admit I'm curious to see his place."

I drove on. The road, though paved with caliche and gravel like most roads in the area, was in excellent condition and had been newly graded. Unlike most roads in the area that connected point A to point B in the most efficient way possible, this one meandered through thick groves of trees and around rocky outcroppings covered with prickly pear and yucca and across the dry rocky bed of a creek as though it had all the time in the world. Around another gentle curve, the trees suddenly opened to reveal a sweep of lawn and a ranch house that in any other location I might have referred to as a manor. Built in the style of a Spanish hacienda, the sprawling home was all white stone and stucco beneath a red tile roof. In the gray light of this fading November day, golden light spilled from arched windows onto stone walkways and landscaped beds of yucca, ocotillo, and agave. Half a dozen vehicles lined the curved drive, including a big SUV, a couple of extended-cab pickups, one black Mercedes, and a glossy yellow Hummer that reminded me of a bumblebee.

I parked beside the Mercedes, and we got out.

Kyla looked around. "This is impressive."

"And new. T.J. must have built all this himself. Those gates are just the tip of the iceberg."

"Guess the exotic hunting business is better than we thought."

Perhaps. I couldn't even begin to imagine how much all these improvements must have cost, but that didn't mean they were paid for. Living beyond your means wasn't something I usually associated with Sand Creek, but it was common enough in Austin. More than one of my students had left school in the middle of the year, family split by debt and foreclosure. I thought again of T.J.'s anxiety at the races and wondered if he was trying to pay for his lifestyle by gambling. Not a financial strategy I could endorse.

The carved wooden front door flew open as we approached, and T.J. stood bathed in the warm light. He wore jeans and a freshly pressed white shirt, cowboy boots, and a tooled belt that somehow on him looked just right. His eyes lit up at the sight of Kyla.

"You came! I didn't think you would," he said, his pleasure obvious.

She looked up at him through her long lashes. "Is the party still on?"

"Of course! I told you, rain or shine, win or lose. I'm so glad you're here. Come in!" He followed her with his eyes as she passed him, then belatedly noticed me. "And Jocelyn."

"Hi T.J. Thank you for inviting us," I said, suppressing a grin. Give him credit, he made an effort to appear pleased to see me. I figured this must be what it felt like to be a celebrity's assistant . . . or pet monkey.

"Come in and meet everyone," he said, closing the door and leading the way down a short, tiled hall.

I had the brief impression of cool Saltillo tile, Spanish wrought iron, and weathered wood, and then we were in a magnificent living room. On the far wall was an enormous stone fireplace, fire crackling merrily behind an ornate fire screen. The room was furnished with oversize leather armchairs and sofas, heavy wooden tables, and bright Mexican rugs. A group of four men wearing camouflage hunting gear stood talking and sipping drinks beneath the glow of a huge chandelier made of antlers and branding irons. Two more lamps made of wagon wheels hung at each end of the room. However, everything else was overshadowed by the animals. I stopped and stared openmouthed at the soaring walls. At least six deer heads stared sightlessly back, each bearing a razor-tipped arrow in multipointed antlers. The long face of an oryx hung beside a bighorn sheep, its curling horns framing its delicate face like a 1950s hairstyle. In one corner, a recessed shelf hosted a grouping of unlikely companions that included a coyote with a mangy coat, a boar with beady eyes glinting above wicked looking tusks, a blackbuck, and a whitetail deer. In another corner, the head and forequarters of a mouflon sheep protruded from the wall as though it were just stepping through

212

the paneling. I recognized longhorn and zebra, antelope and bison. At least forty sets of glass eyes glittered in the flickering glow of firelight and lamps.

Kyla also stopped. "It's a dead zoo," she said.

T.J. cast her one startled glance and then laughed. "Beautiful, aren't they? Of course, some of them weren't taken on this ranch—we've only been going three years after all—but I wanted a display that would show what was available."

"I thought this was your house. Is it some kind of lodge?"

"Right now it's both. The original ranch house is about half a mile away. I can stay there if I need some privacy, but this place is much more comfortable, and I can make sure my guests are having a good time. My rooms are in a separate wing than the guest quarters, so it works out pretty well. Eventually I might decide to update the older place."

T.J. had not yet taken his eyes from Kyla, and he hovered well within what I would have considered the personal space circle. He wasn't actually touching her, but he could not have marked his territory more thoroughly if he had wrapped both arms around her. She did not seem to mind.

"Do you have animal heads in your bedroom?" she asked, looking up into his face with a mischievous smile.

"I don't," he answered in a low tone. "Is that a problem?"

I rolled my eyes and wandered away, hoping that she would remember she was supposed to ask T.J. about Carl's activities, illicit and otherwise. I joined the group of men near an elegant bar.

They parted amiably, including me in their circle, and the tallest asked, "Something to drink? They've got just about anything you could want, and I mix a mean Mexican martini."

I smiled. "How about a beer?"

"You got it," he said and pulled a Negra Modelo from the half-size refrigerator and obligingly peeled back the gold foil and popped the cap for me.

"So have you been hunting today?" I asked.

They laughed. "I was hunting," said my new beer buddy. "The rest of 'em were shooting."

"I still can't believe you missed that blackbuck, Ken," said a short man wearing gold-rimmed glasses. He turned to me and held out a hand. "Eric Palmer. This here's Jim Stolzman, Rick Albrenner, and our crack shot, Ken Staukowsky."

"Jocelyn Shore. I'm here visiting family on the next ranch over," I said, thinking I might as well provide some context for my presence. "What were you hunting?"

Ken grinned. "I'm here for an axis deer, but I'd have taken a blackbuck. Maybe I'll get lucky tomorrow."

"Or maybe not," said Eric. "Me on the other hand, I got my first mouflon. I'm gonna have it processed and taxidermied over at Sand Creek. Gorgeous critter."

They all nodded.

"Processed? You can eat these animals?" I asked, glancing around the walls. I'm not sure why I was surprised, except that with their twisted horns and strange colors, they looked more like fairy-tale creatures than eating stock.

"Absolutely," answered Ken. "It would be wasteful to kill them just for the trophy. Well, the deer-type species anyway. You'd have to be starving before you'd eat something like a coyote," he said with a glance at the mangy mount in the corner.

"Or a snake," grinned Eric.

"I've tried rattlesnake," said Ken. "We killed a big monster—seven feet long if it was an inch—a couple of hunts back out at Big Spring and chicken-fried it in an iron skillet over a campfire."

We all turned to him.

"And?" I asked.

"Yeah, it was as bad as it sounds. The meat had the consistency and color of a tough scallop, and the taste of . . ." He paused, groping for the word.

"Chicken?" offered Rick helpfully.

We laughed, but Ken shook his head. "I wish."

"So are you all trying to shoot something specific or just whatever you come across?" I asked. "I haven't been to an exotic ranch before."

Ken answered, "Well, this isn't like regular hunting. T.J. there breeds a load of different animals, and he can also bring in whatever a hunter wants from somewhere else. I'm sure you saw the high fences on the way in? Those mean that the animals on the ranch stay on the ranch so there's a lot more game here than you'd find on an ordinary place."

"Yeah, and you pay by the kill," added Rick.

"Right. And that ain't cheap, so you don't want to go blasting just anything you see. Plus, if you're after trophies, which we are, the goal isn't finding any animal to kill, it's finding a specific animal, which makes it a lot harder. Specially when you spook a herd of blackbucks and *they* spook the axis deer that you're after," said Ken.

"Oh, is that your excuse?" said Eric.

The man named Jim spoke for the first time. "Tonight

will be special, though. Never hunted something that could hunt me back."

The others turned, and I thought I saw Eric flash him a look of warning.

"What hunts you back?" I asked.

"Mountain lion," said Eric promptly. "There's a big one around here. In fact it's been killing some of T.J.'s stock."

"Mountain lion, yeah," said Jim with a snort.

Ken said, "I'd love to bag that big cat. I'd definitely have the taxidermist make a full body mount for that one."

"That'd cost a fortune," said Rick doubtfully. "And where would you keep it? Bet Linda would have a cow."

"Nope, she'd have a lion," said Ken with a grin.

"There can't be very many mountain lions," I said. "How do you decide which one of you gets to shoot?"

"We're separating. T.J.'s going to drop us at the far corners of the ranch and we'll hunt alone. There's no telling where the cat'll be. It's fair that way."

"The fences don't stop mountain lions?" Even as I asked the question, I already knew the answer. I'd seen one leaping through the undergrowth myself and although he hadn't soared over a fence, I had little doubt he could have.

Ken confirmed my thoughts. "Regular fences don't even slow them down, and they can leap the high fences flat-footed. Besides, they get up in the trees and from there they can get about anywhere they want."

At this, Jim said, "Have to be a mighty big tree."

Ken shot him a glare that should have singed the hair off his mustache.

Puzzled, I asked, "What does that mean?"

"Nothing. Jimbo here doesn't think a big cat needs to climb trees when it's hunting, which is true. They stalk their prey. But they are climbers."

The two men were still exchanging glances, but I decided to let it go. "So how do you know any are still here? Aren't they just as likely to go to a neighboring ranch?"

T.J. and Kyla joined us in time to hear my question. Once again the men obligingly shifted to expand our little circle. Kyla rewarded them with a dazzling smile, and all of them immediately stood a little straighter. I noticed Eric visibly sucking in his gut, and I sighed inwardly.

"What are we talking about?" asked T.J. pleasantly.

"Lions," said Jim promptly. "Jocelyn here wanted to know if they could escape to another ranch."

T.J. just smiled. "I suppose they could, but the eating is pretty damn good here. At least one of 'em has been going through my whitetail like popcorn. Tonight's the night to put a stop to that, and I think one of you boys is just the guy to do it."

They all nodded, grinning and excited. Kyla frowned. "Tonight?" she asked. "But it's already getting dark. There can't be more than another hour of daylight left."

"The darker the better," said Jim with a wink at T.J.

"Mountain lions are nocturnal," explained Ken quickly. "We're far more likely to find one at night."

"Ah," said Kyla, shaking her head. "Well, just be sure you don't shoot each other." She smiled at me. "We probably better be getting back. It'll be dinnertime soon."

The men made a token protest, but it was obvious their minds were already on the hunt ahead. T.J. accompanied us to the front door.

I didn't know what Kyla had asked or not, but I couldn't pass up the chance to speak with T.J. "Did Kyla have a chance to tell you about Carl?"

He nodded, looking grim. "Terrible thing. I couldn't believe it. He just didn't seem the type to commit suicide. 'Course, I didn't know him that well personally, but he did some work for me. Seemed like a nice guy."

"Do you happen to know anyone else he was working for?"

T.J. frowned. "He worked for anyone who would hire him. He had a number of large trailers, and he was always hauling stock or arranging sales for folks around here. Why?"

"Jocelyn doesn't think he killed himself," said Kyla before I could answer. "She thinks his death has something to do with Eddy Cranny."

T.J. turned to me. "That was a terrible thing, too. But I don't see a connection, other than Eddy did some work for Carl."

I wished Kyla knew how to keep her mouth shut. It wasn't something I wanted to go into with T.J., but I supposed there was no harm in pooling our knowledge. "I saw Carl fighting with Eddy on the night he was killed, and I think the two of them might have been involved in something illegal."

"Like what?"

I sighed. "That's what I don't know. I was hoping you might have heard Carl talking about something, or maybe know who else he was involved with."

T.J. was already shaking his head before I finished talking. "Wish I could help you, but like I said, Carl and I weren't close. I have no idea what he did when he wasn't working for me."

We walked to my car, and T.J. opened the passenger door for Kyla. I opened my own door, then stopped. "T.J., why did you let Ruby June stay here?"

He gave a wide grin. "Oh, you know about that already, do you? Hell, I don't know. The girl needed a place to stay, I had plenty of room." He gave a little bark of laughter and glance askance at the two of us. "Plus, I knew it'd piss your uncle off something fierce. Actually, I think that's why Ruby came to me in the first place."

Kyla smiled and laid a hand on his arm in either benediction or forgiveness. Apparently she was no longer worried about family loyalty. Funny what a good-looking guy could do to a sense of duty, I thought sourly.

I wasn't all that worried about the pending feud, either, but I was puzzled by it. "But why? What has Kel done to you? Or vice versa?"

Still amused, T.J. shrugged and lifted his hands. "It's just one of those things." He looked down into Kyla's eyes and then grew more thoughtful. "Nothing that can't be mended at this point, though. Guess I might have to see if we can't come to terms about a thing or two."

She met his eyes squarely. "I think that would be really great."

I sat down in the driver's seat and closed my door. Kyla pushed the passenger door shut with one hip, and lowered her voice to continue her conversation with T.J. I turned on the radio at a low volume so I wouldn't accidentally hear any of their drivel and stared out the side window into the gathering dusk. A small break in the clouds to the west admitted the last traces of the setting sun, casting an odd bronze glow across hills and trees. The leaves on the live oak to my left looked as though they were tipped with gold, and the shadows around the base deepened into a mysterious and impenetrable gloom. Something about November always seemed a little sad, a time of endings and reckoning, a time when the darkness came early. Around the corner was the merry warmth of Christmas, followed by the optimism of the New Year, and then spring. But right now, dusk had come to the day and to the year. And somewhere Eddy Cranny and Carl Cress lay cold and dead, and my uncle waited in a jail cell. I started the engine.

As we drove away, Kyla pulled down the sunshade to watch T.J. in the rearview mirror. He stood there until we rounded the first curve and vanished from sight.

"I like that guy," Kyla announced.

"I noticed," I said. "But why?"

"What do you mean? Have you looked at him? He's gorgeous. And I like the way he looks at me," she said.

I tried not to classify the small smile tugging at her lips as smug. "Everyone looks at you that way. Well, every man looks at you that way. But it's not like you have anything in common with him."

"We have more in common than you'd think."

"Like what? You're not exactly what I'd call an outdoor girl. I can't exactly see you going out and bagging a trophy for the living room."

She laughed and didn't bother to deny it. "I don't think

that's what T.J. is looking for. He's got plenty of other people to do his bagging for him."

"Then what?"

"Money for one thing," she said, grinning. "We both love it."

"And that's a basis for a solid relationship?"

"You might be surprised. The thing is, he's making money the best way he knows. He's not planning on spending his whole life on the ranch. He's actually done quite a bit of traveling, and he's looking to start investing."

"Investing in what?"

She shrugged. "Real estate, I think. Having property—a paying property—out here is a start. He's already got a downtown condo in Austin, and he's living there half time. He comes out here when he's got a big hunt on to make sure his guests are happy. I guess those guys in there are spending a small fortune—you'd never know it to look at them, would you?"

"You would if you looked at their cars," I said, thinking of the yellow Hummer. "You can't honestly be interested in him because of his money, Kyla. That's so . . ." I struggled for the word.

"Cheap? Gold-diggery?" She laughed. "I'm doing all right on my own, if you haven't noticed. And I'm not after him for his money, but a guy with ambition like that? Yeah, that interests me, and I'm not ashamed of it. Anyway, what's your problem with him? You've never cared about the other guys I've dated, and a few of them have made Mr. T. J. Knoller look like a migrant farmworker."

"One, it's hard to keep up with all the guys you date. I'm

not even sure I knew about the rich ones. But two . . ." And here I paused. What exactly was my problem with T.J. after all? Was it because he was a thorn in my uncle's side and because he'd been so quick to accuse Kel of shooting someone? Maybe. Probably. But honestly, wasn't that enough? "Two, what about Sherman?"

"What about him? We're still just dating. He wasn't interested in coming out here, and I wasn't interested in going home with him. Not that he invited me," she said under her breath.

"Ah, so that's it," I said. "Did you ever think that maybe he has reasons that don't have anything to do with you? I mean, maybe his family embarrasses him or they don't welcome outsiders. I don't think you should hold that against him."

"Why not? Anyway, you're a fine one to talk. What about all your boyfriends following you around like puppies on a leash?"

"I've solved that problem. Besides, Alan and Colin aren't suing our family."

"I think that problem is solved as well. Besides, maybe you're just jealous because T.J.'s not flirting with you," she said in that special arrogant tone I hated so much.

This conversation had suddenly taken a nosedive back to those unpleasant high school days that I would just as soon forget. Not a good time in our relationship. I ground my teeth and said nothing.

A couple of moments later, I turned onto a rough caliche road with a crunch of tires on gravel and stopped at the very small and unadorned gates of the Smoke Quartz ranch. We both stared straight ahead for a moment, then Kyla opened the door.

"I'll drop it if you will," she offered.

"Deal," I said.

She got out to open the gates. I knew I should feel relieved that we'd managed to avoid one of our frequent spats, but I didn't. I should feel pleased for her to have found an interesting man to date, but I didn't. The thought of her dating T. J. Knoller made me anxious, but I couldn't figure out why.

Chapter 8

BREAK-INS AND BREAKDOWNS

Dinner preparations and family drama were both well underway when Kyla and I walked through the front door. A fire crackled merrily in the big stone fireplace, which looked almost like a child's toy in comparison to the one in T.J.'s enormous house. Uncle Herman sat in a recliner drawn close to its glow. He'd popped out the footrest and sat ensconced in a fluffy throw, tumbler of amber whiskey reflecting the firelight like a jewel on the table beside him, telephone clutched between one furry ear and shoulder. With his oversize glasses and bald head, he looked more like Mr. Toad of Toad Hall than ever. He was shouting into the receiver, his volume a reflection on neither his own deafness nor any incipient anger but rather the distance of the party on the other end. The farther away someone was, the louder Uncle Herman felt he was required to speak. I wished I could blame it on his age, but it appeared to be an unfortunate Shore family trait. Conversations with my brothers in California could leave both parties hoarse for days.

"Goddamn it to hell, Johnson, are you the justice of the peace for this county or not? My nephew is in jail, and I want you to get over there and put a boot in the ass of that sumbitch Bob Matthews."

I hung my coat on a hook near the door and slipped into the kitchen, leaving Kyla to deal with Aunt Gladys, who was bearing in from the left like a juggernaut.

In the kitchen, the horde of children was gathered around the table, some sitting, some kneeling on chairs to better reach the bounty in the center. Someone had set up a make-your-own dinner spread by tossing down a couple of loaves of white bread, two jars of peanut butter, three squeeze bottles of jam, and half a dozen sacks of chips, and the kids were up to their elbows in junk food. My brother Will was standing beside the stove watching the chaos with a bemused expression.

"It's like feeding time at the zoo," he remarked by way of greeting. "We could film this and use it for birth control commercials."

"You don't want to cause the human race to become extinct," I told him. "We're not eating this crap, too, are we?"

He gestured to the stove where a big pot bubbled gently, putting out a heavenly steam. "Nah, Elaine's making gumbo, and the rolls should be done any minute. She left me to make sure they don't burn."

"And to keep the vermin from killing each other?"

"I have no orders regarding that, nor any incentive to prevent it from happening. Hey, how's what's-his-name doing?"

"What's-his-name?"

"Yeah, what's-his-name."

I could never understand why members of my family were

225

unable to remember names. "His name is Colin. And he's okay, considering. They're keeping him for one more night just to be safe. Where's Sam?"

"He and Christy went for a walk, the cowards. I can't believe they left me alone to deal with this." His gesture seemingly encompassed not only the kitchen but the entire world.

"You're hardly alone," I pointed out. "The house is packed."

"I'm alone if you count sane adults. Or I was until you showed up," he added gallantly. "Have you noticed that everyone we're related to is completely batshit crazy?"

"It had dawned on me," I admitted. "What have they done now?"

"Uncle Herman hasn't been off the phone since he got home from jail. Do you know what his very first call was?"

"To a lawyer to see about getting Kel free?" I suggested, although I knew that anything sensible was a long shot.

Will gave me a pitying glance. "Ha. No. To the racing commission. He wants his winnings."

"What?"

"Yup. His point is that his horse crossed the finish line first. He wants the prize money, and he wants it now."

"But someone shot his competition!" I protested.

"He doesn't care."

I pondered this in silence for a minute. At the table, the kids had gnawed through the sandwiches and had moved onto drawing faces in the peanut butter smears on their plates. I opened the cookies and stepped back just in time.

"How did Uncle Herman get that horse?" I asked. "Has he said anything?"

"Lips sealed tighter than an oil drum. I asked him outright, and he just looked smug." Will suddenly lifted his head and sprinted to the oven. As he opened the door, the smell of baking bread expanded through the room like a puff of steam on a cold day and blended perfectly with the aroma of hot gumbo. My stomach rumbled appreciatively, and Will just looked relieved. "Elaine would kill me if these burned," he said as he pulled them out.

"Why didn't she just set the timer?" I asked.

"It's broken."

I frowned. "See? This is what I mean. Things are really tight around here. I've never seen Kel and Elaine looking so worried, yet Uncle Herman somehow is able to buy a first-class racehorse from Carl Cress of all people. And Carl's the type who would have cheated his own mother out of her dentures if he could have sold them for a profit. So how does that happen?"

"Wow, I thought you weren't supposed to speak ill of the dead," said Will with a grin.

"That's not speaking ill, that's just telling the truth. Carl probably would have been proud if he'd overheard. Anyway, I'm serious. Where did Herman get that kind of money?"

"Who said he did?" asked Will. He turned off the oven, and leaned against the counter. "There are other transactions besides the cash kind."

I looked at my brother with surprised respect. Sometimes I forgot that the snotty-nosed little pest of my childhood was now a financially savvy if somewhat cynical little pest. "Like what for example?"

"There's always bartering. My goats for your horse. But I was actually thinking something a little less direct. Blackmail springs to mind."

"Blackmail? What kind of blackmail?"

"Well if I knew that, Carl would hardly have gotten his money, or rather his horse's, worth, now would he?"

"So for example, Carl did something dodgy, and Herman found out about it? Then traded his silence for Big Bender?" My voice squeaked a little in combined disbelief and consternation.

"That's my best guess," grinned Will. "Do you have a better one?"

"I don't have any problem believing Carl did something blackmail worthy," I admitted, "but . . ."

"But what? You have a problem believing our beloved relative would stoop to blackmail?"

"No, not exactly that either. But what could Herman possibly have found out that would have embarrassed someone like Carl, who I overheard bragging about cheating someone on a lumber sale not two days ago. And how would Uncle Herman have found out anyway? It's not like he gets out of the house a lot."

Will shrugged. "You're wrong there. I know when we're not here he drives into town every morning and has coffee and breakfast with his cronies."

"He still drives himself? He's ninety-five."

Snagging a crusty roll from the pan, Will gave a small yelp and began tossing it from hand to hand to cool it off.

I grinned at him, thinking that some things never changed. He had never been able to wait for anything. He might be taller, a little more sophisticated, but he would always be my kid brother.

"I'm glad you were able to make it."

"Yeah, me, too. Especially since I won't be coming to Texas for Christmas."

"Mom and Dad will be disappointed. Where are you going?" I asked, picturing some exotic vacation and trying to quell a small pang of jealousy. I was currently saving my pennies for another vacation to an as yet undecided destination, but I certainly wouldn't be doing anything over the Christmas break.

"Paris," he said. "It's a promotion. I'll be moving over permanently. Or at least for a couple of years."

"Seriously? Well, I take it back. Mom and Dad will be thrilled."

"Maybe I won't tell them."

I laughed. "They're cool. They won't be interfering with your international jet-setting life. They'll probably just take you out to dinner once in a while."

"Maybe they'll take me to the Au Pied de Cochon," he said thoughtfully.

"Tourist."

"I can't help it. I love that place."

"Maybe I'll come visit you all next summer," I said wistfully.

I wondered if Colin would have any interest in accompanying me, and realized with a little jolt that I had no idea. The unworthy thought that Alan would have jumped at the chance to go skittered across my mind like a dark cockroach, and I firmly stamped on it.

After dinner, I pulled a chair beside Uncle Herman's by the fire. The old man was dozing gently, the glow from the flames reflecting in his thick glasses and off the top of his balding head. Outside, the wind had picked up and the temperature had dropped, making the warmth and crackling of the flames especially welcome. The house was finally quiet. The kids had returned to their trailer for the night and by now were probably asleep or at least slowing down. Kyla and Kris had withdrawn to the bunkroom upstairs and if I listened hard enough I thought I could hear the sound of giggling. Always unpredictable, Kyla had once again surprised me by her unexpected affinity with this acerbic intelligent young cousin. The other adults had withdrawn as well, everyone tired from what had been a very long day. I drew my feet up onto the seat, wrapped a crocheted throw around my shoulders, and waited.

A pecan dropping onto the tin roof with a sharp little ping finally made Herman stir and open his eyes.

"Aren't you ever going to go away?" he asked. "I been faking I'm dead for the last half hour, thinking you'd eventually give up."

I looked at him suspiciously, but his eyes behind the thick glasses were bright and alert as a squirrel's. It was entirely possible he had been pretending to be asleep.

"I have questions, you have answers," I said.

He gave an exaggerated sigh. "It's my birthday. How about a little peace and quiet as a present?"

"Your birthday was yesterday, and I already gave you a present."

"Sweaters don't count as presents."

"That's why I gave you the electronic rain gauge."

He made a sound in the back of his throat that sounded like a cat about to cough up a hairball. I wasn't sure whether it was meant to indicate his opinion of my gift or his annoyance at being corrected.

"Well I'm ready for bed. What do you want?"

"I want to know how you got that racehorse."

The smug, secretive look that crossed his face reminded me so much of Kyla that I almost laughed. It also made me all the more determined to find out.

"That's between me and Mr. Cress," he answered.

"Mr. Cress is dead," I reminded him.

"Then he won't be talking, will he?"

"A man is murdered, and that's all you have to say?"

He blinked, then shrugged. "That was strange all right. Knowing Carl, I mean. He was more like to kill someone else."

"What do you mean?"

"He killed a man when he was young. An illegal found his way up to Carl's place one summer when Carl was still just a teenager and came begging at the door. Carl's story was that the man tried to force his way inside when he realized Carl was home alone. Carl shot him. I always thought that was fishy especially since he was shot in the back. But there's no doubt he was in the house, and a man's got a right to defend his home. There was an investigation, but Carl's old man got him a lawyer."

He sniffed with disapproval, but whether about the killing or about retaining a lawyer I wasn't sure, and I didn't want to be distracted.

"Well, fine. Carl was a weasel at best, but as far as recent history goes, the only two inexplicable things he did was sell you that horse and get himself killed. I think they're related. I don't care what you promised to keep quiet about, he's dead now, and I need to know."

"What do you mean what I promised to keep quiet about?" Uncle Herman looked equal parts amused and outraged. "You think I was blackmailing him?"

"Certainly I do. You don't have the money for a horse like that. How else would you get him?"

Uncle Herman started laughing, a wheezing cackle that ended in a coughing fit. "Fetch me a glass of water, missy," he ordered between hacks.

I did as I was bid, returning with a large glass of ice water and a nearly empty package of Oreos.

He drank a few sips and took a cookie. "All this damn junk food," he complained, pulling apart the wafers. "I remember when we had nothing but homemade."

"Well, you know where the oven is," I pointed out. "I'm sure you'd find an appreciative audience."

"So now I'm a cook, too? Blackmailer and baker. Anything else? Maybe I ride around the ranch at night on a broomstick."

"I wouldn't put it past you. Now are you going to tell me or not?"

He was silent for a long moment. Then he scraped the filling off the cookie with his teeth and followed it with the wafers. He finally said, "As pleased as I am that you think so highly of me, I did not have any what you might call 'dirt' on Carl Cress."

"Then what?"

"Land."

"What land?"

"That strip that T. J. Knoller is claiming as his. I traded it to Carl for the horse."

"How could you do that when the ownership is being contested? And you never sell land," I added. Even though my visits to the ranch had been intermittent, this was the one inviolable rule that was passed down. In good times and bad, the Shores clung to their land like burrs. In fact, Uncle Herman's motto was "I only want my land, and any land that touches my land."

He cocked a bright eye at me. "That's not exactly true. I've never sold an acre off this place. In fact, I've almost doubled its size by buying out my neighbors, but I've bought and sold property in other counties for years. But there's no doubt that we're land rich and cash poor at the moment, and that lawsuit was going to be a problem. The horse trade was Carl's idea. He said he had proof enough that the land was mine to sell and was willing to accept my handshake until we could make it legal."

"He had proof? Why didn't he just give that to you?"

"Carl Cress never does . . . or should I say never did . . . anything for anybody else on this earth that didn't benefit himself in some way. He would've sat on his haunches and watched us go up in flames if he couldn't figure out a way to turn a profit out of it."

Herman sounded philosophical about it, but I had to bite back a few choice words about Carl Cress. He was making it very difficult to feel sorry that he was dead.

"So Big Bender's not actually yours now that Carl's dead. You won't be able to finalize the agreement."

Herman chuckled. "Darlin', I'm not fool enough to have

accepted Carl Cress's handshake on anything more valuable than a wooden nickel, and he wasn't fool enough to expect it. He had those papers drawn up nice and legal before he ever approached me. The horse is mine, all right. The tricky part will be dealing with his heirs. I don't know if Carl told anyone else how to dispute Knoller's claim."

"The horse trade was Carl's idea?" I asked.

Herman nodded.

"Why would he do that right before the race? A valuable horse with an excellent shot at winning?"

"I asked myself that," he admitted. "My thinking is that he either wasn't feeling too good about Big Bender's chances or Knoller was putting pressure on him to throw the race. I suspect a large percentage of his income originates from the Bar Double K. And maybe I'm doing Knoller an injustice. Carl might just have thought beating his best client's horse would be injudicious. He knew I wouldn't feel the same."

"Still, even beyond the prize, the horse is really valuable."

"That's the thing about racehorses. If he wins, he's really valuable. If he loses, his value goes down. Maintaining a racehorse is an expensive proposition. If you're in it for love, that's one thing. But if you're in it for the money, you need to be a breeder selling the foals of winners. That's where you'll see your profit if you're ever going to have any. No, a single racehorse isn't a moneymaker by any stretch of the imagination."

"But you have one now," I pointed out.

"Yes, and I've already got him up for sale. If I can just get that damn racing commission to acknowledge him as the winner, I'll have the two-hundred-thousand-dollar prize and a much more valuable animal to put on the auction block. But

I wouldn't have traded good acreage for a winged Pegasus, much less a racehorse, if that acreage wasn't looking to cost the family cash money. Even if Big Bender lost, his sales price combined with the money we'd save not going to court over the land made it a good deal. The fact that he had a chance to beat Knoller's nag was just gravy. It was a damn shame about that jockey."

I wasn't sure whether he meant that last statement as sympathy for Travis Arledge or chagrin that the race results were being contested. I decided not to ask. Another thought occurred to me.

"What do you know about Sheriff Bob?" I asked.

"I'm tired, missy. How many questions you got?"

"For tonight, just this last one. I think Sheriff Bob's been acting strangely. For one thing, I don't think he's been investigating Eddy's murder the way he should be, and he wasn't very concerned about Ruby June. And now he can't seem to decide whether Carl Cress committed suicide or was killed by Uncle Kel."

Uncle Herman chuckled. "That's what a man does when he's in over his head. And no, not because he's involved himself. Bob is an outstanding member of the community. He's involved in every community fund-raiser, he works his tail off for the Rotary Club, he's good at organizing old ladies, and at keeping the peace. You get a couple of ranch hands fighting in R.T.'s bar on a Saturday night, and Bob's your man. Murder, though—no, that's not his for-tay. This county hasn't had a real murder in decades. 'Bout ten years ago, one o' them Cranny boys killed his wife in a drunken rage, but there was never any doubt who did it. No, poor old Bob don't know which way to turn next. I told him he oughta call the Texas Rangers to help out."

"Bet that made him happy."

"It did not." He grinned. "It's still true, though. I figured having your young man provide some assistance would be a good thing, but that didn't work out too well for either of them."

"No, it didn't." I agreed. "It worries me that Kel is the one who's going to pay for Bob's lack of experience. They won't be able to convict him because he didn't do it, but it will ruin his reputation if the real killer isn't found. People will always believe he might have done it."

"Shores don't care about gossip," said Herman, rising to his feet. "And you should keep your nose out of business that doesn't concern you or any of the rest of us. This, too, shall pass, and things will settle back down."

I rose, too. "Much as I hate to contradict my elders and betters, I can't do that. A lawsuit over two hundred acres will seem like chicken feed compared to being a defendant in a murder trial. You might want to think about that and help me figure out what is really going on around here."

I was tired, but still too wound up to sleep. I wondered if Colin might be awake in his hospital room, and I thought back to the time he had spent most of a night in my hospital room waiting to speak with me. I missed him, I realized with some surprise, and I found myself wishing I could talk things over with him. He had a gift for putting things in perspective, for being able to find angles I wouldn't think of on my own. Besides, he could always make me laugh, and I could definitely use a laugh. But he was almost certainly asleep by now, and making the long drive into town would be of no help to either of us.

I began pacing back and forth in front of the fireplace. The conversation with Uncle Herman had not turned out as I expected and the more I thought about it, the more puzzling it became. What information could Carl have had that would make him think he could prove the strip of land belonged to Uncle Herman? Land deeds, plats, old contracts, sales records—any of those should have been a matter of public record, and although I hadn't asked, I assumed that Kel and Elaine had done their research. As far as I knew, Carl himself had never owned any of the land that made up the Smoke Quartz, so there was no reason to think he would have exclusive access to proof. Yet he must have or why else make the trade? And why would he want that land anyway? In this dry part of the country, two hundred acres, although nothing to sneeze at, was not enough land to run a profitable herd of cattle. And a narrow band of land wedged between two working ranches could not be conveniently accessed and could not be easily resold except to one of those two ranches. Had Carl planned to obtain the land from Uncle Herman and then sell it at a profit to the Bar Double K? But if so, wouldn't that have interfered with his working relationship with T.J.? Or could he possibly have been working at T.J.'s instigation? But again, why trade a valuable horse for something that T.J. felt was his already? No matter how I turned it over in my mind, I could not understand Carl's motivation in arranging the deal.

Feeling more awake, I glanced out the window and saw a sprinkling of stars hanging over the dim outline of the pecan trees. I'd left my own coat on my bed, so I took Kyla's from the pegs by the back door then turned the handle as quietly as I could and slipped out into the darkness. The cold air, biting and fragrant with the smell of smoke from the chimney, enveloped me, clearing my head and making me appreciate my own coat. This stylish camel-colored wool was no match for goose down against a bitter north wind. My feet in their socks made no noise on the wooden porch, and I walked to the edge where I could look up into the night sky, unexpectedly clear after a day of grim clouds. The moon was almost full and floated high in the sky, encircled by a small ghostly halo. Away from its brilliance, the stars made hard little pinpricks sprinkled across black velvet. I drew in a deep breath, marveling at the beauty of the sky, so much more intense here in the country than above the glow of the city lights.

A movement to my right made me jump a distance that would have made a kangaroo proud. I found myself on the gravel drive, stones biting into my stockinged feet, staring at a figure rising from one of the iron chairs. The light wasn't good enough to see who it was, but with a feeling of relief I recognized the small voice.

"Hi Jocelyn," came the quiet words from my cousin, Ruby June.

I expelled a breath and tried to calm the pounding of my heart. "I didn't see you there. You scared the crap out of me."

"Sorry," she said, not sounding particularly regretful.

"What are you doing out here?" I asked, stepping back onto the porch to save my feet.

She didn't answer, but I heard the rustle of her coat, which probably meant she had shrugged.

I realized I had not spoken to her since her disappearance, so I said, "I'm glad you're back, Ruby Juby. We were all pretty worried. And I'm really sorry about Eddy."

She began to cry, not with the silent control of a woman but with the big unrestrained sobs of a kid who has been hurt on a playground. I could almost hear her hot tears splattering on the wood of the porch like raindrops, her sobs amplified by the low roof and wooden floor. Wrapping one arm around her heaving shoulders, I pulled her out into the yard away from the house full of our sleeping relatives, ignoring the rocks and twigs that poked my poor feet. I hoped she had shoes on, but decided that a few sharp rocks would be less painful than having to deal with her mother.

"Poor Eddy. Everyone always hated him. Mom, Daddy, everyone. They never gave him a chance. And now he's dead. And the last thing I said to him . . ." She choked on her own tears, unable to continue.

I dug into my pocket—or rather Kyla's pocket—and found a scarf. I couldn't see the colors but I thought it was probably the pretty rose, blue, and gold wisp of silk that set off her dark hair so well and brought out the color of her eyes. Telling myself I'd have it cleaned, I handed it to Ruby June and heard her blow her nose with an inner feeling of satisfaction marred only slightly by an easily squashed twinge of guilt.

"Don't worry about things like that," I told her. "I'm sure Eddy knew that you loved him."

"I told him I didn't. I told him I wanted a divorce," she wailed between hiccups.

Well, that probably had stung a bit. "I don't see what choice you had. After all, he hit you," I reminded her gently.

"Damn it!" she snapped, anger flashing past grief. "How many times do I have to tell you that Eddy didn't mean to hit me? You and Daddy, you all just don't listen."

"You do have a black eye," I pointed out.

"Yes, yes, okay, he hit me," she said impatiently. "But not on purpose. Not really. He just has . . . had a quick temper. He was real sorry right away."

"He was sorry all right. Sorry when Uncle Kel pulled out that gun. And if you really didn't think he was an abusive SOB, why weren't you standing up for him at the time."

She gave a strangled sound. "I tried. You didn't get there right away, you know. I'd been arguing myself blue. Then Daddy pulled that gun, and honest to God I thought I was going to faint. I thought it was all over, and everything went all gray. I'm worthless. I should've jumped in front of Eddy. I should've done something, anything."

Her voice was full of guilt and regret, feelings that might haunt her the rest of her life. I was reminded again of how young she was, a not very mature nineteen, a kid who could have been one of my pupils. I put an arm around her shoulders.

"None of this was your fault, and if you go blaming yourself for stupid things other people do, you're going to be miserable your entire life. You didn't start this thing, you didn't tell your dad to pull a gun on Eddy, and could've, should've, would've are bullshit statements that'll just drive you crazy. Things worked out okay, at least right then. But Ruby, if you weren't mad at Eddy for hitting you, why'd you ask him for a divorce?"

"Because . . . oh, damn it." She drew a deep breath and blew it out, reminding me of a horse. "Because Eddy was

240

Eddy. It was like living with a twelve-year-old. He just wasn't growing up. He wouldn't take care of anything around the house unless I told him to do it. He'd leave his dirty clothes on the floor, he'd stuff trash into the trash can until it was overflowing, he'd just leave dishes everywhere. He didn't get along with my family, I knew they hated him, and I hated that. He wouldn't even get a real job, but he'd do anything Carl Cress told him to do. I hate Carl Cress. Hated, I mean. I'm not even sorry he's dead—Carl, not Eddy. Nothing was the way it was supposed to be. It was . . . oh God, I sound so petty."

I started laughing and squeezed her shoulders. "It doesn't sound petty at all. I don't know if it will make you feel better or worse, but I think you pretty much just summed up the first year of married life for ninety percent of marriages. It's a hell of an adjustment learning to live with someone else, and it didn't help that you're both so young. Men don't grow up as fast as women anyway, and neither one of you had had a chance to be responsible for your own place before you started sharing one. You guys might have worked it out."

"Maybe," she said doubtfully.

"I know that Eddy quit his job with Carl Cress. Seems to me like he was trying to do what you wanted."

"He really quit working for Carl? How do you know?"

"I saw them have a fight myself, and then I talked to his brother. I don't think Eddy had given up on the two of you."

She was silent for a long moment, and I could feel her shoulders start to shake with silent sobs again. "I was so mean to him," she whispered.

I said, "You had to be. You had to say what you said because you were miserable. The thing is, being mean and saying

241

what you said might have saved your marriage. It might have made your life better for both of you. It was sure a wake-up call for Eddy. The first thing he did was take care of the thing that bothered you the most. Who's to say that he wouldn't have done other things, and the two of you would have worked things out?"

"Do you really think so?" Wistfulness warred with doubt in her voice.

I thought about my own failed marriage, but decided that this was not the time or place for my own particular brand of cynicism. "There's no way to know, but I don't see why not. The real point here, though, is that Eddy hadn't given up, which means he knew you loved him no matter what the last thing you said to him was."

This did not have the effect I'd hoped for. Ruby June dissolved into a semi-upright mass of sobs and snot. There was a very good chance I'd be better off throwing away the scarf and letting Kyla think she'd lost it. Also, I was now chilled to the bone and my feet were feeling bruised.

"Okay, okay," I said, patting Ruby June awkwardly. "Time for us to go in. Listen, Ruby, you don't know exactly what Eddy was doing for Carl, do you?"

She gulped a last choking sob and said, "Sure I do. He was transporting stolen exotics and drugs."

Saturday morning dawned cold, brooding, and dark. Sort of like Kyla's face when I dragged her out of bed at five in the morning in the pitch black of the bunkroom.

"What the hell are you doing?" she asked in a furious

whisper as I tugged on her arm. "It's the middle of the night. Someone better be dying or on fire or both."

I was just grateful she had enough self-control to keep her voice down. "Come on. I need you."

For all her primping, fussy ways, Kyla is capable of swift action if caught in the right mood, which in this case was the half-dazed confusion of someone who was just woken from a sound sleep. She pulled on jeans and sweater in the darkness and followed me down the stairs.

In the car, braced by the frigid predawn air, she said, "Where the hell are we going?"

I started the engine. "Carl Cress's place. We're going to break in."

Give her credit, she didn't open the door and roll from the moving car. On the other hand, I'm pretty sure the look she gave me was a scorcher, and I was grateful for the darkness.

"So having one Shore in jail isn't enough for you. You think Sheriff Bob is just going to look the other way?"

"I don't think he'll ever know. You saw the place. Carl's wife has left him. Manuel lives in town. There's nobody there right now." I hoped this was true, although I hadn't had a chance to verify it. Still no point in telling Kyla that.

I stopped at the first gate. Somewhat to my surprise, Kyla got out to open it.

When she returned, she said, "What are we looking for?"

"Paperwork," I answered. "Ruby June said that Carl and Eddy were selling stolen exotics and drugs. Carl might not have kept any records of the drugs, but exotic animals are a legitimate business. If he was selling to T.J. or to some of the other ranches around here, he'll have receipts."

"You think a rancher would buy a stolen animal? That would have to be a huge risk."

"They might not have known. If we find records, it's likely that Carl was fooling his buyers."

"I hate to break this to you, but even if we do find proof that Carl was up to something illegal, it isn't going to help Kel," she said. "That is what I'm assuming you're trying to do, right?"

I nodded.

Kyla went on. "So say we do find what you're looking for. I don't think anyone is going to be all that shocked that Carl was a crook. It doesn't have anything to do with the murders."

"I think it does. I think someone else was involved besides Carl and Eddy. Someone who had a reason to want both of them dead, and someone who is all too happy to have the blame fall on Kel. I'm hoping we find proof of that at Carl's."

"Here's words I never thought I'd say to you: that's a really good idea. So good, in fact, that you're an idiot."

Offended, I glared at her in the darkness before quickly returning my eyes to the road. We were almost at the turnoff to Carl's place, and I had to pay attention. "What does that mean?"

"You might actually be onto something useful. So why are we breaking in? Why not just report it to the police and let them handle it?"

"Because I think Sheriff Bob might be Carl's partner."

She sat in silence for a minute. "That's ridiculous."

"Is it? Do you think he's been doing a good job around here?"

"I don't think he could find his ass with both hands and a road map, but being incompetent doesn't make him a criminal."

"He didn't do anything about finding Ruby June. He told Aunt Elaine that Colin had gone into Austin, which was a lie, and then he lied about having said it to Elaine."

"To be fair, he was looking for Eddy's killer. Looking for Ruby June wasn't as important," said Kyla.

"If he was really looking for Eddy's killer, the first person he should have been trying to find was Ruby June! I think he wasn't bothering because he already knew who the killer was."

"Kel?"

"No! Kel didn't do it."

"I know that," she said calmly, "but Sheriff Bob might think he did."

I shook my head. "No, Sheriff Bob knows Kel is innocent. At first I thought Carl Cress did it, but now that he's dead, I think maybe Sheriff Bob killed them both."

"But why?"

"I'm not sure," I admitted. "That's why we're breaking into Carl's place."

"I hate playing devil's advocate," she began.

This was a bald-faced lie. She loved playing devil's advocate, and she was extremely good at it. Her mind, although normally self-serving, was also exceptionally sharp and logical. I had no doubt she could chew enough holes in my theory to make it look like cheap Swiss cheese.

"I have no problem believing Carl was up to his eyeballs in crime. I might even consider the theory that Sheriff Bob is a crook. But what in the world makes you think that Carl would have any evidence in his house that Sheriff Bob wouldn't already have confiscated?"

"It's a long shot," I admitted. "But I just keep thinking that anyone as slimy as Carl probably didn't trust anyone else. I have a feeling that he'd try to keep some kind of leverage over his partners. Plus"—I thought of something else—"he had a reason for selling Uncle Herman that stupid horse, and he said he had some sort of proof that the land that T.J. is contesting actually belongs to Herman. At the very least we might be able to find that."

"What are you talking about?" she asked, and I quickly recounted Uncle Herman's tale.

I couldn't see her face, but she sounded disappointed. "Damn, I was sort of hoping the old guy was blackmailing Carl."

I laughed. "Yeah, me, too."

A possum, beady eyes twin flashes of white, trotted through the beam of the headlights and slipped into the brush beside the road as we reached Carl's ranch house. As I'd hoped and expected, the place was completely dark and no other vehicles stood in the yard. I made a circle, stopped at the foot of the walkway to the front door, and turned off the engine.

"Shouldn't you hide the car?" Kyla asked. "What if someone comes?"

"It's five thirty in the morning, and we're half a mile from the main road. If someone comes, we're totally screwed. I'll trade stealth for a quick getaway."

"Good point."

We got out, and I took a flashlight and a tool kit from the backseat.

"What are you going to do with that?" she asked with interest.

"You'll see."

Clicking on the flashlight, I led the way to the front door. The darkness was absolute. Five thirty in the morning in November was pitch black even without the help of the clouds overhead blocking out the faint light of the stars, and in the shadows thrown by the porch roof and swaying live oaks, we might as well have been in a cave. I shivered and felt grateful that at least I didn't have to worry about snakes.

Without any real expectation, I tried the handle of the front door and found it locked. The small window just above eye level was too small for my purposes, and in any event breaking in the back seemed more subtle.

"I'm freezing my ass off here," said Kyla as she followed me. I could hear her rustling through her pockets. "And where the hell is my scarf? I thought I left it in this coat."

"Shhh," I told her. "Keep it down."

"Why? I thought you said no one would be here." Now she sounded alarmed.

"No one is here," I reassured her. "I just don't want to listen to you bitch."

We reached the back door, and as I'd hoped it was the standard builder-grade version, which had a very large nine-paned window in the top half. This time Kyla tried the knob.

"What the hell? I thought people in the country didn't lock their doors."

"This isn't Mayberry . . . or the 1950s."

I put the toolbox on the ground and took out a hammer and one of Uncle Kel's pink rags.

"Now what are you doing?"

"I'm going to break one of these panes, then reach in and unlock the door," I told her. "Look away. You don't want to get glass in your eyes."

She turned her back and put her hands over her ears as I lifted the hammer. Holding the rag over the glass to keep the splinters from going into my face, I swung hard.

The hammer made a dull thud against the cloth and rebounded in my hand. Kyla swung the flashlight around and we looked at the window. Not even a crack.

"You didn't hit it hard enough," she said helpfully.

"Look away," I told her and repositioned the cloth. My next swing was from the shoulder. Thump! went the hammer.

Kyla turned back again, and we both stared at the unblemished surface of the glass.

"What is wrong with you? Hit it."

"I *am* hitting it. It must be the cloth deflecting it."

"Oh give me that," she snapped and snatched the hammer from my grip.

I turned away just as she went into the windup. The crack of the hammer against the pane sounded like a rifle shot in the predawn silence. I turned, expecting to see shattered glass everywhere.

The light of the flashlight revealed a single long crack, stretching diagonally from the lower right pane above the door handle all the way up to the top left pane.

Kyla said, "Oh my God. It's not a bunch of panes. It's one big pane with wood slats over it. How cheap is that?"

"Not as cheap as I'd hoped," I said, examining it. "It's obviously safety glass. We're never going to get through that."

"Oh yes, we will," snapped Kyla, and proceeded to beat on the glass with all her might.

Under her jackhammer pounding, the glass finally shattered into a cobweb mosaic she was able to break apart. As she reached in to unlock the door, her fingers unexpectedly stopped against another barrier. The curse of double glazing.

"Another one?" Her voice rose in outrage. She picked up her purse and fumbled inside.

I saw the gleam of black metal and jumped forward just as she raised her little Glock 19.

"Stop! You can't shoot here!"

"Why not? Get out of my way."

I didn't budge. "For one thing, a bullet from that gun can be traced. For another, it would probably ricochet and kill us both. Now put it away and take the flashlight."

Reluctantly she did as I asked, and I picked up the hammer and finished breaking through the second pane. I reached in with the pink rag and unlocked the dead bolt, and at last we were in.

"Either put your gloves on or don't touch anything," I reminded Kyla, as I pulled on my puffy fur-lined mittens.

She looked at them in silence, then said, "I'm glad you don't do this for a living. You'd starve."

"Yeah, yeah. Just help me look around. Point that flashlight over here, or better yet, give it to me."

She gave an exasperated snort and flicked on the overhead light.

I yelped a protest. "What are you doing?"

"Anyone who could see the light could see the car out front. I think the time for being discreet is long past, and I don't feel like tripping over furniture."

When she was right, she was right. It still made me nervous, but there was no denying searching the place would go a lot faster with the lights on. The house was not large, and it was easy to rule out the common areas such as the kitchen, living room, and den. The whole place smelled musty and stuffy, a cockroach skittered across the countertop, and the kitchen garbage can was making its presence known, but other than that you'd never know that Carl hadn't just stepped out for a few minutes. The house bore the signs of a man living alone. A single dish and glass rested in the drying rack by the sink. On the kitchen table, a Craig Johnson paperback rested facedown, spine broken, beside a crumb-covered plastic placemat. Kyla noticed, too.

"Who would have guessed old Carl knew how to read?" she said.

We moved into the back of the house. The master bedroom held an unmade queen-size bed, but only one side was rumpled. I glanced at the dresser and closet, but chose to move to the next bedroom.

This one had been converted into an office. A metal desk with a faux oak top sat in the middle and a few beat-up putty-colored file cabinets probably salvaged from a business foreclosure stood against one wall. The closet, accordion doors open, was filled with file boxes, a carton of printer paper, and a battered bookcase holding office supplies. A relatively new computer attached to an ancient massive CRT monitor sat silent on a rickety computer desk in one corner. As a model office, it was not pretty, but it was more organized than I would have expected.

Kyla pushed the power button on the computer and then

began pulling open desk drawers while she waited for it to boot.

"That's not going to help. I bet you anything he's got it password protected."

"No doubt," she agreed, still shuffling through papers in the drawers.

In spite of the glare from the lamps, I could see the first faint breath of dawn lighting the eastern sky through the slats in the blinds. I glanced at my watch.

"We need to hurry," I said.

She grunted acknowledgment but continued her search. Lifting a tray containing pens and pencils, she ran a gloved hand under it.

"What are you looking for?" I asked.

"Passwords. Most people write them down somewhere. Your more sophisticated types use an encrypted password keeper. If Carl did that, we're sunk. But somehow I doubt it. Aha!" She gave a cry of triumph and peeled a small card from the back of the big monitor.

She sat in Carl's chair and pulled the keyboard closer. I looked at the boxes in the closet and lifted the lid off one. It was full of old papers and files. Lifting the top page on the stack, I saw it was a receipt for a new tire dated August 1999. Carl was apparently a bit of a hoarder when it came to paperwork. A hoarder, a wheeler-dealer, probably someone who skated pretty close to the line when it came to claiming deductions on his taxes, but was he the kind of man who would store questionably legal valuables on his computer or in his official office?

I poked around in his bedroom for a few minutes. I'd

seen an interview in which a career criminal stated that the most common place people hid valuables was their own bedroom. According to this expert, the "underwears" drawer was a particularly popular hiding place. "Like a thief would be too delicate to paw through your panties," he'd added scornfully.

Mittens on, I pawed through Carl's clothing, underwears and all, but found nothing. I searched under the bed, I looked inside his shoes, I even lifted the lid on the toilet tank. Then I sat back on my heels, thinking.

Kyla's voice came from the office. "This place is Porn Central. I'm glad I'm wearing gloves, and that I don't have a black light."

"Ew," I responded.

"Seriously, I hope Kel has never accepted a disk or opened an e-mail from this guy. This machine is crawling with viruses."

I suppressed a shudder, but the word "crawling" sparked an idea. I sprang to my feet and hurried back to the none-too-clean kitchen.

The tiny pantry yielded nothing but a few more cockroaches and a spilled box of stale Frosted Flakes. The refrigerator, an ancient model from the days when Harvest Gold had been a designer color, had a few half-empty condiment bottles, a greenish steak covered in grocery-store plastic wrap, and a bottom drawer full of liquefied unidentifiable vegetables. I closed the door hurriedly.

The freezer was frosted into a winter wonderland of miniature icicles. The ice tray was half empty, a stack of Hungry Man dinners filled the bulk of the space. I moved them aside, and as I did so, my hand bumped a Blue Bell Cookie Dough ice cream tub, which tipped back. The movement caught my attention. It was the only thing in the freezer not covered by a thick deposit of frost, and it was very nearly empty. Pulling it out, I opened the lid.

Inside was a thick manila envelope, bent and squashed to fit inside the tub. Opening it, I drew out a handful of printed documents. It took me a second to realize what I was looking at, then I hastily stuffed them back into the envelope, returned the tub, and shut the freezer door.

"Kyla! Shut it down. I found what we need."

"Really? What is it?"

"A do-it-yourself blackmail kit."

I heard the electronic pop of someone turning off the power to a computer without waiting for the operating system to shut down, then Kyla appeared in the doorway.

"What's in it?"

"Contracts with Sheriff Bob for one. Did you touch anything?"

She wiggled her gloved fingers. "I was careful."

"Let's get out of here. We'll look at this stuff later." I didn't know why, but I was suddenly filled with a feeling of dread that almost amounted to panic.

Kyla didn't argue. We hurried to the back door with its shattered window. Closing the door, I hesitated.

"What are you doing?" she asked.

"Do you think we should try to cover the hole?"

"Are you kidding?"

"Well, it looks like it's going to rain. Plus, if we cover it, maybe whoever finally notices it will think Carl locked himself out and broke the window to get in."

"Don't be retarded. You know the police have already been out here to investigate after they found Carl, so they already know damn well it wasn't him."

She had a point, but I was now feeling both anxious and guilty, a bad combination if I intended to pursue this life of crime. "But we didn't steal anything. Won't they think that's odd."

"Yes. But . . . and here's the point . . . no one is going to suspect *us*. Even I wouldn't suspect us—a savvy, hot young computer genius and her goody-two-shoes teacher cousin?"

"How come you're hot and savvy, and I'm a Goody Two-shoes?" I protested.

"That's just the way it is."

"I want to be hot and savvy."

"Then why are you wearing that coat?"

By this time, we had collected our toolbox and hurried back to the car. Somewhere behind the heavy gray clouds, the sun was at least peaking above the horizon, illuminating the house, yard, gnomes, and barn. This was the time when country folks would be rising to tend their animals, and it would not be at all surprising to meet someone on the road. We needed to get away fast.

I pulled out onto the county road with a sense of relief. Early though it was, we at least had a right to be here.

"Where are you going?" Kyla asked. "The ranch is the other way."

"We're going into town to get doughnuts. That way we don't have to explain where we've been."

There was a heartbeat of silence, then she nodded with

approval. "Good thinking. Maybe you're better at this than I thought. Give me that envelope."

"You don't have to sound so surprised. I'm very cunning," I said, handing her the envelope somewhat reluctantly. I wanted to look through it myself, but could think of no logical reason why she couldn't examine it while I drove.

Her snort was not complimentary. She clicked on the dome light and pulled out the papers.

A large black pickup truck, headlights on high beam, overtook and passed us as though we were standing still.

"Damn, that guy must be doing close to a hundred."

Kyla glanced at the rapidly vanishing taillights, then returned her gaze to the photographs. "Looked like T.J.'s truck. Maybe he's doing a doughnut run for his guests."

"Are you seeing him tonight?"

"Yup. And I can tell by your snooty tone that you don't like it, so don't bother with the lecture. I'll make it up to Aunt Elaine another time. You know, this doesn't exactly rank up there with the best family reunion in history. In fact, if it wasn't for T.J., I would have gone back to Austin yesterday."

"But Kel's in jail," I said.

"Yeah and what are we supposed to do about it? Don't you think Elaine would probably be thrilled to see the whole pack of us get the hell out of her hair?"

"We're doing something about it right now. Why do you think we broke into Carl's?"

"For this?" she waved the sheaf of papers. "These don't tell us anything. I don't think they're blackmail material."

"Of course they are," I said automatically. "You don't store things in the freezer unless they're important."

"Let's say you're right. What are you going to do about it? Blackmail Sheriff Bob yourself?"

"No, I'll give them to Colin. He'll know what to do with them. He can get the Texas Rangers or somebody else to come investigate Bob. And while they're doing that, they'll send someone competent to investigate Carl's death. And Eddy's. And then Uncle Kel will be able to come home."

The parking lot of the Donut Hole was full, so I pulled into the adjoining Shell station.

"You can get the doughnuts while I fill up," I said.

She frowned, instinctively loathing any idea that wasn't her own, but then shrugged and took herself off.

I started the pump, then took the windshield washer from its bucket of murky water and began wiping the powdery caliche dust from the windows. The water left trails in the dust on my car as I squeegeed it away. A few cars came and went from the parking lot next door. The black pickup that had passed us or its twin was indeed present, and as the pump popped, indicating the tank was full, I wondered if Kyla was taking so long because there was a long line at the counter or because she was flirting with T.J. I dawdled with the wiper a few more minutes, but eventually another car pulled up behind me waiting for the pump, and a truck left the doughnut shop's parking lot, so I moved the car and went in.

A bell jingled merrily on the door when I opened it, and I was greeted by a rush of warm air and the mouthwatering scent of baked bread, fried dough, cinnamon, and coffee.

Patrons crowded around three small Formica tables by the plate-glass front window and piled into the cramped little booths lining the hall leading to the bathroom and kitchen. The bright counter was full of trays of doughnuts, and rolling racks behind the clerks groaned under the weight of kolaches, sausage rolls, and ham-and-cheese croissants. Kyla stood in line behind three men wearing camouflage shirts and bright orange vests, but she was also flirting with T. J. Knoller who stood beside her, holding three large pastry boxes, losing the advantage his speed on the highway had given him.

I joined them, giving a half smile to the grouchy-looking woman wearing foam curlers under a pink headscarf who stood behind Kyla so that she wouldn't think I was cutting in line.

"Hey there," said T.J., acknowledging my presence without actually convincing me he remembered my name.

"T.J.," I said, to indicate that I had the moral high ground of name remembrance without actually indicating I was pleased to see him.

Kyla glanced at me, then became crafty. "Oh good, since you're here, you can order. I don't know what we want." She attempted to get out of line, but I blocked her way.

"No you don't. I need you to help carry. And pay," I added pointedly. After all, I'd just pumped forty dollars into the tank of my Civic, and Kyla, although not cheap, was apt to forget things like chipping in for gas.

"Oh. Well, fine. T.J. was just saying that his hunters did not manage to shoot that mountain lion. They were pretty disappointed."

"I'll bet. Plus that means that thing is still on the loose."

He nodded. "Yeah. You might warn your uncle to keep an eye on his stock."

"I would, but he's in jail," I said tartly before I could stop myself. The woman in curlers snapped to attention like dachshund spotting a rat.

T.J. looked embarrassed. "Oh, yeah. Sorry about that. I forgot."

Kyla linked her arm through his. "Never mind. She's just crabby because she's hungry."

One of the hunters finished paying, and we moved forward a pace.

Raising his boxes as an excuse, T.J. said, "Well, I better get back to it. I'll pick you up about seven." This last was to Kyla.

She smiled and nodded, and he made his escape out the door with a jingle of the bell and a sheepish look over his shoulder.

"I don't know why you need to be rude to him. It's not his fault that Kel's been arrested."

I shrugged. Of course she was right, but everything about the man irritated me. I watched him drive away in his big-ass truck, and decided he was probably overcompensating for something.

"You know, Sherman is a pretty great guy. Why are you"—I glanced at the woman behind us—"messing around with T.J.?"

"Mind your own business."

After getting our order, I drove to the hospital without consulting Kyla. She rolled her eyes when she figured out where we were going but didn't protest.

"Don't take all day," she said. "I have to go to the bathroom."

"Why don't you come inside then?"

Grumbling, she did, and after a brief stop in the ladies' room, we dropped in on Colin.

He was sitting up in bed, a mostly uneaten breakfast of eggs and fruit sitting in unappetizing blobs on his rolling bedside tray. The bandage that had covered his eye had been removed, and although he had a truly impressive shiner, I was more concerned by the strip of tape at the corner of his eyebrow. I suspected it hid a line of stitches.

I also didn't like the gray color in his face or the light sheen of sweat on his forehead. However, he smiled when he saw us walk in.

"How are you feeling?" I asked.

"Brought you some doughnuts," said Kyla at the same time. "Sort of like crack for cops, right?"

"That's a stereotype," he answered her. "And a derogatory one at that."

"Oh, so you don't want them?"

"I didn't say that."

I handed him the little sack. "There's a sausage roll, too. Still hot."

He took it with thanks, and sniffed with appreciation, but I noticed he made no attempt to take it out.

"Seriously, Colin, how are you feeling? You don't look so well this morning."

"How come you can say that, but you get mad when I tell him he looks like shit?" protested Kyla.

Colin grinned. "I'm fine. I'll be getting out of here this afternoon."

Ignoring Kyla, I skewered Colin with my best teacher eye. I always knew when a kid was lying, and Colin, in his current state at least, was doing less well than the average fifteen-year-old. He squirmed a little and focused on Kyla instead.

"What are you two doing today?" he asked her. "You're up awfully early."

She opened her mouth to tell him, but I cut her off for two reasons. One, I didn't think Colin needed to know about our breaking-and-entering activities, at least not yet. And two, I wasn't going to be sidetracked that easily.

"Never mind that. What is going on with you? Really. And don't try to give me some half-ass version either."

"Is she always like this?" he asked Kyla.

She nodded. "Always. And don't ever play poker with her."

He gave a little shrug. "They want to run a couple of more tests. They won't take long, then I'll be out of here."

"Tests for what?" I asked.

He actually looked embarrassed, although for the life of me I couldn't figure out why. Men and their egos were always going to be a mystery to me.

"Internal bleeding," he mumbled.

"Oh, is that all? Well gee, now I understand why you don't want to talk about it. That's hardly worth mentioning." I felt both anger and fear in about equal measures. I wanted to shake him, but I wanted to find a doctor to shake even more. "What kind of internal bleeding?"

"I don't know. It's nothing." He reached for my hand.

I thought it felt hot, and I felt another stab of fear. I'd read the horror stories about people getting infections in hospitals that were worse than the injury or illness that had brought them to the hospital in the first place.

A nurse arrived with a wheelchair at that moment. Colin almost seemed relieved. "Here we go. Look, we'll know more when this is done. How about you come back in a couple of hours?"

He handed me back the sack of doughnuts, and I stood helpless. "Take that back to your family. Someone will eat them. Hell, you'll probably eat them. You can put them on a stick."

I tried to suppress the smile, but he saw. With a smile of his own, he said, "Will you go? I'm not getting up in front of you while I'm wearing this hospital gown."

I came to a decision. "Give me your hotel key," I said, holding out my hand. "Kyla and I will go get our things from the ranch, and then pick up your things from the hotel and check you out. We'll be back here as soon as we can, and then we'll drive you to Austin."

The nurse spoke for the first time. "Sir, the doctor isn't going to release you today."

"We're taking him to Seton hospital in Austin. If he has any records they'll need, we can take those with us or you can fax them over."

She looked alarmed and opened her mouth to protest, but I cut her off. "I bet you send people from here to Austin all the time, so you can make whatever arrangements you need. But one way or another, he's leaving when I get back. And you," I said turning back to Colin, "gimme."

With a grimace of pain, he reached into the drawer of the

bedside table, pulled out a key, and dropped it into my hand. It was a real key, not a card, attached to a battered plastic disk that said "Sand Creek Motel and Bar."

I put it in my jeans pocket and leaned down to give him a kiss. His lips were hot and dry beneath my own.

"Back as soon as I can."

The fact that he didn't argue scared me as much as anything else. Kyla had to trot to catch up with me on the way to the elevator and I punched the button with more force than necessary.

"So we're going back today," she said in a conversational tone. "What about Kel?"

I hadn't exactly forgotten all about Kel and our recent criminal actions at Carl's place, but I admit both had slipped pretty far down on my list of priorities. I stared at her blankly for a moment, then I said, "We'll give what we found to Will. Elaine wouldn't know what to do with it, and Will is used to looking at contracts. He can at least get it all to someone other than Sheriff Bob."

The elevator arrived, and I pressed the ground floor three or four times to make sure it got the message.

"You don't have to go back with me today," I said, remembering her date with T.J. "In fact, someone needs to drive Colin's Jeep home, assuming we can find it. It's probably at the police station, although who knows."

"I can hunt it down, and I'll be glad to drive Monkey Boy's car. We can have Elaine call around and find out where it is while we're packing."

"Great. So you can stay and go out with T.J., then come back whenever it's convenient."

She shot me a sideways glance. "So T.J.'s okay with you now?"

"No, but you're going to do what you want no matter what I say, and I have better things to worry about. Just don't let him . . . annoy you."

I had almost said "hurt you," but I didn't know how that was even possible given the length of time they had spent together.

"No worries there," she answered. "If anyone's going to be doing any annoying, it'll be me."

On the ride back to the ranch, she took out Carl's envelope again and began flicking through the smaller pieces of paper.

She stopped at one and said, "This is weird. It's a receipt from a zoo."

"A zoo?" I thought about it. "Well, Carl was always transporting livestock. Maybe it was an exotic for T.J."

She shrugged and put it back. "Doesn't say what it was. Oh, look!"

I had already seen it. T.J.'s big truck was askew on the side of the road, and T.J. was out and looking at a tire on the far side. Ha. Served him right. I did not slow down.

Kyla said, "We have to stop."

"We don't actually have to. We could slow and tell him we'll call a tow truck."

"Oh for God's sakes, pull over. Colin's not going to be able to leave for hours anyway. You know how those hospital tests work."

"What are you going to do—change his tire for him?" I reluctantly removed my foot from the accelerator and began slowing.

"No, but we can see if he wants a ride."

I hated when she made sense. I pulled the Civic to the side of the road in front of the truck. As she jumped out, I said, "Hurry it up."

She shot me the finger and went back to T.J. I took the envelope from her seat, closed it with the metal prongs, and carefully hid it in the glove compartment. No point in having T.J. see it and start asking questions.

As I was straightening up, a sharp tap on my window made me jump. I turned and found myself staring into the barrel of a pistol.

Chapter 9

KIDNAPPERS AND KINGPINS

I've read that victims of armed robberies make extraordinarily bad witnesses because they are unable to focus on anything except the gun pointed at their heads. I'm here to tell you that's completely true. I was a rabbit caught in the black-death gaze of a metallic rattlesnake. From far away, I could feel my own heart begin to pound in my chest, feel my mouth turn dry, feel every hair on my head stand to attention, but it felt as though it was happening to someone with whom I was only slightly acquainted. Somewhere in the distance, I was vaguely aware of a small clear voice telling me to snap out of it, but I was unable to take my eyes from the gun.

I don't know how long I sat frozen. My heart beat about a hundred times, but that could have happened in a space of about ten seconds. Then the gun rapped sharply on the window again, and the spell broke.

I raised my eyes and found myself looking at something even more frightening than the pistol. T. J. Knoller had Kyla in a choke hold, and he moved the pistol to her temple and gestured to me with his head.

"Get out," he said, his words muffled by the glass.

I opened the door of my little Civic and the chill November air swept over me like a splash of cold water. My brain began to wake up, and I started to breathe again. A quick glance showed me Kyla had a large bruise forming on her temple and a dazed fearful expression that made my heart beat harder for a different reason. A slow burn of rage spread from somewhere deep in my chest, and I seized it eagerly. After all, anything was better than the paralyzing fear.

I stepped from the car keeping my hands up out of instinct.

In a conversational tone, T.J. said, "Before you have a chance to get any bright ideas, you need to know I will shoot your sister here."

"Cousin," whispered Kyla.

He yanked her hair hard and jammed the gun into the soft flesh of her throat. "Shut up," he hissed at her.

I saw her eyes roll in terror, and a single tear slipped down her cheek.

"What do you want?" I asked him, trying to get him to return his attention to me.

He eased up on the hair, although the gun remained in her throat. "I want you to do what I say, when I say it. If you do, you might just get out of this. If not . . . well. Do you believe I'll kill her?"

Well, yes I did. I also believed that he was as crazy as a shithouse rat, but keeping the rat calm had to be my primary goal at this point.

"I know that you could, T.J., but you won't need to. What is it that you want us to do?" My voice squeaked only a little before I regained control and managed a calm, low tone.

His eyes narrowed, and he stared at me appraisingly. "Well, well. Who would have thought it? Little Miss Invisible is the one to watch after all." He swung the gun from Kyla's throat and pointed it at my head.

Goddamn it. The bastard was going to kill me, and he still did not know my name. I could learn the names of two hundred kids in less than a week, and he wasn't able to remember even one?

T.J. released Kyla, who staggered back and then froze. "Get the papers," he told her, not taking his eyes from me.

"What papers?" I asked. There was no way he could know about our activities at Carl's. Or could he? I glanced at Kyla, and saw a look of dawning horror mixed with guilt cross her face. "You told him? In the doughnut shop?"

"No!" she said. "Well, yes. But all I said was we'd found some interesting stuff about Sheriff Bob."

"Just get them," T.J. said sharply.

Kyla hurried around to the passenger side and opened the door.

"They aren't here," she said blankly.

He waved the gun at me in a threatening manner, and I flinched in spite of myself.

"Glove compartment," I told her. After all, there didn't seem to be much point in trying to hide them. And there was a tiny, tiny chance that if he got what he wanted, he'd let us go.

Kyla found the squashed envelope without difficulty and stood.

T.J. said, "All right. You come around here and get into my truck. You're going to drive us where I say."

So much for my tiny, tiny chance. "Drive where?" I asked.

"You shut up. You're going to follow us. If you don't, I'll kill her."

I was close to panicking. Everything I'd ever read about violence against women had said not to let your attacker take you anywhere. Whatever he was going to do to you would be much, much worse if he could do it in privacy. But those self-defense tips had never said anything about what to do if the attacker had a gun on someone you cared about. I glanced at the big black truck, thinking hard.

I said, "You better let me drive with you then. Kyla can't drive a stick shift."

"She can learn," he said tersely.

In spite of my terror, I almost snorted aloud at that. I'd tried teaching her to drive the ranch truck once and thought she was going to grind the transmission into a fine powder. I certainly hoped our lives didn't depend on her learning to shift, but the longer we could delay him, the better the chance that someone else might come along this deserted road, and I figured in the approximately two or three weeks it would take to teach Kyla basic shifting, either someone would come to the rescue or T.J. would lose the will to live.

It was almost as though he read my mind. "I'll drive, then. And you will follow. If you don't, the minute you veer away, I'll drag her from the truck and shoot her like a dog. And you," he spoke to Kyla without looking at her. "If you try anything, I shoot you first, and then I'll go after this one."

Kyla and I met each other's gaze, and I tried to will her to cooperate. I didn't like the panicky look I saw in her blue eyes. Panic could make even the smartest person do something very stupid.

He gestured with the gun and she preceded him reluctantly to his truck. As she started around to the passenger side, he said, "No. This side, then slide over. Keep your hands where I can see them."

It bothered me that his attention was still mostly on me. "You. Give me your purses."

Damn. The hope that he might have forgotten about our cell phones died. I wondered if there was any way I could slide my hand into Kyla's purse and find her gun in time. I moved to the car and opened the door.

"Wait!" he barked sharply.

I froze.

He gestured with the gun. "Move back. I don't trust you."

Keeping the gun trained on me, he moved slowly around the car to the passenger side and removed our purses. There was a brief instant when he had to take his eyes off me, but it wasn't long enough to do anything productive.

He straightened, holding the purses in his free hand. Shutting the door with his elbow, he gestured with the gun again. "Now get in. You follow us, or I swear I'll spatter her brains all over the inside of my truck."

I flinched at the ugly words, but did as he said. His enormous black truck passed me slowly, and I pulled out behind him, willing Kyla to keep her head and willing T.J. to have a heart attack and die.

After a mile or so, we left the main road and turned onto a rutted track that wound through first a cactus field and then into scrubby trees and brush. The suspension on the Civic squeaked in protest as we crossed over first one washout and then another, but the little car gamely rumbled on. I hoped the road wouldn't get much worse, not so much out of fear for my car's suspension but for fear it literally wouldn't be able to keep up and then T.J. would take out his anger on Kyla. My hands gripped the steering wheel so tightly it felt as though it would snap off in my hands. My brain raced furiously, but I was coming up with nothing. T.J. held all the cards. He had our phones, he had Kyla's gun even if he didn't know it, and he was able to use us against each other. I might have been willing to take a chance with my own life, but there was no way I was going to jeopardize Kyla's.

I have a decent sense of direction, but the road wound and twisted for what felt like miles, and by the time T.J. stopped, I knew only that we were miles from the main road and in the middle of nowhere. We had come to a clearing with a few dilapidated outbuildings clustered around a metal stock tank full of brackish water reflecting the gunmetal gray of the sky. T.J. stopped the truck and got out. I waited to see if he would take the gun off Kyla even for an instant. If he did, I would run him over, back up, and run him over again. But he was too careful, and reluctantly I turned off the engine. I quickly slipped the keys into my pocket. If I had the chance, I could jab at his eyes. A foolish thought maybe, but metal would be better than fingernails. I got out of the car.

"This way," T.J. said, gesturing with the gun.

He herded us toward the largest building, an ancient barn of weathered gray wood that looked as though a moderately strong breeze could blow it over.

"Open the door," he told me.

I put my hand on the old-fashioned wooden latch, then stopped. "Why are you doing this? You know people are going to come looking for us."

He gave a small shrug. "I'm betting they won't find you. Now open the door."

I felt a chill go down my back and lifted the latch partway, then stopped again. "Why should I? If you're going to kill us anyway, why should I make it easy on you?"

He cocked an eyebrow at me, considering. "Because it buys you time. I've always been a betting man. Today, I'm betting that when you turn up missing, no one will look my way. If I'm right, well, then, you stay here for a few uncomfortable nights while I liquidate and clear out of here. I can call the cops and tell them where to find you when I'm on a plane to Rio. If I'm wrong, then I can use you as bargaining chips. Your lives for immunity. So you see, if you cooperate, you have a chance of making it out of here. If you don't, I might as well kill you now."

"Is that what you told Eddy when you took him out to that caliche pit?" Kyla asked.

Her voice was shaky, but I could tell she was past the first shock and was starting to think. I was not sure whether that was good or not. Kyla was unpredictable at the best of times, and this was not a best time.

T.J. shook his head. "Eddy killed himself, or as good as. If he'd just left town like he said, he'd be alive today. But he wanted money, and he made the fatal error of thinking that I'd pay for his silence."

"So you shot him."

"You know I didn't. I have an alibi." He paused, then added, "Carl thought Eddy might go to the police."

"So you're blaming Carl? Very convenient, since he's dead. I suppose you're going to say he killed himself out of remorse."

"Absolutely. It's really perfect. Much better, of course, if this all just blows over, but if it doesn't, well, then, I still come out clean. Or almost clean, anyway. I suppose I'll have to let them prosecute me for the illegal animal imports, but I should be able to survive that. Hardly my fault that the man I hired to transport my stock turned out to be a stone-cold killer."

"Except he wasn't."

"No, he really was," said T.J. "That's one reason I hired him."

Almost without thinking, he moved past us and lifted the door latch himself. The heavy barn door swung open of its own accord, helped by the brisk November breeze. An odd odor streamed out—a musky acrid unfamiliar smell—and somewhere inside, something moved.

T.J. gestured with the gun, something that was becoming very old. Hesitantly, we preceded him into the dim interior.

Another movement, followed by a loud whuffing sound.

"What the hell is that?" asked Kyla, stopping abruptly. Even T.J.'s gun pressing into her back did not claim her full attention.

"Move," he said, pushing her between the shoulder blades.

The building had originally been a small horse stable. Four empty box stalls lined the right-hand wall. The left side had been converted into two homemade animal pens constructed of chain-link fencing wrapped around reinforced metal supports set in concrete. The closest pen housed a lion.

A very large, very alert lion. And not a mountain lion either. This lion might have come directly from an African savannah, assuming that the savannah was also home to an all-you-can-eat buffet. Even his mother would have described him as big-boned. Droopy pouches swung and rippled under his belly like furry pendulums. His massive feet looked like soft velvet, his sleek coat shone in the dim light streaming in from the doorway. The eyes, however, told a very different story. Golden, almost the same color as his tawny coat, they had the intensity of a fat kid who has missed a meal and now hears the dinner bell.

Keeping the gun trained on the two of us, T.J. went to the wall and stood beside a pulley system. I followed the chains with my eyes and saw they led to the cage doors.

"Carl designed these. Pretty smart really. When we needed to move one of the lions, we'd back the trailer into the barn, set up some fence panels, and pull open the door. The lion always followed its nose to the hamburger in the trailer. 'Course, Carl had a tranq gun, too, just in case, but he never had to use it. And lucky for you girls, the occupant of this cage," he indicated the second cage with a tip of his head, "got himself shot by one of my hunters last night."

"This is what you were all laughing about when you were talking about a mountain lion?" I asked, trying to ignore his "lucky for you girls" comment. "You're shooting real lions? Where in the world do you get them?"

"Well, that's another reason I'll be missing Carl. And Eddy, come to that," he added as an afterthought. "They were really good at finding older carnivals and roadside zoos that were only too happy to sell their stock to an 'exotic animal rescue' farm without too many questions. A lot of the big cats were older and pretty soft, but it's amazing what a couple of weeks without a meal will do for an animal's motivation."

Kyla's gaze strayed back to the big lion, now pacing back and forth behind its cage door.

"Starving animals, T.J.?" She turned to me. "You were right about him. Much as I hate to admit it, you were completely right. In fact, in retrospect, I don't know what I ever saw in him. I mean, look at him. He's not even all that good-looking."

I looked. "He's not bad on the outside. And after all, he is rich," I consoled her.

"That's probably as fake as his good ol' boy act," she said. "I bet he's up to his ass in debt."

"Probably," I agreed. "After all, he's running a scam just to try to stay afloat."

T.J.'s eyes narrowed. "Carl said you were trouble. I shoulda listened to him."

I nodded. "So why did you kill him? I mean, it sure seems like you relied on him for a lot of things."

"Get in the cage." Fortunately for us, he indicated the empty one.

Neither of us moved.

Kyla just stared at him. "There's lion poo in there."

I tried to think of a way to keep him talking. Without weapons, attempting to overpower him was just going to get us both shot and then eaten by a lion.

"So what did Carl do? Get greedy?" I asked.

"He was always greedy," said T.J. "He got stupid."

"Pretty stiff penalty for stupidity," I said.

"Killing Eddy was stupid. He should've scared the boy

and let him go. No one was going to listen to a Cranny any-way, and we could have spared a couple of thousand to get him a start in a new town."

"That's what Eddy wanted? That's why you killed him? Over a couple of thousand dollars?" said Kyla, shocked.

"I didn't kill him," T.J. reminded her coldly. "But yes, that's what he wanted."

Poor, silly Eddy Cranny. Driven to desperation by the demands of his shady employers and, let's be honest, his wife's family. I frowned.

"So why was Eddy trying to quit? Seems like he had a pretty good job working with you and Carl."

"Nothing was going right. He was convinced that he and Carl were going to be caught, and he didn't want to go to jail." T.J. looked thoughtful. "In retrospect, I might oughta have paid more attention to that point of view."

"So what about Carl? Was he supposed to throw the race so your horse would win?"

T.J. snorted. "Yes he was. But he got greedy, plain and simple. He couldn't stand the thought of losing money on Big Bender."

"So what happened? It was Double Trouble who got shot. Or rather his jockey."

A muscle worked in T.J.'s jaw. "The goddamn idiot hit the wrong target."

I thought that having a horse shot out from under you when you were going forty miles an hour might have hurt a bit, but decided not to argue.

"Carl was the shooter?" asked Kyla incredulously. "Why the hell would he try to shoot his own horse?"

"It wasn't his horse anymore," I said slowly, trying to work it out.

T.J. just shrugged. "It's complicated. Let's just say he had to make sure Big Bender wouldn't win. But he screwed up. No one except a complete idiot would have even considered going for a shot like that."

"Is that why you killed him?" I asked.

"If I wanted to kill Carl for screwing up, he would have been dead years ago. I didn't kill him."

"Then who did?"

T.J. opened his mouth to answer, and then abruptly shut it. "Enough. I've wasted enough time with you as it is. Get into that cage."

Again, neither of us moved.

"And then what, T.J.?" I asked. "What are we supposed to do? Just wait for you to come back and shoot us? Or starve to death?"

To my surprise, instead of answering, T.J. glanced nervously over his shoulder to the open door. As cold as it was in the dim interior of the barn, beads of sweat broke out on his forehead and upper lip, and I realized that he was afraid. Very afraid. And not of us.

The lion in the cage tossed its head and paced back and forth, big paws almost soundless on the concrete. Outside, a breath of wind rustled through the leaves of the live oaks and sent a swirl of dust through the open doors. And with it, the sound of an engine.

"Oh, no," he whispered and swallowed hard. His eyes darted frantically from the two vehicles parked outside, then back. "Shit. You," he pointed the gun at Kyla. "Up in the loft. Hide and don't make a noise, no matter what you hear."

Kyla threw me a wild glance. "Jocelyn, too," she said.

"No. There are two cars out there and no time to hide either of them. If you want to live, get up there and hide."

"Do it," I told her. "You're our safety net. Don't let them see you."

She started up the ladder, but said, "Who are 'them'? What the hell is going on?"

An icy dread settled in the pit of my stomach, but suddenly the pieces clicked into place and I knew. "Los Zetas. Isn't that right, T.J.?"

"Who?" asked Kyla. She was almost to the top, but she paused, looking down.

"Keep going," I told her. "The Zetas are a Mexican drug cartel Colin was talking about. He said there were rumors they were operating in central Texas."

"You're dealing drugs?" she squeaked with outrage, glaring down at T.J. like an elegant avenging angel.

"Probably not," I said, casting T.J. one scornful sideways glance. "Probably money laundering. Not that it matters at this point." Suddenly I felt very cold. Violence and murder, Colin had said. And now they were here. "Seriously, Kyla. You have to hide. Don't let them know you're there, no matter what they do." I fought down a sense of panic.

"'No matter what they do'? What does that mean?" she said, starting to climb down.

"No!" I said desperately. "We need you up there. You may have to go get help, and you're the only one who can do that."

The crunch of tires on gravel outside told us our time was up. Kyla met my eyes, and her own widened as our situation finally dawned on her. Turning abruptly, she slipped into the loft and vanished from sight.

T.J. took my arm and backed us into the nearest stall directly opposite from the lion. "Stay behind me if you can."

Better the devil you know than the devil you don't, I thought. I had no problem with the thought of using T.J. as a human shield, but it felt strange to be considering this complete asshole an ally even temporarily.

Two men walked through the open door, silhouetted for a moment against the bright gray of the morning sky before moving into the dim interior light. Dim, but still bright enough to make out the shapes of the long-barreled rifles they held and to see their faces. The taller of the two was a stranger to me, a big ugly thug of a man with greasy black hair and a hairy growth under his nose that could only be described as a porn 'stache. The other was Manuel, Carl's soft-spoken kind-eyed ranch hand. The gun looked completely out of place in his work-worn hands.

I felt my jaw drop just a little. Manuel was the last person on earth who should have walked through that door.

"Mr. T.J.?" he called in his soft, pleasant voice.

"Right here," said T.J.

In Spanish, Manuel asked, "Why are you hiding, Mr. T.J.? It is just us, your friends."

"Didn't know it was you, and you can't be too careful out here," T.J. replied in fairly decent Spanish. He stepped closer to the front of the stall, but he kept the rough wood of the support post against his left shoulder. He also kept his pistol close

278

to his side with his finger on the trigger. The stall door was still open, and a big part of me wished he would pull it shut.

"Very wise," answered Manuel, taking a pace forward. "But you can come out now."

"I don't think so, and that's far enough," said T.J., gesturing with his pistol.

Manual stopped abruptly, but the stranger looked at T.J.'s gun with contempt rather than fear. I did not like the look in his eyes, a soulless malevolence that I usually associated with cold-blooded predators like sharks, snakes, or toddler beauty pageant moms.

T.J. went on. "I can hear you just fine from there. We don't have anything to talk about anyway."

Over T.J.'s shoulder, I could see the tall stranger turning this way and that, taking in the layout of the barn. He turned to the lion and approached its cage.

The lion paced back and forth and then abruptly lunged upright, rearing on its back legs and resting huge velvet paws against the bars in a parody of a jailed man. The stranger jumped back involuntarily and then gave a harsh laugh. With the abruptness of a striking cobra, he rammed the barrel of his rifle into the lion's muzzle. The big cat gave a startled roar of outrage and whirled away with more speed than I would have though possible for such a large animal. I could see blood on its nose as it turned to face its tormentor, but this time it stayed well away from the bars.

"Not so brave now, *kitty*," said the stranger, also in Spanish.

Manuel frowned at the distraction, but quickly turned his attention back to us. "But Mr. T.J., I think we have a great deal to discuss. My boss has many questions for you. I told him I would bring him answers. Or far better, you can talk to him yourself."

"No," said T.J. "You have the answers, and you have the money, what there is of it. You don't need me."

Manuel looked at me over T.J.'s shoulder with narrowed eyes, and I suppressed an urge to duck my head behind him. "Why do you have the woman here? She was looking for Carl earlier, and I think she knows too much."

"She doesn't know anything. Not about your boss, not about our business. You don't need to concern yourself."

"Yet you brought her to this place. Why?"

"She is my girlfriend. She wanted to see the lion, that is all."

"Unfortunate. For her, that is."

I felt a quiver go through T.J. Asshole though he was, I realized he was doing his best to save my life. Maybe he really had intended to use Kyla and me as bargaining chips after all.

"Not at all. She knows nothing. She doesn't even understand what we are saying. All you have to do is turn around and leave, and everyone goes home safe and sound."

"Of course," said Manuel pleasantly. "Why do we not do that now? You and the señorita can come out, and I shall introduce you to my friend here."

"Thanks, but I don't think so. You walk away. You tell your boss that Carl is the one who made a mess of our business, not me."

The stranger snorted, and Manuel grimaced. "It was your plan. The fact that it was Carl who missed the horse and hit the wrong target does not make you less responsible."

T.J. said, "I'll do what I can to get you the money, but the race winnings are out of our reach, and there's nothing I can do about it. And since you killed Carl, we have the cops sniffing around, and they aren't going to back off. That was stupid, Manuel."

I started, then quickly lowered my eyes, hoping they hadn't noticed. I definitely didn't want them knowing I could understand what they were saying. So T.J. had been telling the truth about not killing Carl. A liar, a con man, a kidnapper, and no telling what else, but he was not a murderer.

Manuel's eyes flashed with anger, but he almost instantly reassumed his mild, pleasant expression. Spreading his hands in a conciliatory gesture, he said, "Carl would have been caught, and then he would have talked. I had no choice. Or rather, my friend here felt he had no choice."

The stranger, hearing himself discussed, turned away from the lion and gave a most unpleasant smile.

T.J. shook his head. "Carl was too scared to talk. He would have gone down first, not that it matters now. Either way though, your boss should cut his losses and pull out. This operation is over."

The stranger spoke for the first time. His smoker's voice sounded like gravel falling into a tin bucket, hoarse, but oddly high-pitched for such a big man. "But what message does that send? Our boss has many competitors who only wait for any sign of weakness to move against him."

Manuel took a cautious step forward. Behind him, the big stranger edged to the side, probably looking for a way to get a clean shot at T.J. Wishing again that T.J. had pulled the stall door shut, I crouched low enough behind him to get my head out of sight, and as I did, my eye caught sight of the metal pulley system that opened the lion cages.

I went down on one knee in the soft dry earth of the stall floor. I could no longer see Manuel or his buddy, but I could see the lion, which had not taken its golden eyes off the two men. It was still pacing, agitated, tail twitching. I considered this a hopeful sign.

The rough slats between the pair of stalls in which we hid had been designed to be easily removable, probably to accommodate a much larger animal than a horse. The lowest slat was some ten or twelve inches above the dirt and sawdust, making a gap almost, but not quite large enough for me to slide through. As soundlessly as I could, I shrugged off my bulky goose down coat and let it slide to the ground. Then, I carefully moved to the back corner and began quietly pushing the dirt away from beneath the barrier, expanding the gap as best I could. For an instant, T.J. glanced my way to see what I was doing.

The sound of a shot rang out, deafening in the enclosed space, followed almost immediately by another. Without thinking, I hurled myself forward, feeling the rough board catch first my hair and then scrape my shoulders. For one terrifying instant, I thought my rear end wouldn't make it, but sheer terror gave me the impetus to wrench through, my feet scrabbling in the dirt before finally finding purchase and propelling me into the next stall. Hauling myself to my knees, I threw myself at the stall door, reached through the opening, and yanked on the lever to the lion's cage.

With a rasp of metal, the cage door rolled back. I had just enough time to see an immense tawny form spring forward before a high-pitched scream and another gunshot ripped through the air. I threw myself down behind the shelter of the wooden partition, then scrambled forward to pull the stall door shut. Wherever the lion was, I didn't want it sniffing its way to me.

From my crouching position, I listened intently—or as intently as I could over the painful ringing in my ears. I thought I could hear a muffled thumping, but no voices, no other human sounds. The smell of dust, hay, and lion urine now mingled with the acrid scent of gunpowder. I waited, half expecting the door of my stall to swing open to reveal the barrel of a rifle, but nothing happened. After a few moments, the ringing in my ears subsided somewhat but I still heard nothing. Cautiously, I put an eye to the gap in the stall door. An empty lion cage, a stretch of dirt floor, but nothing else. Rising to my feet, I cautiously peeked over the door before ducking back down. The brief look had been enough to reveal a pair of cowboy boots, toes pointing to the roof, and a blur of yellow fur. At least one of the two men was otherwise occupied, I thought, but what about the second? And where was T.J.? Dropping back to the floor, I rested my cheek on the dirt and looked beneath the board.

T.J. lay slumped in the corner where I'd left him. He still clutched his pistol in one hand, but that hand, pistol and all, lay motionless in the dirt. A red stain seeped from under his arm, spreading slowly across the front of his formerly white shirt. He was alive, though, and his eyes, dazed and blank, met mine.

"T.J., pull that door closed," I whispered to him. "The lion's out."

He blinked and looked away, but made no other movement. I wasn't sure if he understood. Wasn't even sure he could hear me. After all, he'd been a lot closer to the shooting, and his ears had to be ringing as much as mine were.

Knowing it was not a good idea, I knelt beside the hole between the stalls and spent another couple of moments expanding it, then slipped through again. The first thing I did was slam the door closed, a movement that produced a low growl from a very big throat on the other side. The second thing was to take T.J.'s gun from his hand. Only then did I stand and look out over the top of the stall door.

I sort of wished I hadn't. Manuel lay unmoving on his side in the center of the floor. I could see his open eyes. Worse, I could see the gaping hole that T.J.'s bullet had torn through his neck. The other man, the tall stranger, lay half under the lion. I couldn't see his face, but considering what the lion was doing, I didn't think he was a threat any longer.

From above, Kyla's panicked voice called, "Jocelyn?"

I straightened. "I'm here."

"Oh thank God!" she called back. "Are you all right?"

"I'm fine. T.J.'s not. He's been shot."

"I'm coming down!" she said.

"Um, take a look. I let the lion out."

I heard the tap of her designer boots on the loft floor, then her gasp. "Oh my God!" There was a moment of silence, then she said again, "But you're okay?"

"Fine. A little deaf maybe, but fine."

"I didn't think lions ate people," she said.

"No, I'm pretty sure they do. Especially when you've starved them for two weeks and then poked them with your gun."

"Who poked the lion with a gun?"

284

"The guy currently serving as the main course," I said. "We have bigger problems though. We need to get T.J. to a hospital as fast as possible. Any ideas about how to get past a lion?"

"You could shoot it. I assume you have T.J.'s gun."

"I'm not shooting a lion," I protested. "For one thing, it just saved our lives. And for another thing, I think a gun this size would just make it mad."

"I could drop a hay bale on its head," she offered after a moment's consideration.

"That might hurt it. Could you drop one close to it? Maybe behind it so it would go out the door?"

For answer, I heard the sound of something heavy sliding over the floor, then the sound of a bale hitting concrete. The lion flinched and snarled, but didn't move.

Kyla dropped another bale a little closer with similar results. The third one, however, brushed the lion's tail as it hit the floor, and the big animal gripped the body in its powerful jaws and dragged it out through the open door. I wondered if lions had trouble digesting porn 'staches.

Kyla descended the ladder quickly, and I opened the stall door and pulled her inside before closing it again.

She looked down at T.J., whose face was rapidly fading to the grayish white color of wet caliche. The blood had now soaked through his shirt and was slowly but steadily dripping into the dirt floor. I knew we should be performing some sort of first aid, but getting him to the hospital was the only way he was going to make it. I knelt again and put my hand into his pocket, digging for the keys. He whispered something, but I couldn't understand him.

"I'm going to get his truck. See if you can find something to put pressure on the wound," I said to Kyla.

She looked down at the bloody shirt with distaste, then at the keys in my hand. "Let me go," she offered. "You can apply pressure."

"Don't be silly. You can't drive his truck."

"Then I'll get your car."

"The truck will be able to go faster on that road, and he'll be able to lie flat in the bed of the pickup," I said. This was true. Besides, I didn't know where the lion had gone, and I didn't like the thought of letting her go out there alone. Later I would wonder why I thought it was okay for me to go out there alone, but at the time my reasoning seemed to make perfect sense.

"You don't care if it's better for him," she accused most unfairly. "You just don't want him to bleed on your seats. Which I can appreciate. But how the hell are we going to lift him into that big-ass pickup? We'll have a hard enough time getting him into your car. He must weigh a ton." She nudged his calf with the toe of her boot for emphasis.

She had a point, but I was determined. "Hay bales," I said quickly. "We can haul him up those."

I took the keys and slipped out the stall door, closing it behind me.

"Don't get eaten," she called after me.

"Apply pressure," I reminded her.

I crept to the barn door, stepping carefully around Manuel's body and the pool of blood soaking into the concrete. I peered around the corner, but could see no sign of the lion. That might be good or it might not, especially if it was lurking

286

behind one of the three vehicles now parked in front of the barn. Deciding I would just have to take that chance, I braced myself to dash across the stretch of open ground, shivering a little and wishing I'd remembered to put my coat back on.

The sound of an engine stopped me. I listened as it drew closer, recognizing the sound of tires grinding on gravel and moving fast. Terror streaked through my veins in an icy rush. This was too much. Who could it be, except more allies of either T.J. or his drug-running enemies? I ran for the truck, fumbling with the keys as I went. It was a scene right out of a nightmare. I felt as though I were running through molasses, hands shaking so badly I could hardly fit the key into the ignition. Forcing myself to take a deep breath, I managed to control my hands enough to start the engine. Grinding the gears, I drove the truck right into the barn, snapping the passenger mirror off against the door frame and stopping a scant few inches from the bloody body of Manuel.

Jumping out, I opened the tailgate, then raced to the stall.

To her credit, Kyla had overcome her squeamishness and was kneeling beside T.J., applying pressure to the wound. With my coat. My expensive and favorite goose down coat. Any guilt I might have felt over the Ruby June scarf incident was erased in the twinkling of an eye, but there was no time to scream at her.

"Someone's coming!" I shouted instead.

Her head snapped up, blue eyes wide. "Who?"

"Who cares? We've got to get out of here!"

I manhandled T.J. into a sitting position and gripped him under the arms. I felt a gush of warmth flow over my wrist. T.J. emitted a wheezing gasp.

"Help me," I ordered.

"I say we leave him," she said, although she gamely seized his boots.

I heaved with all my might and together we managed to lift him about six inches before dropping him.

With a small moan, T.J. passed out, which was probably for the best. I gripped his jacket and started dragging him from the stall. I managed to move him about a foot before my fingers slipped and his unconscious head bounced into the dirt again.

"I'm serious," said Kyla, straightening. "We should leave him and get the hell out of here."

"They'll kill him," I protested.

"They'll kill all of us if we don't get out of here."

I hesitated. The sound of the engine was closer, and she was right. The smart thing was to leave T.J. and hope whoever arrived would be more interested in pursuing us than in finishing the job their colleagues had begun.

I couldn't do it. I gripped his coat and heaved again.

Kyla slipped an arm under T.J.'s thighs and put her back into it. Together, we somehow hauled his limp form up onto the tailgate, and then with a superhuman effort rolled him in. I slammed the tailgate shut.

"Get in," I told her.

We scrambled into the truck with the grace and speed of crazed squirrels. I started the engine and ground the gears into reverse.

"Find your phone!" I shouted to her, but she was ahead of me. Kneeling on the seat, she had already retrieved her purse from the back floor where T.J. had thrown it and was digging inside. She removed her hand triumphantly, and from the corner of my eye, I saw she now held her little Glock 19.

I squeaked with outrage. "Your phone! Not your gun! We don't want to be in a shootout, we want help! And buckle up!"

With a glare, she flopped into her seat and clicked her seatbelt, then began digging in her purse again, but I couldn't wait. I hit the accelerator and the black truck shot backward, its tailgate missing my Civic by less than six inches as I spun the steering wheel. I heard a dull thump from the bed of the pickup and guiltily pictured T.J.'s body sliding backward against the cab. As the truck came around, I saw a dark green vehicle approaching fast, caliche dust streaming behind it like a plume of smoke, and recklessly swung directly into its path. For one awful instant, I braced myself for the crash, then the other driver swerved just in time, careening off the road and down into a steep draw. As the green car plunged downward, a massive tawny body sprang heavenward, soaring up and over the hood of the vehicle just in time. And then we were clear, and I was stamping the accelerator to the floor, fishtailing down the road.

Kyla twisted in her seat to stare out the back window.

I wanted to scream at her, and so I did, "What the hell are you doing? Get your phone!"

"I'm trying to see if the lion is going to eat Monkey Boy," she said.

I navigated a sharp bend in the road, the truck sliding on the gravel. I'd never driven so fast or so recklessly in my life. Plus, her words made no absolutely no sense. "What?"

"You should slow down before you kill us," she said

calmly, turning to face forward again. "And, it's up to you, of course, but you might want to go back and see if your boyfriend needs any help with that lion."

"What the hell are you talking about?"

"That was Colin in that Jeep. You remember Colin? About six feet tall, dark hair, broken tooth. Crazy about you, no one knows why."

I took my foot off the accelerator and the black truck slowed.

Ahead of us, I could see flashing lights and hear the wail of a siren as a sheriff's truck approached. I pulled to the side of the road.

Sheriff Bob slowed as he passed, rolling down his window to say something. He took one startled look at me, but I just pointed the way we had come, and he closed his mouth and drove on.

I kept my hands on the steering wheel because I'd started to shake and gripping it helped me concentrate on not throwing up. I knew I should turn the truck around and go back, but I just sat where I was.

"I'm an idiot," I said at last.

Kyla grinned at me. "I've been telling you that for years."

Chapter 10

DEATH AND DECISION

I could have sat there forever, but fortunately for T.J., I finally remembered he was still bleeding in the back of the truck. Kyla called 911 as I drove toward town, and an EMT team met us beside the gasoline pumps at Jo Jo's Fill 'R Up & Kolache Emporium, transferring our unconscious kidnapper to a gurney and into an ambulance. Then, not quite knowing what else to do, we washed the blood from our hands in Jo Jo's restroom and returned to T.J.'s barn.

When we arrived, two more police trucks were on the scene and a tow truck was pulling Colin's Jeep from the draw. A deputy with a gun held up a hand and tried to talk us into turning around when Colin came out of the barn and waved us through.

I've never been so glad to see anyone. His jacket was draped over one shoulder because of the cast on his arm, his dark hair tousled by the wind, a bandage on one cheek only half concealing a bruise, and I thought no one had ever looked so good.

I stopped the truck in the grass beside the barn and ran to him, throwing myself into his arms. I heard him suppress a small gasp of pain and tried to release him, but his arms tightened around me and pulled me close. He kissed me, gently at first then with growing passion, holding me hard, one hand sliding up into my hair to cradle the back of my neck, the other an iron band in the small of my back. Far too soon, he lifted his head and pressed his cheek into my hair, just holding me, and I thought I felt him tremble.

"I thought you were . . . ," he started, but his voice broke and he didn't finish.

"Me, too," I admitted. "It was bad."

I squeezed him again, felt him wince. "Sorry," I whispered.

"Doesn't hurt," he lied, squeezing back.

I suddenly remembered that I'd last seen him in the hospital being wheeled away for tests. "What about the internal bleeding?" I demanded.

"No bleeding. I have a clean bill of health. They were about to release me anyway. Your not coming back when you said you would just speeded up the process a bit."

I frowned at this, not convinced he should be out of bed, much less walking around a crime scene. "So, basically you released yourself and came looking for us? And how did you find us?"

"You can thank Sheriff Matthews for that. When I told him you were missing, he called in favors and got a trace where your phone signal had last been picked up. Then he figured out the closest property with roads and outbuildings. There were two candidates—he took one and I took the other. Luckily, I picked the right one."

"Yeah, thank goodness," I breathed, then remembered something else and winced. "By the way, sorry about running you off the road."

"Ah, yes." He did lift his head at that and looked at me with twitching lips. "Well, you were in a hurry."

Kyla joined us then.

"Damn straight," she said. "We thought you were more of that Lost Zulu gang coming to kill us."

Colin's eyebrows almost met his hairline.

"Los Zetas," I corrected, earning a look of comprehension from Colin and withering scorn from Kyla.

"Whatever," she said. "We were tired of having guns pointed at us."

"So after you ran me into a ditch—a ditch containing a lion, by the way, which is another subject I'd like to discuss—you had a sudden uncontrollable urge to drive into town? You were gone half an hour."

"That's not fair," protested Kyla. "We didn't know it was you until it was too late, and we had to get T.J. to the hospital."

I nodded vehemently. After all, both those things were technically true and sounded much better than "We completely panicked and forgot we had T.J. in the back."

Colin frowned. "T.J. was here? And why did you take him to the hospital? What's wrong with him?"

"The Zulus shot him," said Kyla. "I don't think he's going to make it. And serves him right if he doesn't, the bastard."

He took a second to process what she'd said, then abruptly released me and shouted for Sheriff Bob. I couldn't swear to it, but I thought his eye might have been twitching. After that, things started moving very fast. Sheriff Bob, once he understood what we were saying, sent Colin and a deputy to the hospital to check on T.J., then he drove Kyla and me to the police station on the town square. As we passed the hanging tree, I noticed the decorations had finally been completed and an entire herd of electric reindeer were busy raising and lowering their mechanical heads in time to a tinny rendition of "Winter Wonderland" blaring from a hidden speaker in Santa's sleigh. In Sand Creek at least, Thanksgiving was officially over.

Under the glow of fluorescent lights in his office at the police station, Sheriff Bob looked old and tired. He looked worse by the time we were finished, and we didn't look much better. Over the course of the next few hours, Kyla and I had to explain what had happened to us about six hundred times, Bob asking one annoying question after another, scratching notes on a yellow tablet with one hand and drinking truly terrible coffee from the other. I'd taken one sip myself from the Styrofoam cup he'd given me and set it down in a hurry. He offered nothing else, and I was sorry we hadn't stopped for kolaches when we had the chance.

At last Kyla exploded. "Look, we're the victims here. We were assaulted and kidnapped, and now you're practically water-boarding us. I'm tired, I'm starving, and I want to go home."

She rose and glared at him, as though daring him to stop us. I rose, too. I felt exhausted.

Sheriff Bob looked as though he wanted to object, but finally shrugged his shoulders. "I guess that's enough for today. But I still don't understand why . . ."

Kyla cut him off. "Anything you don't understand, you can bet we don't either. Why don't you ask T.J.? If he's still alive, that is."

"Is he still alive?" I asked.

"Last I heard," said Bob, running a hand over his white mustache as though stroking the ears of a tired and none-too-clean hunting dog.

"Well, ask him then. Now we're leaving."

Kyla stormed out. I remained where I was a moment longer, eyes narrowed, fixing Bob with my best teacher stare. "You're going to release my uncle now, right?"

He sighed. "Already done."

We spent the rest of the afternoon with our relatives, and their questions made Sheriff Bob's interrogation skills look amateurish and pathetic by comparison. Fortunately, however, they very seldom waited for a response and filled in details themselves with endless speculation, theories, and innuendo.

Aunt Gladys shook her head. "Baby doll, you were lucky to get out of there alive. He was going to sell you, that's what he was going to do. Sell you for *you know what.*"

All the younger cousins looked as us with wide eyes, pretty sure they knew what "*you know what*" was, but not entirely positive.

"He was not going to sell us, Aunt Gladys," I said shortly.

"Oh, I don't know," said Kyla, taking a sip of an oversize vodka martini. "What do you think we'd go for on the open market? I'd be worth more than you, of course, but even you'd probably bring in a pretty decent price."

"I seem to recall someone once offering five hundred camels for you," I said slyly, thinking of our trip to Egypt.

"A thousand," she retorted. "It was a thousand camels."

My brothers Will and Sam, and Sam's wife, Christy, left shortly after that.

"Gotta hit the road if we're going to make Austin before it gets dark," said Sam. "We'll have a nice dinner, an early night, then catch the six thirty flight to San Diego."

Christy gave Kyla a hug, while Sam patted my shoulder awkwardly. "Glad you two are okay," he said. "I call you next week for a real update," he added with a wink.

"Me, too," said Will. "I want to hear all about your narrow escape from slavery."

I helped haul their luggage to their rental car. "I feel like I didn't get to see you at all," I complained.

Sam said, "If you promise no more murders, kidnappings, and food on a stick, we'll be back at Christmas."

"You know I can't promise there won't be food on a stick," I returned coldly.

"I can promise," said Kyla. "Better than that, I can promise there will be beer and barbecue. You all have a safe flight."

Kyla and I watched their car rumble up the hill, then returned to the house. Beside the fire, Elaine and Kel sat together on one of the sofas, both looking a little dazed, while next to them in a leather recliner, Uncle Herman sipped on an enormous tumbler of scotch and smacked his lips with satisfaction.

"It's the best news we've ever had," Herman proclaimed, glasses glinting in the firelight. "That sumbitch Knoller admitted his own partner shot his jockey. They'll give us the prize money now. Two hundred thousand dollars." He rolled the words around on his tongue as though they tasted sweet. "That's enough to fix what ails you, eh, Kel?"

"If they give it to us," Kel answered cautiously. "But even if they don't, the lawsuit will be dropped. We'll be fine." He squeezed Elaine's hand.

She squeezed back, then looked across the room to the corner where Ruby June was talking with Kris. The two had their heads together and looked like the pair of teenagers they still were.

"It's been a terrible thing, but Ruby's back and the girls are safe. That's what matters." She smiled at Kyla and me, and if the smile did not quite reach her eyes, I could hardly blame her. I had my own thoughts about Ruby June and Kris.

Might as well get it over with, I thought, rising.

"Ruby June, want to help me in the kitchen a sec?" I asked in that special teacher tone that so clearly indicated it was an order, not a request.

She obediently rose. I felt Kris's kohl-encircled eyes following us with suspicion and mild alarm.

In the kitchen, I closed the door behind us. Ruby June looked at me with studied nonchalance, the half smile on her face attempting to give the impression that she was just waiting to be of service.

"So, are you using?" I asked her bluntly.

She blinked, a moment of genuine surprise, quickly replaced with calculated evasiveness. I suspected the only real surprise was that I had asked the question.

"I don't know what you mean," she said with an air of offended virtue.

"You do."

Her eyes narrowed, and I could practically see the hamster wheel she called a brain beginning to turn. I quickly held up a hand.

"Don't bother. Let me tell you what I think instead. I think that you were Eddy's partner in most, if not all, of his dealings with Carl Cress—especially the drugs. I saw Eddy selling under the bleachers at the rodeo, and I'm guessing the two of you were the main source for all of your buddies at Sand Creek High School. After all, you both graduated only a year ago, and I'm sure you still have friends there. And I'm sure those friends have friends. Probably a pretty good business for the two of you, even with the cut that Carl took."

While I talked, Ruby June reddened, then grew pale, and finally settled down into a sullen defiance.

"You don't know anything," she said.

"So you won't mind if I send Sheriff Bob over to your house to take a look around."

She swallowed hard. "It's just weed."

"It's just accessory to murder after the fact," I said coldly. This sounded quite official. I was pretty sure I'd heard it on a cop show, which must make it a real thing.

"What do you mean?" she squeaked. "I didn't . . ."

"I'm embarrassed by how long it took me to figure it out," I said. "But let's be fair—the timing threw me. After all, we thought you'd vanished before Eddy's murder. But you were just getting ready to leave town, weren't you? Probably visiting friends, maybe trying to make a few final sales to get some cash? Then, you found out that Carl had killed Eddy, and you were afraid you were next. And instead of going to the police, you hid at T.J.'s."

She sat down abruptly on a kitchen chair in a posture that reminded me strongly of the way she'd huddled at this same table while her father threatened her husband. Not a fighter, I thought.

"He woulda killed me if he found me," she said in a low voice. "What would you have done?"

"Call the police! You knew he was a killer, and you knew he was going to come after you."

"Like Sheriff Bob could have done anything!" she said scornfully. "He would just have arrested me for the drugs."

"If you'd gone to the police, Carl wouldn't have had a chance to shoot Travis Arledge, who's going to make it by the way. And Carl would still be alive himself. In jail, true, but alive."

"Now why would I want Carl Cress alive?" she asked. "You have no idea what he was like. I guess I'm sorry about the jockey, but that was not my fault. What the hell do you want me to do about it all? Are you going to turn me in?"

This was the real question. With Eddy and Carl both dead, unless I said anything, I doubted very much if Sheriff Bob would pursue drug charges against a nineteen-year-old widow even if he suspected her involvement. He had enough on his hands with the Los Zetas.

"No," I said at last. "I won't turn you in . . . on one condition. No more drugs. Not even 'just weed.' And if I hear you've been giving or selling to anyone in our family, I will not only tell the police, I'll tell your parents. And you can bet I'm going to be saying a word in Aunt Gladys's ear to keep an eye on Kris. I know the two of you have been smoking."

Her face reddened, but she just nodded. I turned on my heel and left her.

As I returned to the living room, the sound of an engine made everyone turn their heads, and I hurried to the window in time to see a green Jeep rumbling down the hill. Colin had finally arrived, thank goodness. I grabbed Kyla's coat from the peg and ran out to meet him, slamming the door behind me in what I hoped was a meaningful way. The north breeze hit my face, and I knew I was going to miss my own coat. Even if the blood hadn't ruined it, the memories had.

I waved at Colin as I ran. "Don't get out—you have to take me away from here," I called.

He earned major points by slipping back behind the wheel and restarting the engine without question. I jumped in the front seat, and he pulled away just as the front door opened and my relatives boiled forth like bees from a hive. He reversed in front of them as I waved, fake smile pasted on my face, then we were off, and I heaved a sigh of relief.

"You know, in the future when we're around my family, you should always back in to a parking spot to facilitate a quick getaway," I advised him.

"Duly noted," he laughed. "It's good to know there's going to be a future," he added, glancing at my face before returning his eyes to the road.

I felt the warmth of a blush rise in my cheeks, but somewhat to my surprise I realized I didn't want to take it back.

"So where to?" he asked.

I looked around. We were approaching the first gate. To the left, the pasture sloped gently down toward the dry creek bed, the yellow grass bending gently in the breeze. Brown cattle were scattered as far as we could see, like ships on a flaxen ocean. A few of them raised their heads to watch us, probably wondering if we had any feed cubes. On the other side, the rising land became increasingly rugged, dotted with cactus and mesquite, gray rocks breaking through the weeds like the bones of some enormous prehistoric creature. A pair of doves streaked across the sky, moving fast as though blown by the north wind. Dusk was falling over a harsh, beautiful country.

"Can we just pull over for a minute?"

He obligingly stopped the Jeep and cut the engine.

I opened the door and got out long enough to pop the seat forward and crawl into the back. Colin laughed, and did the same on his side. Together on the narrow bench seat, I slid into his arms, slipping my hands under his shirt to feel the warmth of his chest, breathing in the outdoor scent clinging to his jacket, the faint hint of soap and sweat and man on his skin. I'd missed him, I'd longed for him, and holding him now reminded me how very, very glad I was to be alive. We kissed for a very long time, but, fortunately or unfortunately, there was no room for anything else. At last, I rested my head on his shoulder and waited for my heart to stop pounding.

"Might I suggest that you give more consideration to the size of the backseat when purchasing your next car?" I said.

"As a matter of fact, I've been thinking about that very thing quite recently," he answered solemnly.

I chuckled, and he pulled me closer, stroking my hair and kissing the top of my head. I touched the cast that ran from wrist to elbow. "Does your arm hurt?"

"Not too bad."

"Are you just being manly?"

"Yeah. It aches like a son of a bitch."

I raised his other hand to my lips and kissed his wrist. He stroked my cheek.

After a few moments, he said in a more serious tone, "I have some news for you."

I stiffened, then tilted my head to look up at him, but all I could see was the line of his jaw and the pulse beating at the base of his throat.

He took my silence for the invitation it was. He said quietly, "T. J. Knoller didn't make it. He died about an hour ago."

A sharp pang of guilt and regret shot through my chest. "I knew I shouldn't have moved him, but I was so afraid that if we left him, the gang would kill him. If I'd just waited until you got there . . ."

Colin shifted and held me tighter. "You can't think like that. You were trying to save his life, and getting him to the hospital as quickly as you did at least gave him a fighting chance. I figured you'd be blaming yourself, so I asked the doctor. Nothing could have saved him. The bullet had done too much damage."

I said nothing, knowing his words were meant to be comforting, but not feeling comforted. I thought of T.J. telling Kyla to hide in the barn loft, of stepping between me and two armed killers. I reminded myself that he was also the man who'd pointed a gun at both of us, which helped a little. However deserved or undeserved, he had brought his death on himself. Nevertheless, I was sorry.

I said, "It's such a terrible thing. Will we ever know what really happened?"

"I think we've got a pretty good idea. T.J. came around for a while in the hospital and talked. He knew he was dying."

I sat up then, turning in the uncomfortable seat so I could see his face, resting my legs across his lap. "What did he say?"

"He gave us names and details about the gang. Not enough to make up for the pain he caused, but enough to make some arrests, and more than enough to shut them down—in this county at least. He wanted to get rich, and he didn't mind cheating or stealing to do it, but I don't think he was a killer by choice. By the time things turned violent, he was in too deep to back out."

"Do you think he was being truthful when he said Carl was the one who killed Eddy?"

Colin nodded. "I do. He said it again in the hospital, and by then he had no reason to lie, and he knew it. Eddy wanted out and made the mistake of asking Carl for money to keep quiet about it. If he'd asked T.J., he'd probably be alive today."

"But why would Carl leave him where he could be found? And on our ranch?"

"That was sheer bad luck. It was easy for Carl to persuade Eddy to go to T.J.'s place and kill him there. When T.J. found out what Carl had done, he was horrified and demanded that Carl take the body somewhere else. Your uncle's caliche pit was close, and just across a barbed-wire fence. Of course, Carl should have buried Eddy right then, but instead he decided to go into town to establish his alibi. He spent the rest of the evening living large and buying rounds in R.T.'s BBQ and Sports Bar. By the time he sneaked back to finish the job, we'd already found the body."

I frowned. "If he'd just buried the body, he wouldn't have needed an alibi."

"If criminals always did the smart thing, we'd never catch them," Colin said. "In this case, I expect that killing his friend and then moving the body in the darkness shook up old Carl more than he'd expected. I think he panicked, and couldn't bring himself to dig a shallow grave with Eddy just lying there. At least not without a stiff drink or two."

I shivered a little and decided I could hardly blame Carl for that bit. "Okay, fine. That explains Eddy. But what was the plan with the racehorses?"

"Ah, now that's where things get interesting. T.J. needed a way to launder money for Los Zetas. He'd never been involved in the drug-selling side of the business, but he was actually quite clever with money. He was running a series of real-estate deals in about six counties, selling one property, buying another, always moving the money into different banks. I don't envy the investigators who have to figure out that mess. The thing is, Los Zetas were making more drug money than ever, and T.J. decided that horse racing would be an amusing way of laundering large sums of cash. He and Carl had already tested it once by buying a racehorse in New Mexico, racing it a couple of times, and then 'selling' it for quite a bit more than it was worth. They enjoyed the racing so much—acting like rich owners and betting—that they decided to invest in a lo-cal track and run horses here. The purse they managed to finagle was big enough to tempt any gambler, and they decided to stimulate the bettors by a very public rivalry between their two horses. They agreed that whoever won, they'd split the pot, sell both horses, and pass some, but most definitely not all, of the proceeds on to their Los Zetas associates."

"Then Carl got greedy?" I asked.

"More like T.J. got scared. Remember, he'd never wanted Eddy dead, and he was afraid that suspicion was going to fall on Carl and from there onto him. Plus, I think that Manuel was starting to become a factor."

I said, "How in the world did someone like Manuel get involved? He was always so nice and quiet, and he'd worked for Carl for years. Heck, he'd pretty much been Carl's slave for as long as I've known him."

"We're still trying to sort that out. We think Manuel started acting as the liaison between T.J. and Los Zetas. As you say, no one would ever suspect him, and he might have had a relative in the gang, or he might just have started making himself useful. In any event, it's pretty clear that the gang leadership was giving him more authority. I think he was putting pressure on T.J. who had decided that it wasn't safe to be skimming money from the gang."

"And that's when Carl sold the horse to Uncle Herman."

"Right."

I frowned, struggled, and finally admitted, "I don't get it."

Colin laughed. "You're not alone there. It was an idiot move, and even T.J. wasn't sure about all the details. I talked about it with Sheriff Bob. After putting together all the pieces, including that paperwork you found in Carl's house, we came up with a theory. Carl was furious with T.J. for reneging on the money they planned to skim. He had proof that the land T.J. was suing your family for really did belong to Herman, and he figured it must be worth a lot of money if T.J. was willing to sue for it. It's also likely that he was tired of being the hired hand, so to speak. He wanted a bigger piece of the money-laundering action, and maybe he thought he could cut T.J. out altogether if he had enough leverage. So, he traded the horse to Herman for the rights to the land."

"Did T.J. know?"

"Oh, yeah. Carl came to him with his offer for the land. The shit hit the fan at that point. T.J. didn't have any money for the land or for anything else. So he had to tell Carl about the Zetas. Up to that point, old Carl thought T.J. had some fancy investors in his pocket, but he had no idea who they were. T.J. was very good at keeping his various dealings in separate silos."

"Oh," I said slowly. "So when Carl found out he hadn't just double-crossed T.J., but a drug cartel . . ."

"Exactly. He panicked. He absolutely had to ensure that Double Trouble won that race, and he had to get Big Bender back before the Zetas learned what had happened."

"And how was he going to do that?"

"T.J. would have been willing to trade the land and more back to your uncle Herman to get the horse. And you saw what Carl decided to do about the race."

I shook my head. "And so he decides to shoot Big Bender's jockey, but misses and hits Travis instead."

"That about sums it up. T.J. stepped in to do as much damage control as he could, trying to implicate your uncle Kel and protesting the race results. But Carl had really messed up this time. There was no way to keep it from the drug cartel, especially with Carl's own ranch hand Manuel also working for the Zetas."

"So who killed Carl?"

"T.J. didn't know who pulled the trigger, but it was certainly ordered by the gang. Manuel is the most likely suspect. For one thing, he would have been able to get your uncle's gun without too much difficulty."

"And today? Were they planning to kill T.J., too? Or did they really just want to talk with him?"

"There's no way to know." He shrugged, then squeezed my hand. "They didn't plan on you being there, that's for sure."

"Or the lion," I reminded him.

"Or the lion," he agreed. "By the way, the sheriff called the folks who have the exotic ranch over at Llano, and they're out hunting the lion with tranq guns now. With any luck, they'll be able to capture him alive and find a real rescue zoo for him."

I shifted on the seat again, starting to feel cold. "And did you ever find out who attacked you? Was it Carl?"

"It was T.J. I recognized him in the hospital today, although I don't think he recognized me. I guess pretending his car was broken down was a pattern with him."

"But his truck is black," I protested. "You said the guy who attacked you was driving a white truck."

"I'm pretty sure he has half a dozen trucks on that place of his, or he could have borrowed Carl's truck for that matter."

I frowned. "I was so sure it was Carl. Anyway, why would T.J. have wanted to hit you?"

"I never got around to asking." He looked thoughtful. "I wonder if Ruby June wasn't involved in all this a little more than we originally thought."

"I think she was, but what does that have to do with it?"

He shrugged. "He was hiding her on his place for a reason. I was asking awkward questions and getting close. You do the math."

"I'm really sorry. It's my fault you were out there in the first place instead of somewhere warm and safe." That little pill Ruby June. I was almost sorry I'd promised not to turn her in.

"No, not your fault. Maybe my own, for being so careless. But it was T.J. who had the tire iron."

I held his hand, but then another thought occurred to me. "And what about those papers? I didn't have time to look at the contracts and deeds, but Sheriff Bob's name was on them. In fact, I really thought Bob was the one behind everything for a while. What was all that about?"

He just shook his head. "Bob was involved in some land deals with T.J., and somehow Carl found out. He probably took the paperwork as insurance, thinking he could hold it over either or both of them if he needed to. T.J. might have thought there were advantages to having a sheriff as a partner, but he was too smart to draw Bob into any of his shadier activities. It won't look all that good for Bob if it gets out, but there was nothing illegal about it."

"And Bob telling Elaine you'd gone to Austin?"

He grinned at that. "That was dumb, but he just didn't want Elaine telling Kel what I was doing. He figured that Kel would want to go along and might be able to pressure me by using his relationship with you as leverage. It wouldn't have worked," he added.

"I don't know. You don't know my uncle Kel," I answered with a grin. I thought over what he'd told me and added, "You know, between suspecting Bob and trusting Ruby June, I think I've been a gullible idiot," I said finally.

"Yes, you are," he said, his voice carefully light. "But not about that. What possessed you to break into Carl's house? Do you have any idea how dangerous that could have been?"

He was angry and trying to control it. I met his eyes.

We stared at each other for a long moment. I could have become angry in return at his presumption in judging me, but I knew his anger stemmed from real concern. I could have argued or explained or justified. But I didn't feel like it. Besides, it probably wouldn't have worked anyway.

Instead, in my best Kyla imitation, I opened my eyes wide, batted my eyelashes, and said, "I solemnly promise never to break into a drug-dealing, jockey-shooting, goat-fucking son of a bitch's ranch house ever again. Unless of course I need to."

As though from far away, part of me waited in agonized suspense, instinctively realizing this—this insignificant tiny argument—had suddenly become a pivotal moment in our relationship. If he'd argued or stayed mad or become hurt, it would have been all over. He didn't. He drew in one startled breath, and then gave a great shout of laughter.

He pulled me back into his arms and began kissing me again, exuberant, joyful kisses on my cheeks, on my forehead, on my neck, and on my nose. He followed them with passionate kisses on the lips, which I returned with breathless happiness.

When I could finally speak again, I pushed away from him and leaned forward to open the door of the Jeep. Darkness was almost upon us and a single glittering star shone through a rift in the heavy clouds. Drawing in a great breath of clean cold air, I realized that I was stiff, chilled, and happier than I had ever been.

"Where to?" he asked, looking without enthusiasm in the direction we'd come.

I reflected that Kyla was perfectly capable of packing my bag and driving my car, and it was less than three hours to Austin, where I had a warm house, a new bed with fresh sheets, and a fat poodle who would still be at the neighbor's for another whole night. In other words, all the privacy we could want.

"Take me home," I said.